His lips left hers but only to return again, like a flat rock thrown just right, so it would gently skim over the top of a pond.

She'd always been amazed by that, and this was just as incredible. When Lucky's lips settled upon hers for an extended length of time, her knees threatened to give way all over again.

As gentle and perfect as the kiss had started—she was sure this time that it was a kiss—it ended, and Lucky once again folded his arms around her and held her tight. She didn't know when her arms had wrapped around his waist, but they had, and she kept them there, hugging him in return.

They parted by some mutual, silent understanding a short time later. Maddie wasn't sure what to do, how to react, and wondered if she should be embarrassed, letting him kiss her like that, but couldn't come up with a reason why. Not when deep inside she was longing to be as close to him as possible. It was strong, similar to how badly she wanted gold.

But that couldn't be. She didn't want anything as badly as she wanted gold.

Author Note

I've had many people say they have a story idea for me. Usually, I have so many stories already swirling around in my head, there simply isn't room for one more. Not this time. When a friend emailed me after returning from mining gold in Alaska with a story idea, I was intrigued. He set the plot based on a historical couple he'd learned about, and gave me the freedom to embellish it. Which I did—diamonds weren't discovered in Arkansas until a few years after Maddie and Lucky's story.

That's part of the fun of writing fiction!

Thanks, Chris, for the story idea. I hope you and everyone else who picks up this book enjoys how Maddie and Lucky strike it rich.

LAURI ROBINSON

A FORTUNE FOR THE OUTLAW'S DAUGHTER

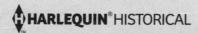

HARLEQUIN® HISTORICAL

Recycling programs
for this product may
not exist in your area.

ISBN-13: 978-0-373-29831-0

A Fortune for the Outlaw's Daughter

Copyright © 2015 by Lauri Robinson

Printed in U.S.A.

A lover of fairy tales and cowboy boots, **Lauri Robinson** can't imagine a better profession than penning happily-ever-after stories about men (and women) who pull on a pair of boots before riding off into the sunset—or kick them off for other reasons. Lauri and her husband raised three sons in their rural Minnesota home and are now getting their just rewards by spoiling their grandchildren. Visit laurirobinson.blogspot.com, facebook.com/lauri.robinson1 and twitter.com/LauriR.

Visit the Author Profile page at Harlequin.com.

To my brother, Norman, for unknowingly
giving me the idea for the name of Lucky's ship.

Chapter One

Life had never been easy for Maddie Stockwell. Being the daughter of the outlaw Bass Mason, a man who'd changed his name more often than he'd changed his socks, had forced her to look out for herself at an early age. She was quick on her feet, too. Quicker than the man with the hands that had just seized her could possibly know.

The fingers digging into her waist sent curse words—things she'd never say aloud but had heard numerous times—running through her mind. They muffled the piano music and shouts of people filling the saloons on both sides of the alleyway. Furthermore, the hand over her mouth stank of fish, and the pressure of that hand pressed grit into her lips and cheeks, igniting her fury.

Whoever he was—this man who'd grabbed her as she left the community well—was big. Strong, too, given the way he hoisted her off the ground, dragging her backward.

Claws of fear dug into her throat, but it was the anger surging inside she focused on. Not again. Did every man think all they had to do was hover in the night darkness and snatch her up as if they were picking peaches or something?

They might be able to do that to other women, but not her.

With movements she'd acquired while fighting off those who had ridden with her father, Maddie kicked one heel backward into the man's knee as she shot an elbow straight back, catching his ribs. She also flung her head back, connecting with what she assumed was his nose by the way he screeched.

She didn't stop there, though. The frustration inside her hadn't played out. As the arms around her went slack, she spun and brought the now half-full water bucket around at full speed. It met the side of his head with a solid thud, and her well-aimed kick targeted right below the belt buckle sent him the rest of the way to the ground.

He was no longer a threat, rolling on the ground as he was, but the names he was shouting, the things he was calling her—as if any of this was her fault—had her temper flaring.

Maddie swung the bucket again, cracking him upside the head. The last bits of water flew in all directions while the bucket splintered into pieces. She froze for a moment when the man went quiet. As swiftly as his hands had grabbed her moments ago, something she couldn't describe gripped her from the inside.

Her entire being shook as if she stood in the center of a Rocky Mountain snowstorm instead of a warm, dark California night. Mad Dog had found her again. This wasn't him, but it was one of his men.

Shouts, muffled by the throbbing in her ears, had

her spinning about. Two men, as big as the one on the ground, barreled down the alley.

Instinct said run, but where?

She couldn't go back to Hester's. That would jeopardize the other girls, so Maddie leaped over the prone body and headed for the street at the end of the alley several buildings ahead. Her heart raced as fast as her feet. The ground rumbled from the weight of those chasing her, and the opening seemed to get farther away instead of closer.

A whoop or whistle had her chancing a glance over her shoulder.

Like the devil riding out of hell, a horse raced right between the two men, knocking them aside.

"Hold out your arm, darling," the rider shouted. "Lucky will save you!"

The two men were scrambling to their feet. The horse getting closer. Her choices were clear: get run over and caught or leap on the horse behind the devil himself.

Instinct, again, had her choosing the latter.

Turning, she held out an arm, and as the man's hand clamped her elbow, she jumped, flinging one leg over the back of the saddle. She'd leaped on behind her father more than once, way back when, before he'd left her with Smitty. He'd been the one man she could always count on, Smitty that was, right up until the end. God rest his soul. Unlike most men, he deserved a place behind the pearly gates.

"Hold on, darling," the man in front of her shouted.

The clop of hooves echoed against the bricks as the horse rounded the corner, entering the street. Maddie wrapped both arms around the stranger to keep from sliding off, and caught a glimpse of her pursuers shaking their fists in the air.

Laughter from the rider in front of her filled the air, and feeling a touch of elation, Maddie shouted, "Are you?"

"Am I what?" the man asked in return.

"Lucky?" She could use some of that. Hers seemed to have run out weeks ago.

"Hold on, and you'll find out."

He took another corner, and then zigged and zagged down streets and up others, turning so many times she was dizzy, and lost, but Maddie kept her knees bent, legs out of his way as the man heeled the horse, keeping it at a full run.

Sea air—a mixture of dirty water, salt, dead fish and wet wood—stung her nose when he brought the horse to an abrupt halt. They dismounted at the same time, and he grabbed her by the back of one arm, propelling her in one direction while slapping the horse on the backside, sending it in the opposite way.

"In here," he directed, hushed and hurried.

The tall building blocked the moonlight, making it impossible to see much of anything. He'd saved her from the other men, but that didn't mean he was safe. Few men were. Life had taught her that. "What about your horse?" she asked, trying to buy time to figure out an escape on her own this time.

"It wasn't mine," he answered. "I stole it."

She dug her heels into the dirt. "Stole it?"

His strength was no match as he pulled her forward. "Don't give up on me now, darling."

"Don't call me darling," she said. "And let go of me."

"Can't. Alan Ridge isn't going to be happy when he

learns you knocked out his henchman. I may have gotten his other men off our tail for a bit, but eventually they'll learn where we went. At least the general direction." He threw open a door. "You can trust Lucky, darling. You're safe with me."

A chill rippled through Maddie. Mad Dog Rodriquez and Alan Ridge were the same man; she'd discovered that in the first town she'd hightailed out of in the dead of the night. Smitty had heard Mad Dog was in Mexico, and that was why he'd sent her to California: to escape the outlaw for good. That plan had backfired and she'd been doing little more than avoiding capture since stepping off the train. Mad Dog had a penchant for stealing girls and selling them at high bounties, but that wasn't the only reason he was pursing her.

"You know Alan Ridge?" she asked.

"I know of him."

She didn't like it, not one little bit, but Lucky, as he called himself, seemed her only alternative at this moment. Given her choices, Maddie followed him, vowing to escape the first chance she got.

He closed the door behind them and let go of her arm but took her hand as he spun around. It was even darker inside, completely black. "Hold on to my belt. I'll never find you in here if we get separated."

Maddie was contemplating that when he whispered again. "But Ridge's men will. Have no doubt about that, darling. When that one comes to, he's going to be looking harder than ever."

"Are you one of Ridge's men?" she asked point-blank, though not really sure what she'd do if he said yes.

"Aw, darling," he drawled. "Would I be trying to save you if I was in cahoots with him?"

Men were a fickle bunch, and not a one of them was above lying, yet her instincts, which she hoped weren't trying to fool her, said she could trust this man. However, her ire was still riding high. "Will you stop calling me that," she hissed, while wrapping her fingers beneath his belt. Men who'd ridden with her father always called her darling. She'd hated it then, and hated it now. Along with everything else about her past.

Lucky started walking forward slowly, as if feeling his way. "I will if you tell me your name."

"Maddie. Madeline Elizabeth Stockwell," she answered. It was a good name. This one she'd settled on. No one could trace it back to Bass. That wasn't likely, considering he'd been calling himself Boots Smith when he died, but she wanted to sever all ties to her former life. California was supposed to have been a fresh start, but since arriving, she'd found herself running more than when living with outlaws.

"Well, ain't that a mouthful?"

Stung, she retorted, "It's better than Lucky."

"Lucky's just my nickname, darling. Real one's Cole. Cole DuMont."

"Who gave you a nickname like that?"

"I did."

"You gave yourself a nickname?" She'd given herself a full name, but that had been a necessity; giving yourself a nickname was just plain silly. Maddie was her real name, as far as she knew. Madeline as well as Elizabeth and Stockwell were ones she'd chosen. They sounded distinguished. Proper. That was what she wanted. A real, proper and distinguished life. She'd have it, too. If she ever got away from Mad Dog and his henchmen.

"Sure enough did." Lucky paused to open a door.

"Figured if I called myself that often enough, it would stick. Luck, that is."

She followed him outside. The air was cool and it had started to rain. Mist really, since it was more as though the water just hung in the air rather than falling to the ground.

"Has it worked?" she asked, curious.

"Sure enough has."

The moisture-filled air was darker, and she wondered how he'd found the next door he opened. Luck, maybe?

They did that several times, entered buildings, weaved around boxes and crates—at least she assumed that was what was on both sides of them, snagging her dress sleeves at times—and exited only to take a few steps before entering another one. Warehouses along the seashore were like that. Long lines of buildings storing the cargo shipped in and out of the bay. She'd explored them during the day in the town she'd first arrived in, but the men she'd encountered along the seashore made her not want to visit the docks again.

Mad Dog's men.

"Was that Ridge's horse you stole?" she asked.

"Don't know," he answered. "I'd just stepped out the back door when I saw you knock down Bubba."

"Bubba?" This building had a sharp, almost sickeningly sweet scent filling it, like molasses, and she glanced around, but might as well have had a burlap bag over her head. She couldn't make out anything in the darkness.

"Don't rightly know if that was his name or not," Lucky said, "but he was one of Ridge's men. I saw the other two going after you, so I ran around front and jumped on the first horse I came to."

They were still whispering, and it was making her voice burn. At least that had to be why her throat felt so thick. "Why?"

"Why what?"

"Why'd you steal the horse?"

"To rescue you." He stopped suddenly and she bumped into his back before stilling her steps. "You do know what Alan Ridge does with the girls his men snatch off the streets, don't you?"

"I've heard." She refrained from admitting all she knew about the alias Mad Dog had taken on. It seemed the outlaw was now the leader of his own gang and had henchmen in every town lining the coast.

Lucky—she still thought that was a silly name—opened another door and scanned the area like he'd done at each one before.

"Don't worry," he whispered. "Ridge won't catch us. Not tonight."

Stepping into the wet night air once again, Maddie squinted, hoping to see something this time. Nothing but blackness, yet she could hear water sloshing. "You sound funny," she said when he opened another door.

"That's because I was born and raised down by New Orleans. A bayou boy. That's what my granny always called me."

"What are you doing here?"

"Shh," he said. "Listen."

She did, until her ears stung from the thundering of her own blood.

"Must've been a rat," he said, moving forward.

Maddie quivered. Rats came in all shapes and sizes, and she knew firsthand how some walked on two legs, pretending to be human.

"Don't worry, darling, rats don't like us any more than we like them. It's not much farther, either."

"Maddie, the name's Maddie."

"Yes, ma'am," he said, as cocky as every other statement he'd made.

After the last building, he led her along a series of docks. Thick fog had settled in, and so had her nerves. An escape route hadn't presented itself. Lucky may have rescued her from that alley, but that was not to say he wasn't as bad as Mad Dog. He could be taking her to a place no better than Mad Dog did the girls he captured. Long ago she'd figured out what happened to those girls before they were sold. She hadn't let that happen back in Colorado, and wasn't going to let it happen here, either. Not with Mad Dog or a man who called himself Lucky.

He stopped and started unlooping a thick rope from one of the posts lining the dock. "Climb down."

She peered over the edge. A rowboat bounced in the water. "Into that?"

"Yes."

"Why?"

"So I can row you out to my uncle's ship. The *Mary Jane*. It's sailing for Seattle posthaste."

Her heart skipped several beats. "Seattle?"

"Yep."

That could be far enough away, but traveling cost money—something she didn't have. The small chunk of gold sewn in the waistband of her petticoat was her seed gold. Smitty had given it to her when she'd left Colorado, along with all the cash he'd had. He'd said he wouldn't need it where he was going, and Maddie had promised to make him proud. To become a woman he could smile down upon while he was busy filling the world with sunshine even on cloudy days. A smile tugged at her lips, remembering how Smitty had insisted if she ever needed him, all she had to do was look up. He'd brighten the sky for her.

"Come on," Lucky said, as he turned around and started climbing down the wooden ladder. "Unless you want to stay here, become one of Ridge's girls."

Something changed, and Maddie glanced up. Strangely there was a momentary part in the clouds. The moon, as big, round and right as she'd ever seen, peeked through and shone down on her. Her heart skipped several more beats as she glanced back toward the rowboat. Still cautious, she asked, "How much will it cost me?"

"Nothing."

It was the first time she got a good look at Lucky's face. Kind of long, with a square, clean-shaven jaw. It was his eyes that caught her attention. Even in the fog they twinkled as if that was where the stars were, instead of high above the clouds where nobody could see them. She glanced up again. The moon was gone. No stars, either.

"Come on, Maddie," Lucky coaxed. "I promise you're safe with me. You'll be safe all the way to Seattle."

There were no others mingling around, no one to hear if she shouted, unless perhaps Mad Dog or his men—if they had followed. She wanted to believe Lucky, climb down and escape this town and all the dangers it held, yet caution had been her constant companion for years. "How do you know I don't have family here?" she asked. "Someone looking for me. Right now, even. Who'll hunt you down, along with Ridge."

His smile made those eyes twinkle brighter. "If you

had family, you wouldn't have been fetching water for Hester."

A splattering of hope rose inside her. "You know Hester?" The older woman had assisted Maddie in escaping Mad Dog's clutches once before and had promised a permanent escape would happen soon.

"That's why I was at the saloon," he said.

The air left her lungs in a gush. "It is?"

"Yes. I'm the rescue Hester promised."

Relief filled Maddie. That explained why Hester had sent her out to fetch water tonight. This was her chance, and she had to take it. "Why didn't you say so?"

He made some kind of reply, but already swinging around, Maddie didn't hear exactly what. She was too busy willing her heart to stay in her chest as she lowered closer to the water. Wet and slippery, the ladder wasn't easy to navigate. A wave of reprieve rushed over her when a firm hold took her by the waist, lifting her the last few feet.

The boat rocked as Lucky guided Maddie to sit on one of the wide boards. Then he flipped a blanket over her head and shoulders before he sat down opposite her and grasped the handles of the oars.

Though already damp, the blanket didn't offer warmth, but did block the wind, and Maddie repositioned it, grasping both corners beneath her chin. Her thoughts went to the two younger girls that Hester had ushered into the attic late last night. When Lucky started to row, she asked, "What about the others?"

"I was just sent after you, but don't worry, if Hester promised them an escape, it'll happen." He made several more big circles with both arms at the same time, moving the boat through the water, before asking, "Are they friends?"

"No," Maddie admitted. "I don't even know their names." Just as she hadn't known the names of the other girls that had come and gone within hours the past few days. Hester had said it would take time to get her out of town, considering her previous encounters with Ridge's men. They hadn't been just run-ins, they'd been escapes. Maddie escaping, that was. Three times, in three different towns. She still didn't know how Hester had learned about her or knew to meet her at the edge of town, but the woman had, and she'd done exactly as promised.

Maddie's happiness faltered. As badly as she wanted to escape Mad Dog, she didn't want to go as far as Seattle. There was no gold there. It was here. In California. That was what Maddie wanted. Gold. Enough so she'd never be hungry again. Never be cold or scared or homeless or penniless. And with enough gold, she could go someplace Mad Dog would never find her.

"Where are you from?"

Maddie lifted her head and questioned answering. The less anyone knew the better. "East of here."

His laugh was quick. "Everything is east of California. Where were you born?"

Her memories didn't start until Wyoming, then Montana, Texas, Arizona. She even remembered a hut down in Mexico. Thus was the life of an outlaw. Until Colorado, where they'd run across Smitty, prospecting high in the hills. Her father had left her with him instead of dragging her along to the next train, stagecoach or bank that Bass thought he needed to rob. That had been five years ago. "Kansas," she said. At least that was what she'd been told.

Cole couldn't say she was lying, and he couldn't blame her for being evasive. She wasn't the first girl he'd been assigned to collect from Hester. She was the last, though. He'd helped with several escapes and liked the adventure of it, but Ridge had caught sight of him last year, and that could jeopardize future rescues. The loss of this woman would bother the outlaw. Her black hair and mature figure, which Cole had tried to ignore since pulling her up behind the saddle, would bring a high price. That was what Ridge counted on. The lovelier, the more expensive.

It was a good thing this would be the last trip for the *Mary Jane* this far south for a while. Ridge had too many eyes on the shore to not put two and two together.

"How old are you?" Cole asked.

"Nineteen."

She was certainly older than the thirteen- and fourteen-year-old ones he was used to moving north, but he'd guess her no more than sixteen. "There's no need to lie to me."

Pulling the corners of the blanket tighter beneath her chin, her blue eyes glistened as she snapped, "I'm not lying."

It didn't matter one way or the other, and Cole decided to let it go. "What brought you to California?"

"Gold."

She hadn't hesitated in her answer, but it was the gleam that instantly appeared in her eyes that he recognized. Knew exactly what it was like. There wasn't another word that affected him like that one did. Gold. Just thinking about it got his blood racing, his heart pounding. He had the fever. Caught it last year, but he didn't let it rule him. Instead, he let it drive him. And it had. All winter. He was now set, had everything lined up, and before long he'd be gathering up more gold than most men only dreamed about. He knew where to find it. Maybe that was why he told her, "There's no gold in California, darling."

"Yes, there is," she argued.

"None a man can freely claim." He wasn't trying to disillusion her. It was something he knew for a fact. The money being made in California was off the miners, not by mining. It was that way other places, too. He just knew where the odds were better.

Her lips were pinched tight and her chin had jutted up a notch.

"Alaska," he said, thinking of his destination. "That's where the gold is."

"That," she said sternly, "is a wives' tale. Alaska's nothing but frozen tundra."

"Now, who told you that?"

"No one in particular."

"Well, go right on believing that, darling. You and the rest of the world." It would leave more for him to find. Tales of discovering gold in Alaska had spread along the coast for years, and prospectors made their way there only to return saying the same thing she did—mainly because they didn't know where to look. He, on the other hand, did. Those thoughts had him slowing the speed of which he rowed. The *Mary Jane* had to be close, and in this fog he might row smack-dab into her side.

"You've seen it?" she asked. "Alaska? Gold?"

"Yes, darling, I've seen it." Something blocked the wind, and he had no doubt it was Uncle Trig's ship. Paddling slow until he could make out the ropes hanging down, he said, "We're here."

The rowboat bumped the big hull of the *Mary Jane*. Cole caught a rope and pulled the little boat beneath the ladder. "You have to climb up first this time. But don't fret, I'll be right behind you."

There was caution in her eyes, but not fear, and he liked that. He'd had to carry more than one young girl up the rope ladder, which wasn't easy. She tucked the blanket under the bench seat and carefully maneuvered to the ladder. He waited until she was well on her way to the top before he tied the side ropes to the rowboat so it could be lifted out of the water by the pulleys once he arrived on the deck of the big ship.

Uncle Trig was at the top and two shipmates were already hoisting up the rowboat when Lucky climbed over the edge.

"Everything go all right?" his uncle asked.

"Yes," Cole answered. "No problems at all."

"Did you see Jasmine?" Trig wanted to know.

"Who do you think motioned me when the time was right?" Cole slapped his uncle on the shoulder. "She's as lovely as ever." Long ago Jasmine had been shanghaied from some foreign coastal town much like Ridge was doing to innocent girls, and though she was now the madam of a similar business, she believed girls should choose to work that profession, not be forced into it. Trig had once been a steady customer of Jasmine's, and though Cole felt there was more—that his uncle had fallen in love with the woman—neither Jasmine nor Trig ever proclaimed anything but friendship. They were cohorts, though, in slipping girls out of town right under Ridge's nose. Although neither of them would admit to that, either.

"I'm sure she is," Trig answered.

"How'd you know about this one?" Cole asked. They'd barely arrived in port when his uncle told him of the mission. Usually there'd been cargo to load or unload and he'd always assumed word had been sent during that time. This time, glancing toward Maddie standing near the wheelhouse, he was curious to know how Trig knew Hester—Jasmine's housekeeper—had this girl hidden and ready for an escape.

"Two lanterns." Trig waved a hand in the general direction of Cole's gaze. "I hung a hammock in my cabin for you to bunk with me until we get to Seattle."

That wasn't new, either. He often gave up his sleeping space for the girls, but not satisfied with his uncle's answer, Cole questioned, "Two lanterns?"

"If there's only one, all is well. If there're two, we're needed."

"Where?"

"Warehouse number seven." Trig, his skin wrinkled and weathered from the sun and sea, squinted thoughtfully. "You thinking about changing your plans?"

Cole shook his head. "You know I'm not. Sailing's been profitable, but not enough to cover what the family needs now. Robbie's waiting in Seattle. He'll take over the rescues." There was a fleeting ounce of regret inside Cole, for he had enjoyed the past four years with his uncle, sailing the seas, mainly the West Coast. They had gone around the cape once and back again. That had been his greatest adventure so far—and most profitable. The funds he'd acquired from buying and selling highly sought after merchandise had allowed him to send a considerable sum home. Yet as much as that had been, he'd heard the family needed a whole lot more. Trig had contributed, too, but the hurricane that had wiped out the family shipyard and warehouses west of New Orleans had done a number on the entire coast, and his uncles back home said Gran was struggling to rebuild the family empire to its former glory.

Cole had set his hope and goal on gold. It would show to his mother that following in his father's and grandfather's footsteps had been the right choice, and prove every man had his own fortune to seek. If his mother had her way, Cole and his brother would still be living under her roof, married to the women she'd handpicked.

He'd left, though, to his mother and Rachel's dismay. So had Robbie. His younger brother by three years had escaped their mother's clutches two years ago, just as Cole had three years before that. It wasn't that they didn't love their mother, just that a man has to live his own life. Gran knew that, and said it, though their mother never listened. Gran had seen through Rachel, too. Even before he had.

Cole let his thoughts skip right over Rachel, as he had for years now. He was glad Robbie had joined him and Trig. It was his brother's turn now to learn the ins and outs of being a sea merchant. He'd stepped off the ship last fall to spend the winter in Seattle in order to drum up cargo he thought they could make a profit from. Trig had given instructions, just as he'd given Cole the first time he'd let him wander on his own, striking deals.

It had been then, when they'd dropped off Robbie, that they'd heard about the hurricane—a message had greeted them when they'd arrived in port. His father's other two brothers, though neither had been overly involved in the shipping industry, had sent a wire saying everything had been lost, but Gran was insistent upon rebuilding.

That was the other reason he needed to find gold, and lots of it: Gran. She'd dedicated her life to the shipping industry and had used her profits to see her sons set up in businesses, and now, as life was catching up with her, she deserved to have her family come together in order for her to rebuild her one true love. DuMont Shipping.

As kids, he and Robbie had loved spending time at her place. They'd sneak away from the house to pretend they were sailors, maneuvering little rowboats around the bayou, both of them dreaming of the day they'd join their father or Uncle Trig on the seas. Their mother had been dead set against that and whipped them soundly the one time she'd discovered where they'd been and what they'd been doing. She'd forbidden them from spending nights at Gran's after that. Even as a young child he'd been torn between the adventures calling him inside and the pain of seeing his mother cry, claiming the sea had stolen her husband. She'd cried when he'd left, too.

Cole sighed. He hadn't wanted to hurt her, but the calling had grown too strong, and now, well, now he had to save the family business. A man lucky enough could make money in Alaska—lots of it, and that was what he needed.

With another friendly slap to Trig's shoulder, and more determined than ever that Alaska was where he needed to be, Cole took a step. "I'll show our guest to her cabin."

Chapter Two

To Maddie it seemed only hours had passed, not days, when a voice on the other side of the door said they were heading into port. At first she'd been cautious, nervous even, but Trig DuMont—Captain Trig—reminded her so much of Smitty, her reservations had disappeared. He was always grinning, and carefree and happy. So was his nephew Cole—although she continued to call him Lucky, still hoping it would rub off on her.

Both Lucky and his uncle acted as if the sun never set, that the world was a glorious place, and all they had to do was flash one of those eye-twinkling smiles and all their dreams would come true. Though comfortable talking with either of them, she still didn't trust men, any of them, and kept to herself most of the trip. The boat was full of other men and she'd readily agreed when Lucky had suggested it would be best if she stayed inside as much as possible. Which wasn't hard.

The cabin was remarkable. Not only did it have a bed—she'd only slept on one of those a few times in her life—but it was full of books and newspapers and magazines—all about gold mining. Due to her limited abilities, reading them had been difficult at first, but the more she kept at it, the easier it became and she found herself wishing they'd never arrive in Seattle. Or better yet, sail right past it. Her luck had shifted—she could feel it deep inside—and she knew what she had to do.

The books she'd read filled her with additional excitement. Alaska was full of gold. There were ways to get it out of the ground, too. Frozen or not, it wasn't so different from what she already knew in a lot of ways. Smitty had taught her all he knew about mining.

Settling the last book back to its rightful place, just as she'd done with all the other ones, Maddie swallowed, forcing her heart to slide back down her throat to where it belonged.

Alaska. That was where gold was, and she wanted gold; therefore, Alaska was now her destination. She wouldn't have to look over her shoulder every step, either. Mad Dog would never follow her all the way to Alaska.

Freedom and gold. Her luck had definitely changed.

Captain Trig smiled brightly as she opened the door. Much shorter than his nephew, the captain wasn't much taller than she. The top of his head was completely hairless and a ruddy red from being exposed all the time, and he had a jagged scar that wrapped around one ear. Yet, like Lucky, his glistening brown eyes made him appear less dangerous than a woeful pup looking for a home. Though her luck had changed, Maddie continued to tell herself she still had to be cautious. Wolves were once pups.

"We're pulling into Seattle," Captain Trig said.

Maddie stepped out of the cabin.

"Hope the trip wasn't too rough for you."

"Not at all," she answered, pulling her eyes off the

gray skies. Seattle didn't appear any more excited to see her than she was to see it. "I could sail for days yet. Months even."

Trig's laugh was low and choppy, but not frightening. Pleasant in its own right. "It would get old to you long before months were up, girlie." He gestured toward the busy shoreline. "We'll dock here. No need for a rowboat this time."

"I didn't mind the rowboat, either."

He laughed again. "Trying to finagle yourself a job?"

Maddie glanced his way.

His eyes sparkled, even as he said, "A ship's no place for the likes of you, darling." Taking her elbow as they walked, he continued, "There's a good woman here in Seattle. She'll provide you with the training to become a nursemaid or servant girl and find you a good family to work for. You'll never have to worry about men like Ridge again. Just follow her instructions."

Maddie bit her lips together. He was right in saying she wouldn't have to worry about Mad Dog ever again, but she'd never be a servant—she'd have servants. Now wasn't the time to share that, so she asked, "For free?" Her father had never figured it out, but she had. Nothing in life is free.

"The cost is covered," Trig answered. "Nothing you need to worry about."

Worry wasn't what she felt. There wasn't a word, not one she knew, to describe how her stomach soured at the thought of being beholden to anyone. She'd given Hester the gun Smitty had given her as payment for getting her out of town. A tiny derringer not worth much, but next to her nugget, it was all she'd had. She'd repay Trig, too, and Lucky, for their parts. The *Mary Jane* was sailing to Alaska when leaving Seattle, and Maddie would be on her. This was her chance and she wouldn't give it up. Once she found her gold, she'd clear her debts and finally be in complete control of her life.

"When are you sailing out?" she asked. "In case I want to say goodbye?"

Trig glanced around at the men doing things with ropes and riggings and such. When his gaze settled on one man, her heart fluttered oddly in her chest. She realized then it was Lucky.

"To me or my nephew?" Trig asked.

She'd barely spoken with Lucky, yet she did think a lot about him. Mainly because she was so preoccupied with all his books. He was her route to the gold, and she had to follow it, yet no one could know that. Not Trig, and not Lucky. Shaking her head, she answered, "You of course. I owe you for rescuing me."

"Think nothing of it, honey. Besides, Lucky rescued you. My ship just carried you north."

"Well," she said, contemplating the truth of that. An answer settled and she grinned. "You told him to."

Trig laughed again. "We'll be sailing out in three days."

Maddie started to count the hours at that very moment. When the time came, it was Trig who walked her down the steep slope created by the drawbridge-type door that was lowered from one side of the boat. He talked amicably about a Mrs. Smother as they walked along the dock then up the stone-lined shore.

Four blocks from the water—she counted and noted distinct landmarks to find her way back—he led her up a set of steps on a large brick building that, despite the colorful flowers lining the walkway, had every shutter shut as if keeping everything outside out and everything inside in.

Mrs. Smother was summoned by the older woman who answered Trig's knock, and soon Maddie was ushered up a set of stairs by the same white-haired lady who'd opened the door while Mrs. Smother, a middle-aged woman with brown hair and faded blue eyes, invited Captain Trig to tea. Maddie had to grin at the thought of the captain drinking tea, but followed the other woman, who introduced herself as Martha.

Maddie was biding her time of course, she couldn't just run away, not until the *Mary Jane* was about to set sail. Martha led her into an extraordinary room. There was a tub for bathing, a commode for, well, necessity and hooks on the wall holding several garments.

"There's hot and cold water," Martha explained. "You can wear anything that fits and leave your dirty clothes in that basket."

A thousand questions danced in Maddie's head, but she didn't want to sound or look ignorant, so she simply nodded.

"Do you need any help?"

"No," she answered, "thank you. I'll be fine."

Years ago her father had left her to live with one of his lovers—that was what he'd called Roseanne—and there had been a room just for bathing there, though not as elaborate as this. Maddie had learned a lot about life that winter, and men and women, and had been glad when Bass had returned. "Make sure you scrub well," Martha said. "It looks as if it's been a while since you've bathed."

Considering there hadn't been a creek handy for several days, it had been a while, but the other woman's tone struck a chord that went beyond that. Maddie held her temper in check and waited until Martha opened the door before suggesting, "I would like to say goodbye to Captain Trig before he leaves."

"It would be best if you didn't," Martha answered, not unkind, but stern.

Maddie bit her lips together and smiled. Three days could prove impossible here. A person knew when they weren't wanted, especially one that hadn't been wanted since the day she'd been born. It was just as well; she didn't want to be here, either.

After her bath, which she figured out just fine, and dressed in a pale blue dress that had fit better than the others—at least she could button the front of this one—Maddie met with Mrs. Smother. She listened and nodded, even answered once in a while, although Maddie had no plans on heeding the "strict set of rules that must be followed at all times." Not stupid, she remained amicable during the evening meal and completed all of the chores requested of her. Then she waited until the house was quiet before sneaking down the stairs and out the door in Mrs. Smother's parlor. The other two doors were guarded. Bass had taught her a few things that had turned out to be useful, like stealth.

A thorough exploration of the docks, which took up most of the night, didn't provide a place to stay until the *Mary Jane* sailed, and a fact occurred to Maddie. Mrs. Smother was sure to contact Captain Trig if she came up missing prior to him leaving port, and he might have the ship searched. As she backtracked and sneaked back into Mrs. Smother's big brick house Maddie pondered how one might possibly board the *Mary Jane* moments before it sailed. Once again, a few of Bass's escapades came to mind.

* * *

Cole cursed as he attempted to roll the wooden barrel up the ramp. The contents inside refused to shift, making the barrel roll back toward him rather than flipping over and rolling up the ramp. Too big around to heft onto his shoulder, he squatted and put all his strength into a hefty shove. It rolled, and Cole hurried upward pushing continuously to keep the momentum going. When it finally topped the ramp, he was breathing hard and calling Robbie a few choice words. Cole had no idea what might be in the barrel, but the scratchy writing, as if someone had used the burned end of stick, saying "the *Mary Jane*" told him Robbie had agreed to ship whatever the barrel contained.

After it quit rocking, he flipped the barrel on end. The faint morning light showed one more set of scratchy writing. "This side up." After rolling it up the hill, flipping the barrel onto its other end was simple. He toppled it end for end and then paused to swipe the sweat from his brow as he glanced around, having sworn he'd heard a muffled moan.

"Cole!" Robbie waved from the dock. "Come help with this luggage, would you?"

Glad to leave the barrel where it sat, Cole headed back down the gangplank. Robbie could take the barrel below, into the cargo hull, that would be easy as the ramp was downhill. Arriving at his brother's side, Cole's jaw tightened at all the tapestry bags and traveling trunks. Disgusted with the "cargo" Robbie had lined up, Cole shook his head. "We aren't a passenger ship."

"We've already gone over that. Alaska isn't yours. People can move there if they want to." Robbie grinned. "Especially paying the price those ladies agreed to pay."

Letting his snort tell his brother exactly what he thought of hauling a dozen dance-hall girls to Alaska, Cole grabbed a trunk and headed back up the ramp.

Robbie, with a couple of carpetbags in each hand bounded up beside him. "Could make for an interesting trip."

Scowling, Cole answered, "*Interesting* isn't the word I was thinking. Don't you remember anything from family picnics? When you get more than three women in a room, there's bound to be a fight. A dozen of them will be dangerous. Ugly, too."

"Not one of those gals is ugly," Robbie argued. "Trust me, big brother."

Cole didn't bother with an answer; instead, he declared, "We sail within an hour. If your ladies aren't here, we aren't waiting."

"They'll be here," Robbie assured. "They'll be here."

Unfortunately, Robbie was right. The women arrived before the mounting stack of luggage had been carried into the hull. The area had been transformed by all sorts of furniture the ladies were paying to have transported. Dressed in outfits and covered in face paint that left their profession in no doubt, the women marched aboard, waving and blowing kisses at the few mates it took to run the *Mary Jane*.

Mainly a cargo ship, the *Mary Jane* only had a few cabins—Robbie had explained that to the women, which was why a portion of the hull had been transformed to make the trip as comfortable as possible. Robbie had set that all up, too, and Cole had been a bit surprised when Uncle Trig had agreed to it.

Trig had, though. In the end, his uncle had been the one to convince Cole there was as much profit to be made off those women as any other cargo they'd haul. It wasn't that Cole didn't appreciate a woman now and again, he just didn't have time for the problems that came along with them. Rachel had been a headache from the get-go. Telling him what to do, what to wear. She'd partnered up with his mother, too, trying to make sure he never took to the sea. When he'd told Rachel he wasn't interested in gaining access to Gran's fortune, but in finding his own, she'd run to his mother again, bawling. The two of them hounding him nonstop had been more than he could take. He'd left despite the fact Rachel and his mother were planning a wedding.

His.

Women wanted nothing more than to rule a man. That would never happen to him. He'd be in charge of his own life.

Cole set down the last trunk, and as he turned, ready to make his exit up the hull ramp, a head of coal-black hair caught his attention. His heart kicked the inside of his chest, making the air in his lungs rattle. The woman turned around to face him, grinning, and he experienced a wave of disappointment. Or perhaps relief. He'd wondered about Maddie since she'd left the boat on Uncle Trig's arm. She'd waved and he'd tipped the brim of his hat, but had wondered how she was getting along at Mrs. Smother's. Maddie just didn't seem like the domestic-servant type.

He told himself he was glad this woman wasn't her and hurried up the ramp. The black-haired woman's profession was the exact thing he was trying to save Maddie from. In all actuality, Hester and Uncle Trig had saved her; he'd just been the runner. She'd been no problem on the trip. Stayed in the cabin, reading his books on mining, although she'd never let on to that. He hadn't let on that he knew she'd read almost everything in his cabin, either.

Cole chuckled as he scurried across the deck to begin preparations to set sail. Maddie had certainly been different than any other girl he'd ever been around. She'd wanted less to do with men than he did women. He'd sensed that. Not only while rescuing her, but during the few times they'd conversed. They hadn't said much to one another, usually just greetings during meal times, yet he'd noted her mind was always going, taking in the surroundings and holding on to every word Uncle Trig had said. That had mainly been about sailing or the places he'd been. Her eyes had sparkled whenever Alaska had been mentioned, and that was probably why he still thought about her. She had the fever as bad as he did.

Cole's thoughts shifted then. It wouldn't be long now, and he'd be finding gold. The thrill of that put a smile on his face.

The *Mary Jane* set sail while the sun inched its way into a clear sky turning a brighter blue with each minute that ticked by. Cole embraced the work it took maneuvering the ship out of the bay and setting their course north to Alaska.

His mind was always on his job, and his heart was right along with it. The day was perfect for sailing, and the women—he figured due to the hour of which they must have crawled from their beds—had settled into the hull as soon as they'd boarded, and with any luck, they'd sleep away most of the day.

The deckhands whispered amongst themselves, but no one made mention of the unusual cargo. To do so would have angered Trig, and no one angered the captain. Cole liked that, too, because it promised a smooth and uneventful trip.

Hopefully.

He still had his doubts.

Late that night, while taking his turn at the wheel, his doubts were confirmed. Cole pinched the bridge of his nose at the commotion coming from the hull. The ruckus had been going on for some time and he'd hoped it would stop all on its own, but evidently that wasn't to be. Since no one else seemed willing to go see what was happening he had no choice. Glancing toward Chester, the other mate assigned to the night shift, Cole nodded toward the wheel. They were in open water, but still needed to be alert. While walking toward the hull, he also glared down the narrow hallway running between the cabins. Uncle Trig or Robbie, who should have been dealing with such rumpus, hadn't stepped out of their doors.

He'd known they wouldn't; it was his job to take care of anything that came about during his watch. With frustration burning his lungs, Cole started down the slope. Women and boats didn't mix. To his way of thinking, women didn't mix with much. They always needed something and whined until they got it. They were clinging, too, as if they couldn't take a step without assistance. Women had their purpose, but he sure didn't have that purpose in his life. That was why sailing fit him so well. Mining would, too.

A man who wanted freedom and peace stayed far away from women.

Cole stopped at the bottom of the ramp. Robbie's cargo looked and acted like a pen of clucking hens. Half of them had scarves made of feathers around their shoulders, which they were flipping and flapping about, leaving an array of red, black, white and pink fluff floating in the air. He couldn't see much beyond that, nor could he hear anything above their squawks.

Sticking a thumb and finger against the sides of his tongue, he let loose a squealing whistle.

Silence filled the hull. He could once again hear the water sloshing against the sides. Praise be. Batting aside a few feathers floating before his face, Cole attempted to release the tension from his jaw before growling, "What's all the commotion about?"

A buxom woman with ash-colored hair streaked with red—a horrible combination—stepped forward. "Where's Mr. DuMont?"

"You're looking at him."

The obvious leader of the pack slapped her hands on her hips and marched forward. As she did so, she exposed a red corset, tasked with the unenviable role of keeping everything in place.

"I mean Captain DuMont," she retorted, stepping close enough to fill his nostrils with the scent of enough rose water to drown a rat. "I demand to speak with him this moment."

"Demand all you want," Cole answered. "He's sleeping." Lord knows how. "I'm in charge right now."

"Well, then," the old hen said, "I demand to know if that woman paid the same price we did to sail upon this ship." Waving a hand toward the group, she continued, "Or if she is a stowaway as I suspect."

Cole stopped shy of saying all the woman had paid when the leader added, "I put out a fortune to have me and my girls transported safely to Alaska and will not abide by others getting a free ride. Put her overboard immediately."

"Overboard?" Did she think the *Mary Jane* was an historic pirate ship, making people walk the plank in shark-infested waters? Proof all women's heads were filled with fantasy and fluff. Just as he'd always suspected.

An eerie sensation and the glare still coming from the woman had him leaning slightly to see around her feathers and hair. His heart dang near dropped to his feet. The rest of the brood had parted, and right there in the middle, chin up and eyeing him with a hint of haughty determination, stood the black-haired beauty he'd been thinking about since she'd walked off the ship. "Maddie?"

"Hello, Lucky."

The way she said his nickname had his knees growing a touch weak. He locked them in place. No woman made him weak, not any part of his body.

"What are you doing down here?"

Rather than answering him, Maddie turned to the pack leader. "I told you I know the boat's owner."

"That doesn't mean you aren't a stowaway," the woman snapped.

Cole had half a mind to wait it out, see how Maddie got herself out of this one, but he couldn't do that. The buxom woman had her claws exposed and looked as if she wanted to tear someone to shreds. He'd learned what was causing the commotion, and it didn't help his mood in the least. Grasping Maddie's arm, he tugged her forward. "What are you doing down here?"

"I—"

Not wanting to spend any more time below deck,

he interrupted, "Come on. I'll kick Robbie out of our cabin for you."

Her eyes grew as round as silver dollars. So did the dozen other pairs staring at him. Robbie should be the one dealing with this, not him, but leaving Maddie down here wasn't an option, not even for a few minutes. Waking up his brother would suit Cole just fine, and he wouldn't be gentle about it, either. He and Robbie now shared the cabin, and his brother deserved to be put out considering the cargo he'd mustered up. Spinning around, Cole pulled Maddie along beside him.

She flashed a smile over her shoulder, toward the momentarily silent brood, and though he didn't mind the quiet, Cole warned, "Don't get too smug there, darling. You've got a lot of explaining to do."

Maddie closed her eyes briefly, just to get her insides back in order. Everything had gone remarkably well until one of the women had noticed her sneaking toward the ramp. If she hadn't had to relieve herself—which she still did—this would not have happened.

"I know," she answered, barely glancing toward Lucky. "But can it wait a few minutes?"

"A few minutes?" he asked, forcing her to march up the ramp.

The urge had her bladder on fire. "Yes, there's something I need to do."

"What? Jump overboard?"

"No." Flustered, she admitted, "I need to use the facilities." There was an area at the back of the boat she'd used before and assumed it was still there. At least she hoped. It had been all day and she was about to burst.

"Go," he said, gesturing toward the back of the boat

once they'd reached the top of the ramp. She didn't take the time to thank him—couldn't.

When she emerged from behind the little wall, Lucky was leaning against the high side of the ship a few feet away. His eyes were sparkling like the stars overhead, but the scowl on his face had her throat swelling.

Maddie had been afraid his brother would be the one to enter the hull to discover what had the women so riled up. Of the two brothers, she was glad it had been Lucky. Though she'd secretly hoped it would be Captain Trig. There was something about him that said he was trustworthy—an aspect she'd rarely sensed in a man. Lucky was that way, too—trustworthy—but she'd much rather deal with Trig. Maybe because of his age. Living with Smitty had taught her how to relate with older men—younger ones were scary.

Lucky pushed off the wall. "A few days ago, I rescued you from becoming one of those women, and now—"

"I'm not one of those women," she insisted, instantly angered by his assumption.

"Then start explaining."

"Explaining what?" she asked more flippant than intended.

There were no sparkles in his eyes now. "How'd you get on the ship?"

Angering him more wouldn't get her closer to her goal. She let out a sigh and shrugged. "In a barrel."

"A barrel?"

She nodded, and refrained from explaining how she'd sneaked out of Mrs. Smother's house every night—after long hours of being "educated"—and searched for a way to board the boat. Last night, when that barrel had sat at the edge of the dock with the moon shining down on it, she'd been convinced Smitty had put it there. She'd stayed nearby, hiding in the shadows until morning was about to break, and then after scratching the writing on the side, rolled it next to the gangplank and climbed inside. Holding on to the lid had left splinters under her nails she still had to dig out. Once it had been rolled on board, an experience that left her head spinning for hours, she'd sneaked out and hidden below deck.

Lucky rubbed his forehead. "*You* were in *that* barrel?"

Although he made no gesture, she knew exactly what barrel he was referring to. "Yes, I was in that barrel. The one you set upside down." She then pointed out, "It clearly said 'this side up.'"

"You wrote that?"

"I saw it on some of the other crates and barrels." Giving him a steady stare, she added, "I assumed you knew how to read."

"I do know how to read, even chicken scratches."

Catching the insult, she went with her gut reaction and stuck her tongue out at him.

He laughed, and the night air seemed to carry the sound away in waves. She shot him a glare that told him just what she thought of his attitude and then turned to look out at the water. The moon was out—a huge orange ball in the middle of a twinkling sky. Its light cast a long yellow reflection into the water, almost in a straight line that ended right where she stood.

Maddie drew in a deep breath and wondered if it really was Smitty up there watching over her, showing her she was on the right path. She could almost hear the old man's laugh, telling her it was him and that he was lighting her way. Smitty had his grumpy moments, too, therefore, young or not, Lucky's ill temperament or his insults didn't overly concern her.

He turned around and set both hands on the rail. Maddie didn't look at him, but she did tell him, "I have to go to Alaska."

"Alaska's no place for women."

The seriousness of his tone had her glancing his way. One of the other girls back at Mrs. Smother's had asked about him, claimed he was handsome. She'd been young and said Lucky had rescued her the year before. Although Maddie had been focused on escaping, the other girl's admission had caught her attention and Maddie had asked why she was still at Mrs. Smother's place. The girl said training to become a proper servant took time, which had increased Maddie's desire to leave. A year at Mrs. Smother's would have turned her batty.

Right now, though, Maddie was supposing the girl had been right about Lucky. He was handsome, but she tried not to look at him because it made her cheeks grow warm. She turned her gaze back to the water. "But it's a place for miners," she said, "and that's what I am. A miner."

His silence said he didn't believe her.

"I am," she insisted. "I mined gold for over four years in Colorado. We didn't hit it big, but only because our claim was paid out before Smitty bought it. We couldn't move on, but with his guidance, I found enough to keep us going." Determination stiffened her spine. "I'll find it in Alaska, too, I know I will."

"Who's Smitty?" Lucky asked. "Your father?"

"No, he wasn't my father." Exposing her past was not in her plan. Yet gold was what she needed to put everything behind her, and Lucky was her way to gold.

Considering that, she admitted, "I did pretend to be his daughter, though. In order to get the medicine he needed. That's why I kept dredging gold, too." Turning, lifting her face toward the moon that appeared even brighter now, she added thoughtfully, "Smitty and I were a team. Two people who didn't have anyone else. We didn't need anyone else, either."

"What happened to him?"

"He died." A strong and invisible power clenched her heart. She hadn't wanted to leave before he died, but Smitty had made her. Said he didn't want her waking up one morning and finding him dead. Therefore, he'd trekked down the mountain beside her, so weak he could barely stand, and in Cutter's Gulch, he'd set her on the train, with boarding passes that would take her all the way to California. Inside, she knew he never made it back to their claim, the cave they'd used as a home for years, and someday, when she had the money, she'd return to Cutter's Gulch, find his grave and place a huge headstone there, for the greatest man she'd ever known.

"Maddie?"

Blinking, she pulled her gaze off the moon and turned toward Lucky.

"I asked when Smitty died."

She nodded, having possibly heard his question while deep in thought. "Last fall."

"You've been alone since then? On your own?"

A lump filled her throat. "Being alone and on your own are two different things," she whispered. Smitty wouldn't want her focusing on the past instead of the future, so she tossed her head slightly, shattering dark and gloomy thoughts aside. "But now I'm on my way to Alaska."

"Trig might have something to say about that," Lucky said. "He laid out good money—"

"I know," she interrupted, holding up a hand. "Mrs. Smother informed me the captain paid for my stay at her place, my training, even the dress I'm wearing, and I'll repay him every cent. I promise." Taking a step back, she lifted her chin and pulled forth all the grit and determination Smitty insisted filled her. "I don't want to be a servant. I want to have servants, and I will someday. I swear it."

He shook his head as if he didn't believe her, and that made her stomach burn. Before he could speak, she declared, "I know how to find gold. I know what to look for, how to pan. I've built sluices and rockers, and I—"

"But are you prepared to live in a tent, in the wilderness, with—"

"I've lived in tents, and caves, and dugouts. In the wilderness and on the plains."

"You have?"

Nothing would stop her. Not her past, and not a man. "Yes, I have. Matter of fact, I've never lived in a house. Not for any length of time. Never had a real bed I could call my own, either." Standing taller, she added, "There's nothing about Alaska that scares me."

He cocked his head to one side and tiny sparks of light returned to his eyes as he grinned. "I believe that, Maddie, but I'd be remiss if I didn't say that you should be scared. It's a wild, untamed country."

"There are a lot of wild and untamed places," she said. "I know. I've lived in some."

Lucky was rubbing his chin, and Maddie was sure he was about to say something else, but a shout sounded first.

"There she is!"

Chapter Three

Cole, in his uncle's cabin, along with Trig and Robbie, plopped onto the chair next to the captain's built-in desk. "What are you talking about?"

"Why'd you tell them that?" Robbie repeated.

"Tell who what? I just went below to see what all the cackling was about."

"Somehow those women got the understanding you and that stowaway are married," Robbie said.

A chill wrapped around Cole's spine like seaweed on a fishing line. "I didn't— I'd never say anything like that," he insisted. "All I said was that I'd kick you out of our cabin so…" The chill increased. "Shit," he muttered. Women always misunderstood things. *Our cabin.* As in his and hers, not his and Robbie's. "I was thinking about waking you up so you could take care of them. Those women were ready to throw Maddie overboard."

Uncle Trig scratched his head with both hands. "Well, they assumed by what you said that she's your wife and that's why she's on this ship. Robbie promised them there weren't any other passengers."

Cole's stomach clenched. He hadn't escaped one marriage just to be shanghaied into another.

"There weren't supposed to be any other passengers," Robbie said from where he sat on the bed, rubbing his eyes and yawning. "Where'd she come from?"

"Hester," Trig said.

"Why didn't you deliver her to Mrs. Smother's?" Robbie asked.

"I did."

"How'd she get on board?"

Cole blew out a long breath. Trig wouldn't force marriage upon him, especially not to a stowaway. "In a barrel." He withheld the grin trying to form and asked his uncle, "What are you going to do with her?"

Uncle Trig let out a raspy guffaw. "We aren't turning around, I'll tell you that. We're set to be one of the first boats to arrive in Alaska this spring." He crossed the small cabin and shrugged out of his coat. While hooking it on the nail on the wall, he said, "The women have settled down, believing she is your wife, and that's how we're going to leave it."

A shudder raced through Cole. "I'm not—"

"You want a mutiny?" Trig asked. "You want to see that girl thrown overboard? If those women find out they're being lied to, that's exactly what will happen." Shaking his head, he declared, "A hundred men, I could handle. A dozen women…" His gaze went to Robbie. "Will never sail on one of my ships again."

Robbie turned a bit sheepish, but Cole still couldn't breathe.

"She's a smart girl," Trig said. "I'll talk to her tomorrow about the importance of letting those women believe their assumption."

Cole held in a protest—it wasn't worth the effort right now—but that didn't stop disgust from lining his guts.

"All right, then," Trig said. "It's settled. Cole, you'll just have to take most of the night shifts, letting Maddie sleep in your cabin. Robbie will bunk with me. During the day, while you get some sleep, she can stay in here."

"We could—" Cole started, convinced he could come up with a better plan if he had time to hash it out.

"What's done is done," Trig interrupted. "It's not that long of a trip, and hopefully once we hit Alaska they'll forget all about it." Waving Robbie off his bed and pointing toward the hammock hanging loose against one wall, he instructed, "Hook that back up. I need to get some sleep." Turning to Cole, he said, "Your shift's not over. Try to keep those hens from clucking any more tonight."

The gnawing of guilt wasn't new to Maddie. A person who'd been born unwanted was used to it. Blaming herself for things for as long as she could remember wasn't new, either, but this time it was different. Lucky was mad, and she was the reason. When they did encounter, his eyes didn't twinkle and there was no perpetual smile on his lips like when she'd sailed from California to Seattle. Trig, though, was as jovial as before, even while explaining the trip to Alaska was over three thousand miles and would take several weeks.

The length of the trip hadn't bothered her, but the other things he told her did. How on earth was she supposed to pretend to be married? She not only knew nothing about marriage, but she didn't want to know anything about it.

There were, however, other things she did need to know.

Five days had passed since the night she'd been discovered. The women's sneers were easy to avoid; she simply retreated to Trig's cabin whenever they left the hull, which unfortunately, was the better part of most days. As long as it wasn't raining.

Avoiding Lucky was about as simple, since he took his turn of steering the ship at night and slept during the day; however, she didn't want to avoid him. His books were no longer answering the questions she had, and all Trig or Robbie, who was rather pleasant to be around, would say was she'd have to ask Lucky.

Captain Trig, after explaining the misunderstanding—about her and Lucky being married—had said her appearance hadn't shocked him. She'd thanked him for understanding and for not throwing her overboard—at which he'd laughed—and after explaining Mrs. Smother's training program would never have worked for her, she'd offered him her nugget in partial repayment for all she'd cost him.

He'd refused to take it, and that was when he'd told her Lucky would be staying in Alaska to search for gold. Maddie struggled to contain her excitement. Being cooped up in the cabin and unable to question Lucky felt worse than waiting out a snowstorm in the dead of winter.

Trying not to cause more anger, she made sure to be out of the cabin early each morning so Lucky could go there to sleep. It wasn't hard, being up so early. The inactivity of her days was wearing and made sleeping difficult. Not even reading helped. Her mind grew tired from her constant ponderings, but not her body.

Maddie shifted her gaze to peer out the little window beside the bunk and let out the air that sat heavy in her chest. Here she was, lying on the bed, staring into the blank darkness again and unable to sleep because of the energy she hadn't been able to use up during the day.

When a knock sounded, she sat up. "Come in."

"Sorry to disturb you," Lucky said. "I just need a coat. It's a chilly night."

"You didn't disturb me." She found the nearby lamp and flint box and lit the wick. "I wasn't asleep."

His gaze settled on her briefly as he walked to the foot of the bunk where nails held a couple of coats. She'd eyed those jackets more than once, expecting she'd need a coat once they arrived in Alaska. There were so many things she'd need, and wasn't sure how to obtain them. She now had an extra dress. The one from Mrs. Smother. She'd kept her old one, once she'd laundered it—that had been her first lesson in domestic chores, as Mrs. Smother had called it—and she'd never parted with her petticoat and the nugget sewn in it. It was what she'd use to outfit herself for gold mining, but that little nugget wasn't going to be enough.

Watching Lucky pull down a coat, the thought of what the women below believed made her insides burn with embarrassment. "I promised Captain Trig I wouldn't say anything to the women about what you told them."

"I didn't tell them anything. They assumed."

She nodded. "He told me that. I'm sorry about putting you in such a predicament."

Putting on his coat, he let out a snort that held disgust. "Predicament? That's not what I'd call it."

His orneriness was a bit irritating. It wasn't as if

she'd done it on purpose. "I don't like it any more than you do," she responded.

He scowled.

She let out the air once again heavy in her chest. "I will never get married, and even pretending to be galls me."

"It galls you?"

"Yes, it galls me." The cabin was tiny, and made smaller by his large frame filling half of it, yet he didn't make the space feel uncomfortable, just stuffy with his attitude. She swung her legs over the edge of the bunk and the book she'd been reading earlier fell onto the floor.

It landed next to his feet. He picked it up and handed it to her. "I thought every woman wanted to get married."

Running a hand over the cover, she said, "Maybe the foolish ones. I plan on having gold. Lots of it. Why would I want to have to share it with someone? A husband, I mean. They'd claim it was theirs as much as it was mine and spend it as they chose." Her father had done that with the gold she and Smitty had found. Claimed it was partially his since she was his daughter. She set the book on the bed. "I won't have that." Not wanting to sound completely callous, she said, "I won't be a miser. I'll spend my money. Pay Captain Trig back and buy the things I want. Even share it, but I don't want anyone telling me what I *have* to do with it. What I *can* do with it."

"What if you don't find any gold?"

"Not find any gold?" She stood. "I'll find gold, Lucky. I promise you that." Encouraged by the tiny half smile that appeared on his face, she added, "I'll find some for you, too."

He laughed. "I don't need anyone finding gold for me. I'll be finding my own." When she started to follow him toward the door, he asked, "Where are you going?"

Not embarrassed to tell him, she said, "To the back of the boat."

He waved toward the wall of the cabin. "You better grab my other coat. It's chilly out tonight." Then without waiting to see if she did or not, he opened the door and left.

After using the facilities and thankful the oiled canvas coat blocked the wind, Maddie took a stroll along the rail to use up some energy before attempting to sleep again. Lucky stood behind the big wheel, both hands wrapped around the wooden handles that jutted out all the way around the wheel. The fact he'd spoken to her a few moments ago gave her the courage to walk over and stand beside him.

Smitty had been the only friend she'd ever had, and a raw hole had appeared inside her since she had left him in Colorado. Captain Trig's kindness had helped, but a friend wasn't what she needed right now. A partner was. One person could scratch up enough gold to live on, but two people could find enough to set a future, and that was what she wanted. A future.

"I meant what I told you," she said when Lucky glanced her way. "I'm sorry to have caused such trouble."

Considering she only came up to his shoulder, Lucky glanced down at her, and though he didn't say anything, the distrust in his eyes made her insides churn. She tugged the big coat tighter, wrapping the open front around her almost like a blanket. "I meant the other part, too, about never getting married."

His gaze went to the open water ahead of them, even while he said, "Don't be saying that too loud, darling. Those women below would still like to toss you overboard."

The moon was out again, big and bright, and a swirl of frustration rose inside her like smoke leaving a fire to disappear into the air. "I know."

Sounds from the ship, creaks and thuds, the splash of water and other subtle, unidentifiable noises, filled the quiet void as he stared forward, and Maddie, unable to hold it, let out a long sigh.

"One of them say something to you?" he asked.

"Yes." More than one. Every time one of the women noticed her they hissed a slur of some kind or another.

"What?"

"Nothing of importance," she answered.

"What did you say in return?"

"Nothing. I just walked away."

He nodded before he said, "You best head back to the cabin. The temperature is dropping. I predict we'll see rain in a few more minutes."

Maddie, full of questions, wanted to protest, but her good sense prevailed. She'd have to be cautious where Lucky was concerned. "Good night."

"Night," he responded without glancing her way.

She made her way back to the cabin. Even though they hadn't said more than a few words, she still felt hope rising inside her.

Maddie held on to that hope, and each night, long after the boat settled into the quiet darkness, she'd venture out to the wheel after using the facilities at the back

of the boat. Though Lucky never appeared happy to
see her, he didn't appear surprised or angered, either,
and her hope continued to grow. More so when several
days later, Captain Trig said he was pleased to see she
and Lucky were on speaking terms again. He said the
women below had noticed their late-night meetings and
no longer doubted the marriage ruse as much.

One night, while standing near the wheel, she said,
"Tell me about Alaska, Lucky. Please."

"Alaska or gold?" he asked a few moments later.

"Both."

"You have gold fever, darling."

Though she'd hated it before, she didn't mind when
he called her darling. It suggested his anger might be
diminishing. He'd make a good partner, considering
all he knew from the many books he owned. With all
Smitty had taught her, the two of them could find a lot
of gold together. They'd have to have separate claims,
of course. She'd meant what she'd said. Her days of
sharing—certain things anyway—were over. He was
right, though; she did have gold fever.

"I've had it for years," she answered. "How long
have you had it?"

"Who says I have it?"

"Me. I know it when I see it." In truth she wasn't
sure he had the fever. She'd seen men with gold fever
and Lucky wasn't like that. Those men had been dangerous, full of desperation and more often than not,
full of whiskey.

Lucky was so quiet she couldn't even hear him
breathing, leaving her to wonder if he was still mad
and wasn't about to share anything with her. Then, gazing over the water, he started, "It's an amazing place.

Alaska. Last year we sailed up the Yukon River to Dabbler. There's only a few months out of the year that can happen, but when the waterway is open, a sailor can make a fortune. That's what Uncle Trig is counting on. The hull, the part not full of women, is stuffed with cargo the miners need. Mainly foodstuff they can't get. Raisins and—"

"Raisins?"

"Yes. Miners claim raisins are all they need to survive. It's not true, of course. No one can live off just raisins, but they are easy to haul and they're paying top dollar a pound."

"Is a boat the only way to get to Dabbler?" she asked, not overly interested in the cargo—raisins or women.

"No, there are trails, but they're long and dangerous. Sailing in is the rich man's way. Trig could have made a lot of money taking on passengers, but he doesn't like hauling people. They're more work than cargo, and the *Mary Jane* isn't equipped for it."

She'd heard that much. Trig wasn't impressed with Robbie for agreeing to haul the women, and she'd learned the large woman in the hull had paid a small fortune for herself and her girls to sail on the *Mary Jane*.

"I plan on going northeast of Dabbler," Lucky said, "farther into the Klondike. That's where the gold is."

Maddie's heart leaped inside her chest. "How do you know? Have you seen it?"

"Yes. Last year we hauled gold back to Seattle," he answered. "The purest, richest gold Trig had ever seen. An old friend of his, Whiskey Jack, brought it in, knowing he could trust Trig to get the best price. Knew he could trust me, too, and gave me a map."

Her heart hammered so hard she could barely breathe.

"It's not in my cabin," he said, turning back to gaze over the water.

Slightly flustered, yet not enough to quell her excitement, she said, "I wouldn't steal your map."

"How do I know? You sneaked on board."

"Yes, I did, but I had to. I couldn't stay in Seattle."

"Not the kind of gal that can be penned up, are you?"

A flutter happened inside, and she determined it was because he was teasing her, not mean like the outlaws used to do, but in a fun way. Grinning, she shook her head.

"Even that cabin's driving you crazy, isn't it?"

"Yeah, it is," she admitted.

"How you gonna survive living in a tent for months on end, then?"

"That'll be different," she said. "You know it will."

He nodded. "I guess I do."

"How much gold did that man Whiskey Jack find?" she asked.

"Plenty, and he said there's lots more to be found."

Maddie's entire being hummed with excitement.

"Settle down, darling," Lucky said as if he knew exactly what was happening inside her. "We still have a long way to sail."

"I know," she admitted. A warmth filled her then, and she wasn't sure if it was from the moon shining down on her, or because of the sparkles in Lucky's eyes. Either way, she'd never experienced anything like it. Not as a child or an adult. She knew one thing, though— with Smitty guiding her and Lucky as her partner, she'd soon have the life she'd always wanted.

* * *

Each night thereafter, when she'd join Lucky on the deck, they would talk about Alaska, gold and a few other things. Some nights, they'd stand by the rail of the boat with the moon shining down on them as they gazed north, talking of all the gold just waiting to be found. When the wind grew chilly, he'd take off his coat and fold it around her shoulders, and Maddie had never felt so protected, so shielded from the elements.

Part of it might have been because she had no worries of Mad Dog finding her, but other parts of it came from inside, a place she'd never really been happy before.

Standing in the dark, whispering, she told Lucky about living with Smitty, how he'd taught her to find gold. What to look for. Lucky told her things, too, about growing up in New Orleans and all the places he'd sailed. She never asked if she could go with him into the Klondike, and he never offered, but Maddie had no doubt it would happen.

Her late-night excursions meant she slept during the day, often curled up on Captain Trig's bunk, but sometimes, if she was sleeping when Lucky entered their cabin, he wouldn't wake her, just go into the captain's cabin himself. Guilt rolled in her stomach on those days, and she tried to make sure it didn't happen often.

It was a long trip, and one particular day, Captain Trig entered his cabin and sat down in the chair. "So you've mined gold before?"

"Most of my life." She'd already told him about mining with Smitty, and figured he was going to try to talk her into sailing south with him again, probably back to Mrs. Smother.

Scratching his chin, he said, "Well, then, I've got a proposition for you."

Maddie's mind raced with excitement. "What's that?"

"Well," he started, "seeing how you're so dead set on staying in Alaska, and Lucky needs to find gold…"

Cole had listened to Maddie talk about searching the ground, looking for different shades of dirt, and other things he'd never heard or read about, and all the while a battle formed inside him. He had to find a way to tell her that she wasn't staying in Alaska. As the *Mary Jane* floated closer to Dabbler, his thoughts became more twisted. That was how it had been lately. He found himself thinking about her more and more. Which had to stop.

Now.

He was still furious at how she'd sneaked on board and had all those soiled doves thinking the two of them were married. That was how women did things. Sneakily. She was sneaking into other places, too, inside him, and he didn't like that. Not at all.

Rachel had done that, sneaked inside him, and at one point, had almost made him change his mind. Had she said she'd wait for him, let him try sailing, he might have married her.

That would not happen again.

Yet as he gazed toward the shore, he couldn't help but admit he was partially to blame for Maddie's behavior. She'd been so skittish at first, like a lone kitten found in a barn, and he'd used little tidbits to entice her out just as he would have offered little treats to a stray. So in a way, he'd led her to believe there might be a chance he'd let her follow him into the goldfields.

His gaze settled on Dabbler. The town had grown considerably since last year. It now boasted all sorts of establishments, and people. Many of them were probably preparing to head into the Klondike, too, which could very well hamper his chances of finding gold.

It wouldn't hamper Maddie, though. She'd convinced him she knew what she was talking about, and her determination wouldn't let up until she found gold. Yet the Klondike was no place for a woman, and there was less room now than ever for a woman in his life. His family was counting on him. That was what he needed to focus on.

"There sure are a lot of boats."

Despite the war going on inside him, Cole had to smile. Leave it to Maddie to refer to the array of the ocean liners as boats. The traffic on the waterway had grown steadily in the past few days, but he, too, was surprised by the line waiting to dock. "Yes, there are," he said.

It was early morning, no one else on the *Mary Jane* had stirred, and though it had only been a few hours since he'd told Maddie to go get some rest, she was back and dressed for the day. Lovely, too. He'd come to accept that, as well. The ladies below, flashing their goods and batting their lashes—which had gotten old before any iota of interest could have formed—had made Maddie all the more pretty. And vulnerable. The men in Dabbler would attack her like sharks.

Leaving the rail, Cole walked back to the helm, though no attention was needed, anchored as they were.

She followed, as he knew she would. "I'm so excited, I could swim to shore."

"I wouldn't advise that," he cautioned. "You'd freeze to death before you got ten feet from the boat."

"I'm not going to do it," she said somewhat saucily. "I'm not stupid."

Air snagged in Cole's chest as he dragged in a breath. "I know you're not stupid, Maddie." Gesturing toward the queue of ships, he said, "Most of these are passenger vessels. Hundreds of people, thousands actually, will debark here."

"All hoping to find gold," she answered while nodding.

He nodded in return before he said, "It's going to be dangerous, Maddie. No place for a woman."

Her face fell. So did his insides.

"I'm not going south with Trig," she said. Folding her arms, her gaze was expectant when she looked up at him. "I've suspected you were going to suggest that."

"Alaska's no place for you, Maddie. Go south with Trig. He'll find you—"

"Lucky..."

When she said his name like she did—all soft and wistfully—it almost took his breath away, and irritated him to no end.

She grabbed hold of his coat sleeve. "Haven't you learned anything about me in all this time we've been traveling?"

He pulled from her hold to grab her arms. "Yes, I have. That you're a pain in my backside." It was true. He thought of her all the time, and that was painful. The other truth was, if she'd been a man, he'd have already asked her to pair up with him.

Her mouth gaped, and his insides stung. He did know her, and simply telling her she couldn't go with him wouldn't work. She was far too stubborn for that. He had to show her she wasn't wanted. "That's right. A royal pain in the butt. I'm going to be busy, Maddie. I won't have time to worry about you." He didn't want to worry about her. Not now. Not ever. With one hand he gestured to the mountain ridge beyond the town. "You see those mountains? I've got to cross them. You'd be like a weight around my neck, making the trek that much harder, that much longer."

She wobbled and he let her go, and told himself not to catch her as she stumbled backward. Any other woman would be shedding tears, but Maddie wasn't prone to crying, or letting her emotions show. She wasn't whiny or constantly complaining, either, and for a moment he wished she was. All this would be a lot easier, then. Walking away from Rachel sure had been.

Maddie's eyes grew cold, bitter, and her chin came up. "I'll never be a weight someone has to carry. Not for you or anyone else."

He had one stab left, and he had to seal the deal. "What do you think you've been all this time?" he asked. "A paying passenger? No, you've been a lie I've had to cover up since the first night we set sail. A burden I don't need or want."

Her lips puckered and her nostrils flared, yet her chin never quivered as she spun around and stomped across the deck.

Sickened, for he didn't like hurting her, Cole sent his gaze back to the line of ships ahead of them. He couldn't say he liked who he was lately. Maddie had changed something inside him, and it wasn't any good.

Just as he'd known it wouldn't be. When a man lets a woman into his life, everything changes. He'd sworn that would never happen to him, and it wouldn't. Yet, it left him feeling as if he'd eaten a bucket of crab apples.

"So you told Maddie she can't go with you, did you?"

Cole didn't glance at his uncle, who'd appeared at his side. "The Klondike's no place for a woman."

"And that is?" Trig asked, obviously talking about Dabbler.

They were close enough to see how misshapen tents and crudely slapped-together buildings covered acres upon acres of land along the shoreline. "No, it's not," Cole said. "That's why she needs to sail out with you."

"She won't," Trig insisted gruffly. "I asked, but even then I knew the answer. That girl wants gold worse than you do. That's why I said I'd finance her."

A shiver shot up Cole's spine. "What?"

Trig's grin looked crustier than ever, as if he was as pleased as a pauper sitting in a king's chair. "I know a good investment when I see it."

"You're a fool," Cole said.

"Maybe, but I don't think so."

"You can't leave her here," Cole insisted.

"I have to. I've financed her expedition—for a ten-percent profit." Trig's laughter chased a flock of floating gulls into the air. "That girl has gumption and guts. And knows what she's talking about. She knows more about gold mining than ninety percent of the people attempting to strike it rich up here right now, maybe ninety-nine percent. You want money to rebuild Du-Mont Shipping, and so do I. So I hired her to find it."

"You what?"

"I figure your idea is a good one. I make good money sailing, but it'll take years to earn enough to build the warehouses back to their glory. Gold, though, a good solid find, could have things back to what they were in no time."

Fury flared inside Cole. "Traitor." Finding gold was his plan, his way of making things right with the family and his mother.

"I'm not telling you to partner up with her," Trig said. "I'm sure I'll find someone else. Probably have plenty of takers."

"No, you won't," Cole snapped. The thought of Maddie pairing up with someone else was worse than that of having her by his side. And the idea of not being the one to find the money his family needed sparked flames in his guts.

Trig laughed as if Cole hadn't spoken. "She drove a hard bargain. I was lucky she finally settled on ten percent. Almost had me over the barrel at eight."

Anger had Cole at a loss for words. "You can't do this," he muttered.

"Yes, I can," Trig said. "And I did."

Less than a week later, when the *Mary Jane* headed downriver to the Bering Sea and, ultimately, to the Pacific Ocean, Cole left Dabbler, taking a well-worn path heading northeast and leading two pack mules.

Behind him, Maddie led two others.

Chapter Four

Maddie would never, ever, let Lucky know just how badly he'd hurt her. For one, it didn't make sense. No one, other than Smitty, had ever wanted her, and she didn't expect people to start now. For two, if she did admit he'd hurt her, she'd open herself up to more hurting. She'd had enough of that in her life. All that really mattered was that she was here, on her way to the richest goldfields in the world. The talk in Dabbler, from miners, town folks and new arrivals, all said it was so, and she believed it.

Her wandering gaze, taking in the mountains they had to trek, the mud covering the trail, the tall pines and spruces, settled on the man in front of her. He was lucky, all right. Lucky she was with him. Especially after the things he'd said. She'd tell him that, too.

Someday.

Right now, they weren't talking. They weren't even looking at each other, which was fine with her. She was completely capable of trekking through the mountains without him, and took every opportunity to show him that. From the first night they'd set out, she ignored his offer to share a fire. Instead, she built her own, several yards away from his, and set up her own tent, too.

In fact, if not for the deal she made with Trig, she might have already ventured out on her own. She wouldn't, though, not with an additional 40 percent of her gold hanging on the line. That was what it would cost her if she left Cole high and dry. Fifty percent of her findings would go to Trig if Lucky wasn't at her side when they left the goldfields, but only 10 percent would go to Trig if they were together.

They'd be together, all right. Even if it meant she shackled him to her. Lucky, of course, didn't know that part of the deal. Trig said it would be better that way, and she believed him.

That first night, her feet had throbbed from her new boots and her arms were rubbery after pulling on the stubborn mules all day, but she wasn't about to let Lucky know that. She'd thought about just bedding down on the ground, but seeing him set up a tent had forced her to set up hers, too.

The days that followed were long; not just in the miles they walked but in how the sun barely left the sky before it rose again. One of the books she'd read said there'd be days when the sun never set. She hadn't quite believed that, but did now, and found it frustrating. A person needs darkness. Not only to rejuvenate, but to think. She did her best planning, her best dreaming, while lying awake at night. But when it was light out, her eyes didn't want to close, and that kept her mind busy.

It was midday, on their fourth day on the trail, when they had to stop to let the mules rest after a particularly steep section. She yawned while settling onto a rock to rest her own feet.

"Having a hard time sleeping at night?"

Surprised Lucky had spoken, she glanced up. They'd been civil to one another since leaving Dabbler, but since the day they'd docked they'd barely shared words, nothing like they had while on the boat. Not so sure she was ready to talk to him now, Maddie reached down and checked the laces of her boots.

"It's easier when its dark, isn't it?"

The urge to know if her voice still worked was too strong to ignore. "You must be used to it, considering you manned the helm at night and slept during the day."

"That didn't make it any easier. I can't say I liked it, either." He pointed toward the trail. "I'm going to scout up around the bend, see if there's a place to set camp."

"Why? It's early yet."

"I know," he said. "But the mules are exhausted. We can't chance losing one."

Maddie didn't say a word as he headed up the trail. Holding a grudge made her insides feel all dark and cloudy. Always had. She'd learned that years ago. Trouble was, when she'd let go of her grudges, mainly those against her father, he'd always reciprocated with another act that left her more vulnerable than the one before.

The deal she'd made with Trig already had her vulnerable enough. She'd attempted to bargain with the percentage, but he'd held strong. Her instincts said there was more behind Trig's doggedness than he let on, for Lucky certainly could take care of himself, but nonetheless, she'd agreed. In part because she didn't want to be alone. Serious gold mining took two people.

She was still in the midst of pondering things when Lucky reappeared. His solemn gaze had her rising to her feet.

"It doesn't get any better around the bend," he said. "But there is a small space someone else used as a camp. We'll spend the night there, let the mules get a good rest and start off again tomorrow."

The short reprieve had refueled her energy, but she respected his judgment, especially when it came to the animals. "Is there water?" she asked.

"Yes, and grass."

She moved to check her packs, as Lucky did, making sure everything was still secure, and then gathered her lead mule's rope.

"Ready?" Lucky asked.

"Yes."

"It's not far," he assured her.

It wasn't far, but the area was little more than an indention in the side of the hill with a tiny pool of water and small patch of grass. She was staking down her mules when Lucky walked over.

"There's not enough room for two tents. We can share mine."

"I don't need a tent," she said, focusing on driving the wooden stake farther into the hard ground.

Lucky took the hammer from her hand and finished the job. "It's cold up here, Maddie. We need the shelter of a tent if we don't want to freeze."

"Sharing a tent wouldn't be proper."

"Proper? We've shared a cabin for months."

She opened her mouth to tell him that wasn't the same, but he was faster.

"Don't you think it's time we called a truce?" Lucky

asked. "What's done is done. There's no sense dwelling on it."

"I wasn't the one dwelling on it," she insisted.

"You weren't?" he asked. "You've barely spoken since we left Dabbler."

She took the hammer from his hand and tied it to the pack. "Because you've barely spoken."

Lucky was right behind her and took her shoulders to spin her around to face him. "I know," he said. "And I don't like it. Can we call a truce?" A grin formed on his lips before he asked, "Please?"

Though she tried, the smile forming on her lips was too strong to hide. There was something about him that made her feel all light and airy, especially when he grinned. And no one had ever said *please* to her before, not like that. "All right."

"Good." His hands slid off her arms. "How about I get a fire going and then you can cook supper while I put up the tent?"

In an attempt to ignore all the silly things happening inside her, Maddie asked, "Is that the only reason you wanted a truce? So I'd cook for you?"

"No," he said. "I'll cook while you put up the tent if you want."

The twinkle in his eyes tickled her, and that made staying mad impossible. "I smelled the beans you burned last night. I'll cook."

"That's my girl," he said while touching the tip of her nose with one finger. "I knew you were still in there."

She frowned, wondering exactly what he meant. He certainly made her think a lot. About many things. He had her feeling things, too. Silly and odd things.

With the afternoon ahead of her, Maddie made a stew

out of jerky and rice for supper, and after setting it to cook in the heavy lidded pot, she took advantage of the water trickling down the mountainside and pooling near the base before flowing out along a miniature stream. She heated several pots full and washed her clothes, as well as the spare shirt Lucky dug out of his bag when she asked. She laid everything out on the rocks to dry and couldn't help but think of those women back on the *Mary Jane*.

They'd been washing clothes constantly, hanging them all over the decks, even their bloomers, for the wind to dry. Dull and plain, her dresses were nothing like theirs had been. Bright and colorful with bows and ribbons and fancy buttons, she could only dream of having such things.

She smiled then. Dream. Someday she'd have dresses as fancy and frilly as those women had. One of every color. Maybe two. Once she found her gold, all her dreams would come true.

"Sure smells good."

The packsaddle he'd been working on now sat next to the other one. As he approached, Maddie gathered the tin pans and forks she'd unpacked earlier. "It should be done. I hope you like it," she added. "I made enough for us to have tomorrow, too."

"Like it or not," he said, "I'll eat it."

Maddie removed the lid, but paused in dishing up the stew. "Why do you say that?"

"Because we aren't here to worry about what we're eating, darling. We're here to find gold."

She grinned then. "You're right. We are." As she handed him the plate, she added, "I still hope you like it."

That night, long after everything was put away and they were both stretched out in his tent, the day was repeating itself inside Maddie's mind. Lucky had said he liked the stew and considering he'd eaten two plates full, she figured he'd been telling the truth. He always did, though, tell the truth that was, which was what she was pondering now.

"Still having a hard time sleeping?" he asked.

"I guess so." Shifting on the hard ground, she turned to look at him. There was barely enough room for the two of them to lie between the angled sides of the tent. "It's different here than on the ship."

He grinned. "Sleeping during the day is easy when you've been up all night."

"Do you always work all night when sailing?"

"Usually."

"Why?"

"It's my duty."

She knew all about duty, and rolled onto her back again, staring at the canvas billowing from the wind. It was chilly this high in the mountains, and tonight seemed colder than the previous ones, which left her with the desire to shake a shiver from her shoulders. "Do you always do that?" she asked. "Fulfill your duties."

"Yes. Every man does."

"No," she argued, as an invisible and heavy weight filled her chest, "they don't."

"Why do you say that?"

Unable to hold it at bay any longer, she let the shiver go and snuggled deeper beneath her blanket before saying, "History."

He scooted closer, pushing an arm beneath her head.

Growing stiff, she turned his way, questioning such behavior.

"You're cold," he said. Curling his arm so her head rested on his shoulder, he pulled his blanket over so it covered both of them. "We'll share our blankets. Maybe then we'll both get some sleep."

She'd shared shelters with men before, plenty of them, out of necessity, and told herself that was what this was, too. No different than sharing the cave with Smitty, or dugouts with her father and the men riding with him had been.

Inside, though, it felt different. Lucky's chin rested on top of her head, and that, as well as his arms, was uniquely comforting. Heat was penetrating her clothing, too, from him, and she turned onto her side, snuggling her backside up against him to gather more.

Needing something to concentrate on besides his warmth and comfort, she asked, "Why do you want gold, Lucky?"

"Just 'cause I do."

"But—"

"Go to sleep, Maddie," he whispered. "We have a hard trail to travel tomorrow."

"Worse than today?" she asked. Even with her head full of questions, the warmth was relaxing and her eyes wanted to close.

"Probably not," he answered.

They both chuckled and Maddie sighed afterward, feeling herself slipping into sleep.

The trail the following day was no worse, but no better than the day before. At this height, snow covered the ground, so they made one bed that night, sharing the blankets beneath and over them, as well as their body heat. From then on, Maddie began to look forward to the nights. She was sleeping sounder than ever and waking up refreshed, ready to face whatever they encountered.

The days were more fun, too, than in the beginning. Lucky was much more jovial. They talked and laughed and planned how they'd mine gold. She told him about sluice boxes and exactly what they'd need to build one. She'd never felt more pride than when he'd said he'd build one first thing.

Going down the other side of the ridge was no easier than going up had been. The ground was rockier and the trail full of sharp pebbles and gravel rather than sand and mud. Fearful of a mule getting stone bruised, Maddie walked with caution, picking routes for the animals to step.

They'd just topped a miniature ridge when Lucky slowed his mules and waved her up beside him. She clicked her tongue, encouraging her mules to pick up their pace. Arriving at his side, she asked, "What? This doesn't look like a good stopping place to me." There wasn't an iota of flat ground; besides, it wasn't time to rest the mules, not yet.

"Look." He pointed down the hill.

Tents and buildings along with a river appeared in the valley below as if Lucky had waved a magic wand rather than pointed.

"Home, sweet, home," he announced.

A shiver tickled her spine. "That's a town."

"Yep. Bittersweet."

"I didn't expect a town," she said.

Lucky started down the hill. "With any luck, darling, we'll be sleeping in real beds tonight."

A chill, not from the wind, seemed to start in her toes and didn't stop tingling until it hit her head, setting a good number of thoughts into motion. The only reason Bass had taken her into towns along the trail had been to leave her there. A warning from Trig flashed through her mind, too. *Don't let him go off on his own,* his uncle had said. *He likes to do that.*

Her gaze settled on Lucky's back. If he thought she'd just trekked halfway across the world, tugging two stubborn mules in her wake, just to be left in town while he went out looking for gold, he had a whole other think coming. She didn't care if she ever slept in a real bed. She would, of course, once she was rich, but until then the ground was just fine. Had been all her life and would continue to be for a while longer. She didn't need his shoulder for a pillow, either. But she would not let him sneak away. Would not.

Hours later, for the town was much farther away than it first appeared, as it usually was when looking down upon things, Maddie had worked herself into a good, steaming fit of anger. Lucky was dang near running toward Bittersweet.

Trig had outfitted her for the excursion, including pocket money, and she was good at finding gold, but Lucky had the map. Therefore, she was trekking just as fast.

Several other sets of prospectors had left Dabbler before them. Their camps had littered the trail, but it hadn't been until the downward trek that she'd seen how many others there were. All afternoon the trail ahead of them had been dotted with people, scurrying toward the town as quickly as she and Lucky. A glance back up the hill told her how many traveled behind them, too. All the time she'd thought it had been just the two of them in this vast wilderness, they'd just been two among many. Another thought had forced its way into her mind, too. Mad Dog. She hadn't thought of him for weeks. That wasn't like her. She still didn't believe he'd follow her all this way, but others were here, and they were after the exact same thing she was. Gold. She had to get to it first.

"Let's see if there's a livery where we can put up the mules and then find a place for ourselves," Lucky said. "Hopefully everything's not full."

"It most likely is," she said. "With the number of folks ahead of us, I think we'd be best just to continue on."

His grin had the effect of cactus needles on her— biting deep and leaving a sting. "Can't hurt to check," he said, all bright and cheerful.

Swallowing a growl, she kept her frustration out of her voice, but did tell him, "If you're that tired we'll just pitch our tent on the edge of town. There isn't any reason to spend money frivolously."

"Yes, Maddie, my girl," Cole said, "there is." He wanted a room—two rooms—almost more than he wanted gold. One more night of cradling Maddie in his arms might just be the death of him. He woke every morning, stiff and sore, neither from the hard ground, and desperately needed a reprieve.

If his uncle had been anywhere at hand, he'd have belly punched him. Putting a man in this type of predicament was flat-out evil.

Luck, which usually followed Cole, seemed to have deserted him. They'd walked from one end of town to the other, and there wasn't a stall to be found for the mules, nor a single bed, let alone two. And Maddie. Aw,

Maddie. Stomping along behind him, lips pinched and eyes snapping, she was about as adorable as he'd ever seen her. Who'd have ever thought he'd find an irate woman becoming? Not him. Yet, she was. Becoming, that was. Feisty, too, glaring at men who'd dared lift a brow as she walked past.

He liked how she could make it clear as glass she didn't want anything to do with men. He'd seen that in Dabbler, back when he'd been avoiding her. Trying to anyway. He'd tried ignoring her on the trail, too, but being next to her every minute of every day had worn him down. Besides, resenting her for wanting gold had been foolish. She couldn't help it any more than he could. Right now, what he was trying to control was how he wanted her. Suggesting they could share a tent had been a foolish idea.

"Let's try the general store," he said.

"What for? Our packs are still full. If you'd quit wasting time, we could —"

"We're spending the night here," he said, stopping her rant. It would be easier to tell her Whiskey Jack had said he'd leave a message in Bittersweet with directions to his camp, but since Cole had yet to find out who might have that message, he didn't mention it to her. "Come on. There's one thing I haven't tried yet."

Her glare was icy as she wrenched on the mule's rope to follow him toward the dry-goods store. Once there, Cole grabbed one of the bags hanging off his front mule and handed her his rope. "Stay close to the door, where I can see you." The town was full of new arrivals and those looking to pick anyone clean. He'd told her the same thing everywhere they'd stopped. Once again, she rolled her eyes at him, but took the rope.

He couldn't help but chuckle as he bounded up the steps. One thing about her, she definitely made life more fun.

The solid wood door opened as he reached the top step.

"I was just closing up," a man said, reaching for a sign hanging on a nail and flipping it to say Closed. "Come back in the morning."

"Just a minute," Cole said. "I'm hoping to make a deal with you."

"No deals. Cash money or gold," the man said, pointing to another sign that said as much in crooked, faded writing. Dressed from head to boots in wool—the shirt red-and-black plaid, the pants a dull gray—the man could have been another miner instead of a merchant. "I'll be open by seven in the morning."

"Just a minute," Cole said, pulling open the drawstring on his bag. "You'll like what I have in here."

It took a moment, but just as he'd thought, curiosity won out and the burly man stepped closer to peek into the bag.

"That's not gold," the merchant said, drawing back.

"Almost as good," Cole said. "It's raisins."

Again, precisely as he'd imagined, a gleam appeared in the man's eyes.

"Raisins?"

Cole nodded.

"A man can't survive on raisins," the merchant whispered.

"I know," Cole said. "But rumor has it, a man can."

The grizzled character glanced around, scratching the chin beneath his thick beard. "Don't know who started that rumor, but it's spread faster than tales of half-pound nuggets. Men are acting as if they're pure gold themselves." Nodding toward the bag, he clarified, "Raisins, that is."

"I've heard that," Cole said. "These will bring you a goodly sum. They're fresh from California. Sailed in on the *Mary Jane* only a few weeks ago." He held out the bag. "Try one. They're still soft."

About to pluck a raisin out of the bag, the merchant stalled. "The *Mary Jane*?"

Cole nodded.

"You aren't Cole DuMont, are you?"

Surprised, Cole nodded. "Yes, I am."

"Well, why didn't you say so?" the man asked, grinning broadly. "Whiskey Jack told me to expect you."

Old lady luck was back. Cole had known it would happen; she never left him for long. "You know Whiskey Jack?"

"Sure enough do. He financed this here store for me. Was in town just a couple of weeks ago. That's when he told me to be on the lookout for you. To give you directions to where his claim is." The man stepped sideways then, eyeing Maddie. "He didn't say nothing about a woman, though."

Standing as she was, holding the reins of four pack mules and wearing a flat-brimmed man's hat and the thick coat she'd bought in Dabbler didn't begin to disguise Maddie was a woman. A fine-looking one, at that. One of quality, too. Cole had thought that right from the beginning. Her frame and stance, the way she held her chin up and head straight, gave her a regal appearance. She was full of stamina and determination, too, and though her background may have been hard, harsh even, she carried none of the weight with her. Not on the outside. He could see her being a rich lady. She'd be a powerful one, too. Not just due to money. She had it in her. A lot like his grandmother.

The hem of her dress was stained by the mud splatters of the trial, but it didn't deflect from the nobleness of her character. It came through no matter what she wore. Perhaps because of the care she gave her personal appearance. Even after hours spent trekking up the mountainside, each night she heated a small pan of water and entered the tent before him to wash. This time of year, streams were plentiful, water melting off the peaks and running down the slopes, and yesterday, when they'd stopped by one such miniature waterfall to rest the mules, she'd warmed enough water to wash her hair.

Cole's lips went dry and he licked them, recalling how she'd left her hair down so it could dry in the midday sun as they'd started walking again. Each time he'd turned around, those long black tresses, sparkling in the sunshine and fluttering around her face and shoulders had sent his pulse beating inside his skin. Her eyes did that to him, too. They were as blue as the gulf waters, and when they filled with merriment, or caught him looking at her, they shone so bright a man could be blinded.

He huffed out a bit of hot air and turned back to the merchant. "Maddie knows more about mining gold than any man." His throat felt as if it held more gravel than the dirt beneath his feet. Partnering up with Maddie had more consequences than any male he could have paired up with, and he was smack-dab in the center of realizing most of those consequences.

The merchant scratched his chin again. "Whiskey

Jack told me to ask you a question. One only you'd know the answer to, just so I wouldn't be giving his location out to anyone."

"Go ahead," Cole encouraged. "Ask away." He needed something—anything—to alter his thoughts.

"How old was Captain Trig DuMont when he started sailing?"

Cole laughed. "He was born sailing." In order to assure the merchant he was the man Whiskey Jack was waiting on, Cole added, "Captain Trig DuMont is my uncle. He and his twin brother, my father Adam DuMont, were born on a ship captained by their father, Belmont DuMont, my grandfather."

Nodding, and smiling, the man held out a hand. "Name's Truman Schlagel. It's good to meet you, Cole DuMont."

"Likewise," Cole replied, shaking hands.

"Now, how much do you want for those raisins?" Truman asked.

"Room and board for our mules and Maddie and me."

"Barn's out back. So's the cabin Whiskey Jack stays in when he's in town. It's not much, but better than a lot of others. Has a real bed and stove, and yours for as long as you want it. Or until Whiskey Jack comes to town."

Maddie desperately wanted to know what all the whispering was about. Cole's laughter, and the other man's, were easy enough to hear, but anything else was drowned out by the sounds of the bustling town, growing louder as evening turned into night. Not by the sun—it still hovered in the sky—but the people, who upon entering town had headed straight for one of the six saloons she'd counted as Lucky had her traipsing from door stoop to door stoop.

She wouldn't deny a man a taste of spirits now and again. Smitty said nothing compared to how a couple sips could warm a man on a cold night, but she'd never abide by all-out drinking. Men who rode with her father had done that—Bass, too. The stench of their breath still had the ability to haunt her at times. She'd known what those men had wanted from her, and how drinking had made them foolish enough to believe they could take it. The memory had her glancing over her shoulder. One had fought hard and got too close once, and she'd shot him. Just in the thigh, but she'd never forgotten it. The brief glimpse she'd gotten of Mad Dog down in California said he still walked with a limp.

Shortly after the shooting, Bass had left her with Smitty. Something she'd always be thankful for.

She was thankful for the gun Trig had given her, too. A fine six-shooter. Mad Dog might never find her here, but it would do every man glancing her way in this muddy little town—aptly named Bittersweet—good to know she wasn't afraid to shoot them where they stood.

"Maddie, this is Truman Schlagel."

Turning her gaze from the busy street to Lucky and the merchant now standing near the mules, she nodded. "Mr. Schlagel."

As bald as a turnip, yet with more gray hair on his face than a bear, the older man grinned, leastwise it appeared that was what happened under all those whiskers.

"Nice to meet you, Mrs. DuMont," he said. "Welcome to Bittersweet."

Her stomach muscles tightened. Though her upbringing had been full of them, she'd never participated in telling lies, and didn't appreciate how Lucky let this one—about them being married—keep going. Just as she opened her mouth to set the tale straight, Lucky opened his.

"There's a cabin out back we'll spend the night in, Maddie, and then head out to where we'll make our claims in the morning." Grinning, Lucky took the rope to his mules. "And Truman invited us to supper. Let's get these animals round back so we can join him."

She nodded her thanks toward the shopkeeper and followed in the wake of Lucky's mules, tugging hard for her tired animals to step up. Still worried he might try to leave—habits were hard things to overcome, and she hadn't trusted Smitty at first, either—she couldn't help but keep glancing back toward town.

"What are you scowling about?" he asked.

"Just wondering why you were so insistent we spend the night in town."

"Because it may be the last chance we get," he said over one shoulder as he led the mules into the barn. "Once we set out to meet up with Whiskey Jack, we may not be back this way for months."

Once all four mules were tied up, she began unloading their heavy burdens. "Why should that matter?"

He stepped closer and hoisted the heavy pack frame off the mule as if it weighed nothing. "I figured you'd like the chance to sleep in a bed."

"I've told you before, I—"

"I know," Lucky interrupted. "But I am used to sleeping in a real bed, and I like it."

His nearness, and his grin, had her heart picking up speed. That had been happening a lot lately, especially at night, when they snuggled to stay warm. No one had ever held her like Lucky did, and she liked it, which went against every grain inside her.

Maddie moved to the next mule, unloading bags and bundles so Lucky could remove the pack frames. Ever since Mad Dog's attack, she'd hated men—except for Smitty—so why didn't she feel that way about Lucky? He didn't scare her, not like others always did. She didn't mind looking at him, either. Actually, she liked looking at him. Even now, with short stubbles of whiskers covering his jawline. They appeared each night even though he shaved every morning. She liked that. The men that rode with her father rarely shaved. They never cut their hair, either, and though Lucky's hair was long, he bound it at the nape of his neck with a leather strap, and as unusual as it was, it fit him.

His hair was thick and dark brown, his eyes that color, too. They were her favorite things about him. The way they twinkled, she could almost hear them laughing. Eyes couldn't laugh, of course. Couldn't make any sound, yet his sure seemed to. They were kind, too. Sometimes when he looked at her, her insides did funny things. Grew all soft and warm and, well, somewhat giddy. To the point it made her cheeks flush and her heart rush. Especially when he winked at her. Which he did often enough. Probably because he knew it made blood rush to her face.

Thinking of such things, she glanced over, and had to turn away to hide the flush of her cheeks when he winked, almost as if he'd known that was exactly what she'd been pondering.

Once the mules were seen to, Lucky took her by the elbow. "Let's go see what this cabin of Whiskey Jack's looks like. We may decide to sleep in our tent after all."

"Why would we do that?" she asked.

He laughed. "You sure are different than every other woman on this earth, Maddie, girl. That's for sure."

"The world would be a dull place if we were all the same," she declared, while trying not to think overly hard about what he might mean.

He laughed again and a few steps later they stopped in front of a tiny cabin made from huge logs. Lucky had to duck in order to walk through the door. She followed, blinking at the darkness. Light flickered. While he replaced the lamp chimney, she turned around to close the door. Not much larger than Captain Trig's cabin back on the ship, there was a bed, a table and two chairs, and a stove.

"Looks fine to me," Maddie said, although she tugged her coat tighter. Being closed up, the air inside the cabin was colder than that outdoors.

"I'll get a fire started," Lucky said. "Then we'll go over to Truman's. He said he has a pot of stew bubbling on the stove."

She crossed the room and pushed a hand deep into the mattress. Though she'd never had a bed of her own, she had grown used to the one on the *Mary Jane*. "When I strike it rich, I am going to get the biggest bed money can buy."

"Are you?"

Spinning around, she plopped onto the bed. Maybe that was why she liked Lucky. He let her talk about all her dreams, even encouraged it, as if he, too, believed they'd all come true. "Yes, I am. The softest, biggest bed ever, with lots of pillows."

Lucky grinned, but didn't say anything as he added more kindling to the flames. She leaned back to rest on her elbows. The other thing she was going to buy was a bathtub like Mrs. Smother had back in Seattle. At the time, she'd been too preoccupied with escaping to appreciate the luxury it provided. After the cold streams of Alaska, she found herself thinking about that big tub with its hot and cold water more and more.

Staring up at the crossbeams of the ceiling, she imagined she'd have no trouble falling asleep tonight. With only one little window above the headboard of the bed the daylight wouldn't bother her at all.

Maddie scooted across the bed to get a better look out that one window. What she noticed had her jumping to her feet and digging in her coat pocket at the same time.

Out the door in a flash, gun in hand, she shouted, "You there, get away from that barn."

Two men, looking about as rough as those who'd ridden with Bass, spun from the door. Lucky shouted her name and arrived at her side, yet she never took her eyes or the aim of the six-shooter off the men.

"Get away from the barn," she repeated, slower and more meaningful.

The men, hands in the air, backed up, and then, like two whipped dogs, spun around and fled. Maddie would have fired shots over their heads, just so they'd know not to come back, but Lucky snatched the gun from her hand.

"What do you think you're doing?" he asked, lowering the hammer on the trigger.

"Protecting our belongings," she said. "They were going to steal them."

"How do you know that?"

"What else would they be doing?"

Lucky handed her back the gun. "That's probably what they were thinking about doing, but you don't go running out the door."

"What do you do, then?" she asked. "Stay inside and let them steal you blind?"

"No." His gaze was in the direction the men had ske-daddled, and he frowned slightly. "Sometimes, Maddie, being a bit neighborly will get you further than running out with guns drawn." He waved a hand in the general direction of the barn. "Those men could have had guns, too, and shot you."

"That's why I had to get the jump on them," she said. "Everyone knows that."

He smiled and scratched a brow. "Sometimes," he said, as if he had to agree with her. "But sometimes a person's better off to act kindly. You know, not upset anyone."

She checked the chamber of her gun to make sure he'd properly uncocked it before putting it back in her pocket. "Tell me how that works for you, Lucky," she said. "Right after some man shoots you full of holes."

"Maddie," he said slowly.

There was a hint of scorn in his tone, and that smarted. "I've mined gold, Lucky, but even before then I knew when men were considering stealing from me."

He opened his mouth.

She shook her head. "I know when it's time to be neighborly, too, so don't try giving me a lesson in manners, or whatever it is you're trying to do. Those men were up to no good, and no amount of your sweet talk is going to make me believe otherwise."

"Sweet talk?" He shook his head. "I'm not trying to sweet-talk you, Maddie. This country is full of men,

and we'll be a lot better off making friends than ene-
mies with the lot of them."

"Well," she said, taking note of the seriousness of his
gaze, "I'll gladly make friends with any of those who
don't try to steal from me."

"Already had some thieves sneaking about, did we?"
someone behind them said.

"Yes, we did," Maddie assured, turning to where
Truman Schlagel stood on his back stoop. She also tried
to keep a smirk off her lips.

"Well, don't worry," the man said. "Gunther will be
here shortly. He'll keep them at bay."

"Who's Gunther?" Lucky took her arm and steered
her toward the stoop.

"My night watchman," the merchant explained.
"Don't have much trouble until newbies arrive in town.
Then Gunther guards my place all night. I'd be stolen
blind otherwise, probably killed, too."

Maddie couldn't help but look up at Lucky. "Still
want to make friends with those men?"

Chapter Five

Cole didn't answer Maddie's smug little remark, nor did he comment on how she befriended Truman while they ate. The two of them chattered nonstop like two long-lost friends. She was something. Ready to shoot one man and then charm the next. Admitting she had a knack of knowing which one to pick—between the good and bad—didn't make Cole feel any better.

Gunther arrived during the meal. A huge Alaskan with skin as brown and wrinkled as dried-out leather whom anyone would question going toe-to-toe against. The guard gobbled down a plate of stew and left without grunting out more than three words. Cole felt like doing the same thing—grunting.

He wasn't in any better of a mood once he and Maddie entered the cabin again, either. The bed looked smaller than the little settee in his mother's parlor. He and Maddie would be sleeping on top of each other. Spinning, he grabbed hold of the doorknob.

"Where are you going?"

"Out," he answered, wrenching open the door.

"Are you still mad at me about those men?"

"No, I never was mad at you," Cole answered. "Just stay inside. I'll be back."

She rushed past him and plastered herself against the door. "You aren't leaving."

He started to move her aside, but then saw the fear in her eyes. His heart tumbled, landing near his feet. "No, I'm not leaving." It hurt that she'd think so low of him. He lifted her chin to look her square in the eye. "I wouldn't leave you here."

Her cheeks grew rosy as her gaze fell.

"I'm just going to check on things. The mules and such." He released her chin and waited for her to step aside. When she did, he said, "You stay inside where it's warm. I won't be long."

Truman was outside, smoking his pipe and leaning against the side of his store. Built of huge logs, the building looked as if it would be there through the next two centuries. Likely, it would last longer than the town. He'd seen that before. Towns that used to be but no longer were all along the seashore. There were all sorts of reasons for communities to build up and then empty out just as quickly. Shipyards were like that, too. Not DuMont Shipping, though. That was what he had to remember. Had to focus on.

"There's nothing to worry about," Truman said, pausing to take several short puffs of his pipe. "Gunther's in the barn. He can see anyone coming up the road."

Cole walked closer and then knocked a clump of dried mud off the side of his boot on a chunk of wood. He had plenty of worries, but they didn't include the barn or Gunther.

"I ain't figured out if you're a smart man or a fool."

Looking up, Cole waited for the other man to continue. It was obvious Truman would as soon as he was done drawing in smoke. Cole considered spinning around and leaving, but didn't, and he couldn't say why. Other than he wasn't ready to be shut in a cabin with Maddie. No matter how hard he tried to concentrate on other things, four walls and a ceiling seemed much more intimate than a tent, and that tiny bed had sent desires throbbing in his loins.

Truman waved his pipe toward the cabin. "That little darling of yours is going to cause a stir. Plenty of men might try to steal her right beneath your nose."

"I'm aware of that," Cole admitted.

"So," Truman said questioningly, "are you a smart man or a fool?"

Cole let his gaze rest on the cabin for a few minutes. He wasn't exactly sure himself. "Maybe a bit of both, but most of all I'm lucky." His confidence was as strong as ever—it had just shifted, and he wasn't quite sure what to make of that.

Truman laughed. "I'd agree." After a few more puffs on his pipe, he knocked out the embers and sighed heavily. "There are a few women up here, but not wives. The gals up here are looking to make it rich, just like the men. They don't plan on panning gold, though. They plan on finding it in other places, mainly in men's pockets. You best keep a close eye on the one you have there."

"I plan on it," Cole answered.

Truman changed the subject then, started talking about where the most color had been found and a variety of other topics. After more than an hour, when the merchant said he had to turn in, Cole agreed and made his way back to the cabin. The bed hadn't grown. He and Maddie would still be crowded, but Truman was right—she was as much a sought-after commodity as raisins were. Trig had known that, too, which was why he made Cole promise to look out for her—and return her to Seattle safe and sound.

Maybe he wasn't so lucky after all. Downright foolish might be a better description.

Once inside the cabin, Cole went to the stove to add a log, but a whisper came across the room.

"Please don't. It's plenty warm in here."

It was rather toasty. He shut the little cast-iron door and moved to a chair to remove his boots. "You covered the window."

"With one of the blankets off the bed," she answered. "We won't need it. Don't really need any of them."

"Sleeping in the tent got us accustomed to the cold." Hot from head to toe—but not because of the woodstove—he crawled onto the bed and stretched out.

"There's a blanket at the foot of the bed if you need it."

"I'm fine," he answered, folding his arms beneath his head.

"Me, too."

"Good night."

She didn't reply; instead, the mattress shifted as she rolled onto her side. The cabin still wasn't dark enough to hide the glimmer of her eyes. "How much gold do you think we'll find?"

"As much as we need," he answered, trying to keep his gaze on the ceiling.

"How do you know that?"

"Because we won't stop looking until we do."

She went quiet again, before finally asking, "How will we know when we have enough?"

"We just will," he said. "Go to sleep now, Maddie. We'll want to get an early start."

He'd thought she had gone to sleep until she asked, "Why'd you let Truman think we're married?"

"To keep you safe," he answered without thought.

"Thank you." Then, soft, like a feather falling from the sky, her hand landed on his chest and stayed there long after she whispered, "Night, Lucky."

Lady luck did live in his corner, and would continue to. He'd just never known what that meant before, or the penalties she carried. Bringing a woman into the goldfields was one thing, but being responsible for her another.

Maddie made it easy, though. She was good company and carried her own weight, even when he suggested she let him take care of certain things. Guilt still churned in his stomach for what he'd said to her back on the *Mary Jane*, about being a weight around his neck. She'd been let down before, left—the fear he'd seen in her eyes earlier proved that, which was a whole different problem. He was the last man who should be responsible for her. He'd left his mother and Rachel when they'd begged him not to, and there was nothing to say he wouldn't do it again.

The big logs used to build the cabin hadn't had time to warm, and as soon as the little stove went cold, so did the darkened space. Chilled, Cole bent down to pull the blankets over both himself and Maddie, and tucked her tight against him when she snuggled closer. He fell asleep then, as if it had been impossible until his arms were around her.

* * *

Warm and content, Maddie fought waking up. She'd thought sleeping next to Lucky in a tent on the hard ground, had provided her with hours of wonderful rest, but snuggling in his arms in a soft, comfortable bed, well, she doubted even clouds in heaven could compare. Gliding her hand all the way across his shirt, she grasped his far side, nestling just a bit closer for a few more minutes.

"It's time to get up," he mumbled above her head.

"I know," she answered. "I just don't want to. Not yet."

"Well, darling, you don't have a choice."

He moved so quickly, throwing back the covers and sliding off the bed, her head rolled onto a pillow before she had a chance to lift it off his chest. She flipped onto her back, stretching her arms overhead as he pulled the blanket off the window.

"We need to hit the trail before anyone else," he said, tossing the blanket at the foot of the bed, "and stay ahead of them."

Maddie scooted to the edge of the bed and bent down to pluck out the socks she'd rolled up and stuffed inside each boot last night. That was from habit, to keep unwanted crawlies from sneaking their way in while she slept. It was too cold for crawlies in Alaska, but she couldn't help from doing such each night. "Are others going toward Whiskey Jack's claim?"

Lucky had tugged on his boots and stood from the chair he'd taken. "Can't say. Truman said he only gave us the directions, but others might try to follow, or just be going that way. It's upriver."

After clipping her socks to her garters, she pulled on

her boots and fastened them. "I'll make up the bed, then get some breakfast fixings from our packs."

"No need," Lucky said. "Truman said to visit his kitchen this morning. He has a few things to send with us for Whiskey Jack."

"I hope it's not much," she answered, already straightening the covers. "The mules are already packed tight."

Lucky let out a chuckle, and she glanced his way, wondering what he found funny. He did that now and again—laughed at something she said as if he knew something she didn't, like last night when he'd chuckled about not staying in the cabin. It flustered her, and she still didn't understand what he meant about her not being like other women. It most likely was true, considering she'd never known many women, therefore didn't know if she was like others or not.

While she gathered her coat and such, he hauled in an armload of wood, saying it was the neighborly thing to do, replace what they'd used up. Maddie pondered that, as she had many things he'd said or done since the night they'd met. She didn't know much about being neighborly, or about women—the two days she'd been at Mrs. Smother's house had been spent doing laundry and scrubbing floors, which hadn't taught her much—but she had lived around men all her life. However, Lucky wasn't like any of the men she'd known. He wasn't gruff or rude, nor did he insist she was wrong all the time.

Actually, he was gracious in a lot of ways, like now, the way he held the door for her to exit the cabin.

Breakfast was a noisy affair. Gunther's two sons joined them for the meal. Truman explained they kept people honest during the day, and considering Gunther was small compared to his sons, Maddie understood how that might happen—keeping people honest. She had to wonder if people actually dared enter the store with these two men sitting next to the door.

Before long she and Lucky had said their goodbyes and had started up the path leading to the ridge—above the opposite side of town from which they'd entered yesterday. The trail wasn't as well-worn, and no one appeared to be ahead or behind them. It seemed to take forever for them to top the ridge and start along a narrow trail. "Seems to me," she said, whilst looking down into the valley where one could see the entire town laid out along the riverbank, "plenty of folks are taking boats upriver. Why didn't we do that?"

"Because we have mules," Lucky answered, "and this is the route Whiskey Jack said to take." He paused long enough to glance her way. "You getting tired?"

"No." She hadn't meant to sound as if she was complaining, just curious. "How long will it take us?"

"Truman said the better part of the day."

She nodded, glancing back to the river and hoping those folks wouldn't make better time. Finding the right claim was a lengthy process, and having a crowd searching the same area would make her feel rushed or miss what she was looking for.

"Keep your eyes on the trail," Lucky said. "All the miniwaterfalls coming down this mountain are making the ground slick."

Maddie was about to say she'd noticed that when the ground disappeared beneath her and she was on her bottom, sliding downhill fast.

Her stop was so sudden, she screeched at the pain of both arms practically being wrenched from their sockets. Realization hit as she drew in a breath. She was hanging over the edge of the mountain, holding on to nothing but the lead mule's rope, which was slowly slipping from her grip. Seizing a brief moment, she took in her predicament. Less than five feet on either side of her was solid ground. Rocks and boulders, but all out of reach. Right smack in the middle, where she was, there was nothing below, not for a long way.

The rope started jerking uncontrollably, which meant the mules were bucking, and holding on grew more difficult by the second. Both arms stretched over her head, and burning from the strain, Maddie squeezed her eyes shut, focusing until she managed to wrap the rope around each wrist. Concentrating again, using all her efforts, she flipped around to face the hillside instead of the nothingness of sky. Mud and water splattered her face, and she couldn't see the mules above her, just the edge of the ridge that had given way.

Lucky's face appeared, peering over the edge, but too far away to reach her. "Don't let go, Maddie!" he shouted. "Don't you dare let go."

Dare had nothing to do with it. She'd seen what was beneath her. Not much for several yards, then jagged, wicked rocks. Kicking her feet proved the years of water trickling down the hillside had left nothing but wet, slick rocks her boots couldn't cling to.

Lucky disappeared and the jarring on her arms eased. She blinked at the water trickling over the edge and bent her head backward as far as her neck allowed, watching the spot as fear set in.

He was back a moment later. "I'm going to pull you up!" Lucky shouted. "Don't let go!"

Claws of panic dug into her throat and prevented

any words from forming, and the constant spray of water didn't allow her to nod. Inside, though, she was screaming, *Hurry, please, hurry.* Her fingers were tingling, going numb as the rope cut into her wrists, and her shoulders stung from the weight of her body. Her lungs were burning, too, and although she told herself to breathe, it was impossible. The water hitting her face kept stealing her breath. Lucky was gone again, and there was no sensation of moving. Not upward, and she wanted to scream, beg him to pull her up, but that was as impossible as everything else.

She did start to move then, upward. All of a sudden Lucky was only a few feet away and grabbed hold of her elbows. In a rush, he tugged her over the edge, where he rolled with her, one over the other until they collided with the mountain wall.

Maddie lay there, gathering her wits and air, and praising the solid ground beneath her. Lucky was untangling the rope from her wrists. She tried to help, but her arms felt heavy and didn't want to move no matter how hard she attempted to use them.

He wiped the water from her face then and grasped her shoulders. "Where are you hurt?"

"Nowhere." The word burned, and sensation returned to the rest of her body, making her moan. "Everywhere."

"Where's everywhere, darling?" he asked, running both hands down her arms.

Feeling as if they'd been asleep and awakened by his touch, her arms begin to tingle, as if being poked with a million pins and needles. Her entire body started trembling and wouldn't stop.

His hands ran over her rib cage and down her legs

before he leaned over her again and cupped her cheeks. "Where's everywhere? I've got to know if something is broken."

Closing her eyes, she concentrated on her limbs, her body. Both shoulders ached and her backside stung, but there was no severe pain. "Nothing's broken."

"You sure?"

"Yes, I'm sure." Remorse hit then, hard and fast. "I'm sorry, I didn't—"

"Shh," he said, leaning down and pressing his forehead against hers. "Nothing to be sorry about, darling," he whispered.

Prepared for a reprimand, for she hadn't been paying as close of attention as the trail demanded, his kindness made her eyes sting. "But I should have—"

"Hush now," he said softly.

He kissed her forehead then; at least that was what it felt like. She'd never been kissed anywhere, so she couldn't say for sure. His hands grasped her shoulders again and he lifted her into a sitting position. Maddie's mind was spinning, especially as his arms folded around her as he held her tightly. Hugged her. She'd only been hugged one other time, by Smitty when they'd said their final goodbye. Her chest started burning and it wasn't just her lungs—it was her heart warming. Her arms, no longer useless, wrapped around Lucky's waist, held on to him. Held on tighter as water dripped from her eyes. She never cried. Never. Not even when she'd said goodbye to Smitty.

"Shh," Lucky whispered again. "It's all right, darling. You're safe. Lucky has you."

She knew that, and for some unexplainable reason more tears formed, rushing down her cheeks.

They stayed like that, wrapped in each other's arms for some time, until her tears ran dry and her breathing returned. The burning in her chest eased, too. Turned into a soft, warm sensation that eventually allowed her to exhale.

He released his hold, and she let go of him as he leaned back. His grin was as brash and charming as ever. "Feeling better?"

Not overly sure what she was feeling, yet inclined to answer, Maddie nodded.

"You scared the life out of me, Maddie, girl." He leaned forward and kissed her forehead again. While his lips were still pressed against her skin, he whispered, "The very life out of me."

He was so kind and understanding. Had been right from the start, and that was unusual for her life. She was used to looking out for herself, and had been amiss in not paying attention, watching the valley instead of the trail.

Everything returned in a rush, though this time worry overtook her instead of fear. "The mules."

"They're right there." He pointed to where all four animals stood against the mountainside a few feet away before he took hold of both of her elbows. "Do you think you can stand?"

"Yes," she answered. "I'm fine."

Although her legs felt as rickety and unsteady as a three-legged chair, she willed her knees to do their job as he helped her to her feet. Lucky didn't let loose of her elbows, even after she nodded, silently telling him she could stand on her own.

His smile grew remarkably tender, and his gaze held something Maddie couldn't describe. She'd never seen anything like it and had to close her eyes, hoping to seal it in her memory so she could analyze it later, because right now it was causing her heart to miss beats uncontrollably.

"Aw, darling."

She opened her eyes at his whisper, but he was too close to see, and the next instant his lips, warm and moist, connected with hers. The sensation was like being struck by lightning, or something out of the realm of the world she'd known all her life. Her eyes closed once again, as if her mind, without telling her why, wanted to seal this, too, into her memory.

His lips left hers but only to return again, like a flat rock thrown just right, so it would gently skim over the top of a pond. She'd always been amazed by that, and this was just as incredible. When Lucky's lips settled upon hers for an extended length of time, her knees threatened to give way all over again.

As gentle and perfect as the kiss had started—she was sure this time that it was a kiss—it ended, and Lucky once again folded his arms around her and held her tight. She didn't know when her arms had wrapped around his waist, but they had, and she kept them there, hugging him in return.

They parted by some mutual, silent understanding a short time later. Maddie wasn't sure what to do, how to react, and wondered if she should be embarrassed, letting him kiss her like that, but couldn't come up with a reason why. Not when deep inside she was longing to be as close to him as possible. It was strong, similar to how badly she wanted gold.

But that couldn't be. She didn't want anything as badly as she wanted gold. "Why—why'd you do that?"

"Do what?"

Her cheeks burned. "Kiss me."

He stared at her for a long time, but it wasn't a harsh or unkind stare. It was thoughtful and that confused her, or maybe scared her, a bit.

"That wasn't a kiss," he finally said.

"Yes, it was," she argued. "You kissed me. Why?"

He sighed. "Because I'm glad you're all right, but that wasn't a kiss. If I were to kiss you, really kiss you, you'd know it." He turned her around by her shoulders. "You walk ahead of me. I'll bring the mules."

More confused than ever, but having no idea what to say or do, she replied, "You can't lead all four mules."

"Sure I can."

She had no doubt he could. He seemed capable of doing most anything, yet she had to pull her own weight. Always had. "No, I'll follow you. I can lead my own mules."

He laughed and she spun around. There was a teasing glimmer in his brown eyes. "I know you can, darling, but this one time, you're going to do what I say." He spun her back around. "Until we're off this ridge, you'll walk in front of me and I'll lead all four mules. Now start walking. Just go slow and stay next to the wall."

"But—"

"Maddie," he said sterner than before. "Start walking."

For a moment she considered protesting again, but he had just saved her life; therefore, she put one wobbly foot in front of the other. Considering how her entire being trembled, not leading mules was probably smart, at least for a short distance.

The distance turned out to be much more than short.

By the time they rounded a corner where a grassy pla-
teau stretched out before them, Maddie was not only
thankful to be off the tedious trial, she'd regained a
goodly amount of strength.

"Let's stop over there," Lucky said, "near that clump
of trees."

Maddie led the way, seeing to her two mules while
Lucky saw to his. Her animals didn't appear affected
at all by Maddie's recent suspension from the edge of
the cliff. Not even the rope was frayed. Her insides
were, and might never be the same. She glanced toward
Lucky as he dug in a pack, and her heart skipped a beat.
Whether he wanted to admit it or not, he'd kissed her,
and whether she wanted to admit it or not, she'd liked it.

Joining her on the rock, he handed over a napkin
full of raisins, a chunk of bread and a strip of jerky.
"How're you doing?"

"Fine," she answered, nibbling on a few raisins.
She'd never tasted them until this trip and was glad he
hadn't sold them all to Truman. They were sweet and
moist and she could understand why the miners liked
them so much. Yet the raisins didn't distract her from
thoughts of his kisses for too long. She needed to stop
thinking about it, though. "How much farther do you
think it is?"

"Not exactly sure," he answered. "There should be a
large outcropping of rocks soon, and we're to turn left
shortly before reaching them, then there'll be a creek
to follow until we come to the river."

"That's where Whiskey Jack is?"

He shook his head and finished chewing his bread
before answering, "Nope, we have to go someway upriver until we come to his camp." After a swallow from

the canteen, which he then handed to her, he said, "We can make camp here. Rest for a while if you're too tired."

"No." She glanced at the sky, but hadn't been able to figure out the time of day up here, not by the sun anyway. Walking though would give her time to think. "I'd rather keep going. We can still make his camp today, don't you think?"

"I suspect so, but I don't want you going on if you're hurt."

"I'm not hurt." Gesturing toward her coat and skirt, which were now dry, but dirtier than anything she'd ever worn since growing old enough to wash her own clothes, she said, "I may look a mess, but I'm fine. Really, I am."

Lucky eyed her critically for several moments before he nodded. "All right, after the mules have rested we'll take off again."

They ate the rest of their meal in silence, other than the noise of the mules munching and stomping now and again. Once Maddie was done, she folded her napkin into a small square. She was contemplating the kiss again. What had he meant when he'd said she'd know a real kiss when it happened? That had been a real kiss.

He shook out his napkin before folding it, as well. "So," he asked, "besides buying the biggest bed possible, what are you going to do with your gold?"

The breath she drew in was as wistful as the dreams that filled her head. "I'm going to build a big house and fill it with furniture, including a bathtub. It'll have a big kitchen, too, with a never-ending supply of food, and I'll hire someone to cook all sorts of things."

The smile had slipped from Lucky's face, and Maddie held her breath, wondering why.

"Where are you going to build this house?" he asked.

Surprised by his question, she shrugged. "I don't know. I'll return to Colorado, to put a marker on Smitty's grave, but I don't know if I'd want to live there." If she went south again, Mad Dog might find her, and she wasn't ready to contemplate that. "Will you go sailing again? After you find your gold?"

Chapter Six

"No," Cole said. He'd head straight to New Orleans. Not to live, but to turn over a goodly sum of money. Show his mother leaving had been a good thing. For him and the family. For Rachel, too. Robbie had said she'd married James Hinz two years ago. Other than feeling a bit sorry for James, the news had been of little interest.

It was hard to say what he'd do after visiting his family. He might return to sailing with Trig, but that had lost some of its appeal. Yet living in one place wasn't for him. Unlike Maddie. The fear from seeing her hanging over the edge of that cliff was still as fresh in his mind as the taste of her lips on his mouth. Not even the sweetness of the raisins had diminished that. Cole sprang to his feet. "We better get moving before the mules decide to take a nap."

Arriving at Whiskey Jack's camp was more important now than ever. The desires he felt were getting too hard to ignore. Being alone with her had long ago grown testing, but it was now downright dangerous. Kissing her had been more foolish than sharing a tent. It had been an impulse. A foolish, reckless whim. But seeing her in such danger and then knowing she was safe had done something to him.

There was no trail, but the ground was even, leaving plenty of room for them to walk side by side, which seemed to give Maddie free rein to chat. And she did. About the big house she'd build, all the servants she'd hire and how warm and comfortable the big bed she'd buy would be.

Cole, shy of moaning, commented now and again while his mind toyed with other things. Like how comfortable he imagined that big bed she spoke of could be. He could imagine she'd get that entire house, servants and all. It was also easy to imagine kissing her again. Really kissing her. Like he'd wanted to, but had held back.

They were so different. Him and her. He already had all the things she wanted. A fine house. Big, comfortable beds. Servants. Food. They'd just never been enough for him. And they never would be. He wanted adventure. Always had. Gran had said he was just like his father and grandfather and that he shouldn't try to change that.

"Look," she said, catching his attention. "Do you think that's the outcropping?"

In the distance, a large set of jagged rocks stretched out from the mountain as if they were trying to start their own range. "I do believe that's it," he said.

Little more than a mile later, they crossed the creek and they started following it downstream. The landscape changed again, taking them through a wooded and swampy area full of scrawny tamarack trees. The trees gave way next to a river, its shoreline wide and sandy, and much to Cole's relief, for Maddie's steps had grown slower, as had the mules', they arrived at Whiskey Jack's camp less than an hour later.

The old man saw them coming and shouted, "Ahoy!" loud enough that it echoed along the valley over and over.

"Is that Whiskey Jack?" Maddie asked.

"Sure enough is," Cole answered.

"He's a friend of Trig's?"

"A friend of the entire family. He sailed with my grandfather years ago." Cole hadn't shared a lot about his family, or Whiskey Jack. At first because he hadn't planned on taking her into the goldfields with him. Later, he'd kept quiet because he hadn't wanted Whiskey Jack to scare her out of her pantaloons. However, considering how feisty Maddie was, there probably wasn't much that could scare her.

Maybe that was why her scream startled him so much. Snapping his head her way, he snatched the gun from her hand before she fired. "Damn, you're quick with that thing," Cole said, uncocking the lever as he had last night.

Protecting her head with both hands, she cowered slightly while Homer zoomed above them. "What is that?"

"A bird," Cole answered.

"I've never seen one like that," she squealed, ducking as Homer swooped lower.

Whiskey Jack whistled and the bird made a graceful arch, changing directions to fly back toward his owner.

"Homer's a macaw," Cole explained while untwisting the lead rope she'd managed to wrap all the way around her wrist. "Whiskey Jack's had him for as long as I can remember."

"It's as big as a goose," Maddie said, taking the rope belonging to her mules.

"Almost," Cole agreed. It was the little things he liked about her. No matter what the situation, she remained steadfast, kept her head and wits about her. "Just a lot more colorful," he added, referring to Homer's bright red, blue and yellow feathers. "Stay calm around him," Cole warned as he handed back her gun. "He doesn't like fast movements and is very protective of Whiskey Jack and his possessions."

"He must be awfully old," she said gesturing her chin toward the short man standing near a fire ring. "Both of them."

"Yes, they are," Cole answered, chuckling. The man hadn't changed in years, except for his clothes. Right now, he had on a hide coat, and it was hard to tell where the human hair stopped and the fur started. There was no way to guess how old Jack might be, either, considering that he'd seemed ancient decades ago, when he'd visited the family with Uncle Trig.

Homer was strutting back and forth in front of his owner like a guard dog and Cole, having witnessed the bird snap some good-size branches in two with its beak more than once, had stopped Maddie and the mules from taking any steps closer.

"You made it," Whiskey Jack said in greeting.

"Yes, we did," Cole answered.

"Who's the gal?"

"This is Maddie."

Whiskey Jack scratched at the long black-and-gray beard hanging from his lips to his chest while squinting, casting his gaze from Maddie's toes to her nose. Cole held his breath. He'd wondered what the old man's reaction would be to having a woman in the camp, but ultimately had decided that if she wasn't welcome, they'd go out on their own.

"Homer," Whiskey Jack finally said, "you best be on your best behavior. No cussing around the lady."

"No cussing," the bird repeated. "No cussing."

Maddie, eyes wide, turned his way. "It talks?"

"Yep," Cole answered, laughing.

"More than I want at times," Whiskey Jack said. "Put the mules over in the paddock with Emily." He gestured toward a mule in a small fenced-in area. "No sense unpacking all your goods. I've got plenty and you can use my extra tent until you stake your claim." Waving toward his smoking fire, he added, "Just frying up some fish for supper. Got more than enough. Hurry up, it's almost done."

Relieved by their welcome, Cole did as instructed, with Maddie helping him. There were a total of four tents and a small shelter made of tree trunks for the mules to be out of the weather when necessary. The main tent was twice as large as the others and had a wooden base a good three feet high. He'd have to take a closer look at that one in order to build a similar one for him and Maddie when they needed to set up camp.

After they'd carried the last of their possessions inside a small storage tent, Cole untied a bag of raisins. As they walked toward the scent of frying fish, he handed Maddie a palmful of the dried fruits. "Feed these to Homer. He'll remember and like you."

"Does everything like raisins?"

"Just about," he answered, chuckling again. He liked that about her, too—how she made him laugh.

"Weather's been good," Whiskey Jack said as they approached. "River's flowing stronger every day."

Cole turned over a stump and indicated Maddie could sit on it. "Bringing gold with it, I hope," he said while taking a seat on another stump.

Whiskey Jack let out a chortle and Homer shrieked, which not only stung Cole's ears, it startled Maddie almost off her stump. He reached over and laid a hand on her knee. Mud had crusted on her skirt, but still his palm stung. If not for the shimmer in her eyes, he might have withdrawn his hand.

"There's gold, that's for sure," Whiskey Jack said. "Lots of color in this area. More than I can gather. Sharing it with Belmont's grandson seemed the right choice. He shared his riches with me on more than one voyage." A smile showed the old man didn't have many teeth left, yet his weathered face turned serene when he asked, "How's your gran these days? I ain't seen her in a long time. A very long time."

"She's doing well," Cole answered. His insides took on a splattering of warmth, and he withheld the news about the hurricane for now. "Still running the warehouses, though mostly from a rocking chair on the front porch of her house."

Whiskey Jack laughed. "You know, son, there's women and then there's ladies. Your gran's a lady. Always was. I remember the first day we ever laid eyes on her, Belmont and I. We'd just shored our schooner at a small town several miles north of Boston. Something had spooked the two fine white horses pulling her carriage. Belmont took after them as though he was half horse himself."

Cole grinned, having heard the story several times.

"What happened?" Maddie asked.

The way she was pitching the raisins, one by one, toward Homer without looking at the bird had Cole biting his lip. She knew about animals, too.

"Belmont stopped the horses," Whiskey Jack said. "And before we set sail two months later, Belmont and Annabelle were married. She gave birth to Cole's father on that first voyage, along with his uncle Trig. I remember that day, too. Those were two fine-looking babies."

Whiskey Jack pulled the pan off the fire and slid the fish onto three plates he'd balanced on the rocks. Using a nearby stick, he shooed Homer from getting too close as he asked, "Got any more of those raisins you're giving my bird?"

Maddie glanced his way and Cole nodded before he reached for the bag by his feet.

"Yes, we do," she answered. "I'll wash my hands and serve some with the fish."

Cole hid his grin again as Whiskey Jack lifted both brows until they almost touched his cap. The old man rose off his stump. "Well, come on, boy, guess we better wash, too." He waved his stick at his bird. "Don't touch my fish or you'll be in that pan for breakfast."

The bird squawked and strutted toward the water along with everyone else.

"Women like to do that," Whiskey Jack said. "Turn everyone into raccoons. Washing hands. Washing food. Washing clothes."

Already having enough to think about, Cole held his opinion, and shortly they all walked back to the fire, where they ate fish and raisins.

Maddie enamored Whiskey Jack as quickly as she had Truman Schlagel back in Bittersweet. She captivated Homer, too. The bird rubbed his head against her knee like a housecat looking for a scratch.

Gran would be impressed. She'd told him to watch out for silly and prissy women. Gran had been the only one who understood how smothered he'd felt by his mother. Rachel, too.

Cole was lost in imagining Gran and Maddie meeting when a squawk brought his attention back to the present. Maddie and Whiskey Jack were laughing at how Homer was saying Maddie's name and squawking with self-imposed pride at getting it right.

"You have a protector, now, girl," Whiskey Jack said. "Not even a grizzly bear would dare get close to you. Homer will see to that."

Maddie laughed. "He can be a bit frightful."

Before Whiskey Jack started in praising his bird again, Cole rose to his feet. "I'll be back in a few minutes." He winked at the concern in Maddie's gaze and grinned as her cheeks turned red. Getting such reactions out of her gave him an inner thrill. However, this afternoon still weighed heavy on his mind. Maddie could have died falling off that ridge.

In the first tent he found her bag of clothes and then gathered up their blankets. Bundling everything together, he carried it all into the next tent. There he cleared out a space on the canvas covering the ground and, using some of the furs piled in one corner, made a pallet, adding their blankets to the top and setting her bag of clothes on top of them. She'd want to change out of her muddy dress before going to bed, and a flash of her wearing little more than her underclothes danced in his head. He wouldn't mind snuggling up to her dressed like that, or not dressed at all.

Cole shook his head, trying to shatter the idea, but it had stuck, and would take a very strong will to make it disappear.

He returned to the fire. "Everything's in the tent," he said before nodding toward the sun that was level with the earth, yet neither sinking nor rising. "It's been a long day."

A tremendous sigh gathered inside Maddie. She didn't want to be rude, but she was exhausted. Thanking Lucky for his thoughtfulness with a nod, she brushed a hand over Homer's head one last time before gathering her skirt to rise off the stump. The crusted mud was hard beneath her palm, and she turned to Lucky, wondering how to tell him she'd need some time alone.

"I assumed you'd like to change," he said, taking a seat on the stump he'd sat on earlier. "I put your bag in the tent."

A rush of warmth flooded her system, including her cheeks. She'd never met anyone as considerate as him.

"Take your time," he said. "I'm going to visit for a while."

A bit tongue-tied, Maddie nodded before managing to whisper, "Thank you."

The endearing warmth she felt heightened as she entered the tent. Lucky had also laid out a pallet for them to sleep upon, complete with their blankets. The sight of her bundle of clothes made her feel a bit misty-eyed. Smitty had watched out for her, but not even he had been as caring as Lucky. She didn't know what to think of all that, nor how to act.

Kissing him this afternoon still hovered in her thoughts, which was frustrating. Now that they'd arrived, gold should be the only thing on her mind.

Convinced she could control whatever was going on inside her, Maddie pulled her clean clothes from the bag and shook the wrinkles from the dress Mrs. Smother had provided. It was a colorless gray—the blue one she'd put on after her bath had disappeared after that first night. This one was a lot like her old one and as serviceable. She'd added the cost of it to the funds she owed Trig. Other dresses came to mind once more, colorful, fancy ones, and this time she wondered what Lucky would think seeing her dressed in such clothing.

"Maddie?"

She dropped the dress and wrung her shaky hands together as she walked to the flap to stick her head out.

"Here." Lucky handed her a bucket. "It's warm water."

Her cheeks grew hot. He certainly knew her habits. "Thank you."

With her heart fluttering, Maddie carried the bucket across the tent, where she removed her dirty clothes and washed thoroughly before donning her clean outfit, right down to her socks and pantaloons. She folded the dirty ones—which she'd take the time to wash tomorrow—before replacing everything in her bag. After brushing out her hair, she carried the water outside, dumped it behind the tent and went farther into the brush to take care of business before she brought the empty bucket back to where the men sat.

They were quietly conversing, but stopped as she neared. "I didn't mean to interrupt," she said as they turned her way. Unsure what to say when they both remained silent, staring at her attentively, she said, "Thank you again, Jack, for the fish. They were delicious."

"My pleasure," he answered.

Still not sure why they looked at her so, Maddie glanced down at her dress. Having left her coat inside the tent, she ran a hand over the buttons, assuring they were fastened. Finding nothing out of the ordinary for them to be curious about, she nodded. "Good night, then."

Once in the tent, she removed her boots again, and her socks, stuffing them inside the boots before climbing beneath the covers. Rubbing her cold toes together, she curled onto her side, wondering when Lucky would retire. She'd grown used to his warmth, and after her cleansing, felt chilled to the bone by the night air.

A fleeting thought entered her mind, and she glanced toward the tent flap. Perhaps Lucky wouldn't join her. He might have told Jack they weren't married. That could have been why they were both staring at her so. A great wave of disappointment rose inside her. Pretending to be Lucky's wife had given her a sense of security she'd never known. She'd felt contented last night when he'd explained that he'd continued the ruse for her protection. Which was about as confusing as his kisses.

Maddie rolled over onto her other side and tugged the covers over her shoulder while trying to make her mind center on gold. And finding it. Soon.

Though he tried, Cole couldn't keep from glancing at the tent every few minutes. Figuring there was no sense putting it off, he stretched and roused up a yawn. "I think it's time for me to turn in."

"Can't blame you," Whiskey Jack said. "If I had that warming my bed, I'd probably never leave it."

Pin prickles shot up his spine, and Cole considered admitting he and Maddie weren't married, or anything close to that, but in truth he didn't mind letting the tale continue. At least for a bit longer. It was safer for others to believe they were married—for her—and he didn't mind being the one offering the protection. "See you in the morning."

Whiskey Jack laughed, Homer squawked and a hint of guilt rolled inside Cole as he walked to the tent. He certainly didn't mind people believing she was his. That he was that lucky. She'd unbraided her hair, leaving the long black tresses hanging down her back, and when the light of the fire had caught in the glistening strands, they'd sparkled as if sprinkled with gold. Her cheeks had glowed, too, and her eyes looked so blue they'd practically mesmerized him.

He'd noticed her attractiveness the night he'd pulled her onto that horse, but as time went by, he'd come to realize few women, if any, matched her beauty. Maybe that was what was growing on him. Though he'd lived a sailor's life the past few years, he'd grown up surrounded by fine and beautiful things and hadn't noticed he missed them until Maddie.

That was exactly where his mind should be. Home, and finding the gold his family needed. He hadn't wanted a wife when he'd left and still didn't. Especially not once he found his gold. His mother would prosecute him if he came home with one after walking out on Rachel.

Lucky entered the tent and quietly removed his coat and then his boots. Though he was trying not to, he couldn't help but think how lying next to Maddie each night had become a refuge he'd never encountered and an adventure he'd come to look forward to, even though it spiked his desires insurmountably.

She rolled when he lifted the blanket, glancing up at

him with those remarkable eyes, now glossy from sleep.
A smile touched her lips, too, and everything inside him
listed like a ship hitting ten-foot swells.

"It's cold," she said drowsily.

"I'll warm you," he whispered, crawling in beside
her.

Her little murmur of contentment fueled and worried
him at the same time. He was playing with a loaded gun
and would soon have to set it aside or fire. Trouble was,
he wasn't sure if he could live with either choice. They
both had a list of consequences. Long lists.

The next few days flew by. They staked their claims
and chose the spot to set up camp. Though the ground
was different here, Maddie used what Smitty had taught
her about how to trust her instincts, sense when something tugged inside her. Similar to how she knew when
a storm was about to hit. But she'd had a hard time of
it recently. Lucky's effect on her meant that finding
the tug, that little thrill that said gold was near, took
deep concentration, and she wasn't overly confident
she'd found it. Others were moving in, though, miners
from all over. Knowing they had to stake their ground,
she'd picked out a tract of land that had made her heart
skip a beat.

She hoped that meant there was gold. Truth was, when
she'd seen Lucky standing on the little hill next to the
riverbed, with the sun shining behind him and the water
glistening before him, gold may not have had anything
to do with the fluttering of her insides. Lucky hadn't
kissed her again, and wanting him to was consuming her.

Jack had said she'd chosen a good spot. So had
Lucky, and the two of them had wasted no time in

building a tent—complete with a wooden floor of logs they'd sawed in two. More logs had been used to build the base of the tent, which stood almost as tall as she did. The canvas they'd used for tents on the trail made up the rest of the walls and the roof. They'd built furniture, too—three-legged chairs and a table, as well as a bed. It was all rough looking, with bark-covered logs making up the legs and the entire bed frame, but Maddie grew a bit misty-eyed every time she entered the tent. In all actuality, this was the finest place she'd ever called home.

Lucky had added rope stays to the bed and piled them full of furs from Jack, providing her with her first real bed. She doubted, not even with loads of money, could she buy one more comfortable or warm. Most of the warmth, though, came from Lucky, when they snuggled close together at night.

That, however, hadn't happened the past couple of nights. Lucky was mad at her again. Not talking, like when they'd first left Dabbler. He refused to look at her, too.

She knew why, but they were here to find gold. Not build a homestead, which was what he seemed to be focused on. Having a warm, comfortable spot to bed down every night and wood already chopped and stacked nearby to throw on the fire was handy, and she appreciated it, but all that took time away from what they should be doing. She'd told him that; his answer was that once they started mining gold, it would take all their time, so they needed to have everything else done already. Although this made sense to Maddie, it wasn't how she was used to doing things, and that grated on her nerves.

He'd even made a trip to Bittersweet to buy more supplies. The trip by river—there and back—took far less than a day. Jack had a small boat Lucky had used. Explaining which tributary to take off the main river to find his claim was almost impossible, Jack had said, which was why he'd suggested they take the land route the first time in. But once you rowed out of it, he said, finding your way back wasn't a problem.

Though Lucky had asked, she hadn't gone with him. Thought it a waste of time and money, and when he'd returned, with six laying hens—so they'd have eggs— she was even more irritated. Eggs were as precious as gold in the Yukon. Only a foolish man would pen up chickens. Their clucking could bring in all sorts of things. Not just hungry animals, but thieves.

Maddie tossed a couple of handfuls of grain—also brought from town—on the ground for the hens to peck at, and then whistled for Homer to follow her. The bird had taken to flying upriver to visit—and eat a few raisins—on a daily basis. Considering their claims butted up to Jack's, it wasn't far for Homer to fly, and she truly didn't mind his company. *He* was still talking to her.

"Leave those chickens alone," she told him when he strutted along the edge of the fence.

"Leave chickens," the bird repeated, along with a few loud squawks, but followed along behind her to the tent.

He waited on the step while Maddie replaced the cup in the bag of chicken feed and then retrieved a few raisins for him. Once outside again, she knelt down to feed him. The sound of a hammer pounding grated on her already frazzled nerves. Today Lucky was building an outhouse. An outhouse, of all things. They were surrounded by a million acres of woods. Claiming he was used to such things—outhouses, a roof over his head, cut firewood, eggs, a bed—Lucky seemed to find a million things to do besides look for gold.

"That's fine," Maddie said to Homer. "I don't need him to find gold."

"Don't need him," Homer repeated.

Pleased the bird agreed with her, Maddie picked up her shovel and gold pan and headed for the water. Unlike Lucky, she'd searched for gold every day. As of yet, she hadn't found so much as a glitter, but that didn't mean it wasn't here. She just needed to look harder. A sluice box would help, too, but when she'd gathered the hammer and nails, along with some of the hewn lumber, Lucky had confiscated them, stating he'd build a sluice box when everything else was done.

"At the rate he's going, we'll be too old to pan gold then," she told Homer. "Some partner he's made. Seems to me finding gold is last on his list."

The bird squawked and Maddie nodded, pretending Homer was agreeing with her. "You're a better partner than him." That of course wasn't true, nor what was really bothering her. Lucky not talking to her meant other things weren't happening, either. Things she wanted to happen. Him holding her at night. Kissing her.

Homer squawked again. Though she grinned, Maddie kept her eyes on the riverbank, looking for something, anything, to tell her where to dig, anything to keep her mind off Lucky.

The ground here was different than in Colorado, and she wished for the hundredth time that Smitty was with her. He'd know where to dig, always had. He said he couldn't describe it, how he sensed the difference in the ground, knew where the gold was hiding.

Smitty had said she had it, too, that inner sense, but she'd panned dozens of scoops of riverbed and hadn't seen a hint of gold. Not in the rocks, sand or dirt. "What am I missing, Smitty?" she asked softly. "I really thought this was the spot."

A flash or flicker happened out of the corner of her eye and she glanced around. There was nothing out of the ordinary, and she deduced it must have been a bird flying overhead. But it happened again as she dropped her gaze to the water.

This time, she scanned things more intently, and when it happened again, she pinpointed where it came from. Several yards ahead of her and a couple feet out from the shoreline. The water was cold, and she didn't relish standing in it, but that was what miners had to do—get wet—so she stepped into the river, keeping her eyes on the spot she'd seen glistening brighter than the rest of the water.

The current was strong, and the water up to her knees when she arrived. It was a rock, a boulder, really, the top of it just beneath the water. Sunlight caught on the wet stone as the waves washed over it. Disappointed, Maddie stuck the blade of her shovel into the riverbed to lean against the handle. The shovel went down farther than she anticipated and she almost lost her footing.

The water was clear, showing that the base of the boulder was surrounded by sand rather than rocks. She shifted, examining the rock and the sand more closely. There was a whirlpool, a miniature one, and the sand at the base was streaked with black.

Maddie's heart started racing.

Chapter Seven

Cole thought about telling Maddie to get out of the water, but it would be a waste of breath. She was stubborn and set on finding gold. Which was the reason they were here, so he couldn't fault her on that. Besides, he could see her. She was close enough that if she fell, he could make it to her side immediately.

He'd start mining as soon as their camp was set up. That had become his goal when she'd told him she'd never had a home with a floor. Such a little thing, one he'd never thought of before, yet to her, it had been significant. Tears had misted her eyes, and at that moment, he'd wanted to make her happy more than he wanted anything else.

Almost.

He wanted her. In a way a man wants a woman, and that want had grown so strong he no longer dared hold her at night. Working, physical labor that left him exhausted, was how he managed to still sleep in the same bed as her. He made sure when his head hit the pillow he was so exhausted nothing could keep him awake.

Try as he might, it wasn't working all that well. He'd

taken it a step further, too. Ignoring her again. Which was like ignoring the sun.

He pulled his gaze off her to resume hanging the door on the front of the outhouse with leather hinges, but her swift movements had his gaze snapping right back. She'd scooped up a shovelful of riverbed and was hurrying to the shoreline, where her pan and Homer waited.

She filled the pan with water and then dropped in handfuls off the shovel to swirl about, and then repeated the actions several times. When she lifted her head and looked around as if to see if anyone was watching, he averted his gaze and took off his hat to wipe the sweat from his forehead.

Miners now lined the banks, mostly on the other side, which didn't make a lot of sense. The water was deeper and faster moving on that side, leaving little or no sandbars for the gold to collect upon. Still, a group—the Fenstermacher brothers, Abe, Albert and Tim—had made camp directly across the river from them. Those men were busy panning, mostly the little creek that trickled into the river next to where they'd set up their tent.

Maddie had pointed that out to him, how they'd set up a tent and started mining immediately. He'd chosen to ignore her statements rather than argue with her. She'd see sooner or later, when the first rainstorm hit and the Fenstermachers' camp floated downriver.

Built high above the water, on a nice little knoll complete with grass for the mules and chickens, their camp would remain dry. She'd appreciate his hard work then.

Flagging a hand at the squawking Homer, she stood, and though she appeared to be walking normally, Cole caught the glimmer in her eyes. He set down his hammer and moved toward her, his heart thudding, which happened every time he was close to her now.

Homer was the first to speak. In a raspy bird whisper, he said, "Gold."

"Hush, now," she said to the bird before telling him, "Come into the tent."

Cole followed, grinning to himself. He hoped she had found a nugget. She'd been working hard enough.

At the framed-in wood door, she said to Homer, "You go on home now."

The bird squawked, but ran for a few feet before his wings caught air and he flapped his way downriver.

"Shut the door," Maddie whispered, already standing near the table inside the tent.

Cole did as instructed and moved closer, watching how her hands shook as she lowered the pan onto the tabletop. Holding back the desire to lay a hand on her shoulder, just to steady her nerves, he focused his attention on the pan. Wet, shining black dirt covered the bottom of the pan, and mixed amongst it was gold. Not big flakes or nuggets, but a splattering of fine grains. He dipped a finger in the dirt and examined the gold more closely.

"It's gold, Lucky," she said. "Gold."

A hint of the fever filtered Cole's bloodstream—something he'd contracted back on the *Mary Jane*, when Whiskey Jack had opened a bag of dust and poured a little out in his palm. He recognized it right away. How his mouth went dry and his heart raced. How he couldn't pull his eyes off the fine specks.

"Will you tell me?"

Cole snapped his head up. Maddie had crossed the

room, stood by their bed and was staring at him with woeful eyes.

"Tell you what?"

Her arms fell to her sides as if heavy and useless. "What I've done to make you so mad at me," she said. "So angry not even gold excites you. Makes you happy."

Cole brushed the dust off his finger back into the pan with his thumb and crossed the room to where she stood. He was happy, happier than he'd been in a long time, but the gold had little to do with it. Letting out a tiny chuckle, he shook his head. "I haven't been mad at you, Maddie."

She frowned, but then grinned. "That's gold, Lucky. What we came here to find."

The shimmer in her eyes sent him right to the end of his rope. "It sure enough is, darling," he whispered, dipping his head while tilting hers back to line up their lips. The connection was startling. Her lips were softer, sweeter, than his memory could recall, and when her arms wrapped around his torso, he ran his tongue over the entire length of her lips.

Her sigh mingled with his breath, and he kissed her cheeks, her chin and the corners of her mouth before teasing her lips apart and kissing her more deeply and thoroughly than he'd ever kissed a woman.

Images of lowering her onto the bed behind them caused him to ease out of the kiss.

Glassy eyed, she blinked and then grinned. "That was a real kiss, wasn't it?"

He took a step back in order to keep her at arm's length while admitting, "Yes."

Her lips twitched as a smile formed and her cheeks turned red. "You're right. There was a difference."

There certainly was, and places inside him were throbbing in response. Although he wanted to kiss her again, he laughed and pulled her into a hug.

Maddie attempted to draw in a breath of air, but her lungs seemed to be locked tight. The thrill of being in Lucky's arms was like coming home after trekking through a snowstorm. "I've missed you holding me at night," she whispered.

"I've missed holding you at night."

His gaze had gone to the bed, and Maddie knew why. She rested her cheek against his chest. Before leaving her with Smitty, Bass had left her many other places, and more than once that had been with one of the women who'd been smitten by his black hair and blue eyes. Lately she'd been remembering the winter she'd spent with Roseanne and the houseful of women similar to those in the hull of the *Mary Jane*. Though once repulsed by what had taken place in their bedrooms, experiencing such things with Lucky had taken on an intriguing appeal.

He leaned back and frowned at her, as if he knew exactly what she was thinking about.

They weren't married, even though people still thought they were, but those women hadn't been married, either.

"Maddie?"

She didn't want a man taking what was rightfully hers, telling her what to do, but she didn't want to be alone, either. Lucky wasn't like other men, hadn't been from the very beginning, and there were things she wanted to share with him. Like kissing. That was something she sincerely wanted to do again.

A thrill shot through her, and Maddie took a chance. Stretching onto her toes, she pressed her lips to his.

He didn't move—not even his lips twitched beneath hers—and Maddie's heart threatened to stop beating right then and there. She wasn't a quitter, though, not when it was something she wanted, so she reached up, grabbed the sides of his head and pressed her lips harder against his.

A smile formed on his lips; she felt it, and her heart took to racing. She grinned, too, and then giggled.

"Aw, darling," he said as his arms wrapped around her. "What am I going to do with you?"

"Kiss me," she suggested.

He lifted her feet off the floor and spun around in a wide circle until they were both laughing. "Like this?" he asked as his lips danced over hers playfully.

Growing dizzier by the second, even though he'd stopped spinning, Maddie laughed. "I didn't know there were so many ways to kiss."

"Too many to count," he said, nibbling on her bottom lip.

It was amazing, and made her want more. She grasped his shoulders, pulling herself onto her toes again, and parted her lips. His parted, too, and she swept her tongue inside his mouth, as he'd done earlier. A quiver raced through her, and she nestled in closer, completely swept away by the game of tag happening between their tongues.

The game was utterly fascinating, as was the way his hands roamed her back. Every caress, every swirl caused other things to happen inside her. Her nipples tightened at being pressed against his shirtfront, and deep down, in her most secret spot, heat spiraled as if there was a miniature whirlpool inside of her.

A squawk along with a gruff voice stating, "Don't mean to interrupt," brought everything to an abrupt stop.

On the outside. Inside Maddie was still as worked up as she'd ever been.

Lucky's nose bumped hers as they both glanced toward the doorway. To her own surprise, no hint of embarrassment rose up as Jack, along with Homer, entered the tent. There was no room, Maddie suspected, for such feelings when her entire being was overflowing with joy.

"The bird told me you found gold," Jack said.

"She sure enough did," Lucky answered, hugging her to his side with one arm. "Come take a look."

Arm in arm they walked to the table, and the thrill of the gold specks glistening in the pan was ten times greater this time than when she'd first seen them. Especially when Lucky kissed the top of her head. She glanced up, and the gleam in his eyes was enough to make her joy overflow. Though she covered her mouth with one hand, her happiness let a laugh escape.

Lucky laughed, too, and hugged her again while Jack whooped.

"That's some mighty fine color, there, girl," Jack said, examining the pan closer. "Mighty fine color." He turned his wrinkled, smiling face to Lucky. "Looks like we need to get that sluice built right quick-like."

"Looks like we do," Lucky agreed, tugging her closer yet. "Looks like we do."

"Well, let's get at it," Jack said.

"Gold," Homer squawked. "Gold."

"Blabbermouth," Maddie muttered. The men laughed again, but a tainted and dark memory slipped into her thoughts to destroy her bliss. "What if the men across the river see us?"

Lucky frowned. "The Fenstermacher brothers?"

She nodded.

"Of course they'll see us, girl," Jack said, chuckling. "Most likely they'll be green with envy, too."

"Exactly," she said. The Fenstermacher brothers were huge German men who were always yelling at each other. Though they'd been over a few times to talk with Lucky, she'd stayed away from them. "Maybe we could mine at night."

Lucky turned her to face him by grasping both of her upper arms. "Maddie, honey, you need to learn to trust people."

Trust was not something that came naturally to her. "Why should I trust them?"

"Because we're all in this together, girl," Jack said. "Mining gold. They may be green with envy, but they'll protect your plot as much as they will their own."

That made absolutely no sense and she turned her gaze back to Lucky. "They could steal it, our gold."

He shook his head. "No, they won't. They'll be happy to know there's gold in this part of the river. If it's on our side, chances are it's on their side, too."

Her insides quivered so hard her stomach flipped. "But stealing ours would be easier than mining their own."

"Now, listen here," Jack started. "Miners—"

"There's a stack of boards behind the tent," Lucky told him. "I'll be out in a minute."

Grumbling, Jack left, taking Homer with him.

Maddie attempted to take a step back, but Lucky's hold tightened. He was frowning. Her past hadn't been all that pleasurable, but it had never hurt quite like it was right now. Perhaps because she and Lucky were so different. His upbringing had been nothing like hers. He hadn't told her about his family, Jack had, and about the mansion he lived in, how his grandparents had made the entire family wealthy beyond most. In her mind, it all came down to how Lucky didn't understand people like she did. "Most every man tries to steal something or another."

Lucky pulled her toward him gently, as if she might break if he tugged too hard. "No, they don't, honey," he said softly. "Besides, I'm here. I won't let them steal your gold."

Maddie wanted to believe him with all her heart, but it was hard. She was conscious, too, of the precarious position she was in. If she and Lucky were truly married, she might feel more secure, but as it was, he could cast her aside on a whim. She'd seen that, too.

"You trust me, don't you?"

Though trust wasn't something she was overly familiar with, and the little bit she had known was most likely rusty from not being used, she did trust Lucky. Had from the moment he'd raced down the alley and rescued her. "Yes," she admitted. "But I don't know that I can trust the Fenstermacher brothers."

He grinned, and a moment later his lips met hers, unhurried and tender.

When the kiss ended, her insides were all warm and swirling again. Even her fears had diminished into little more than a mingling thought in the back of her mind.

The fact Lucky could affect her so, just by kissing her, had a blush creeping over her face.

"We'll find a safe place to hide your gold. A real safe place, where no one can find it. Will that help?"

Tongue-tied by her twisted thoughts, she nodded.

He kissed her again, just on the end of her nose. "All right, then. Let's go get that sluice box built."

They hadn't been outside more than ten minutes when the Fenstermacher brothers arrived, having rowed across the river in a boat much too tiny to hold all three of them, yet to Maddie's disappointment, it didn't sink.

Lucky was a tall man with broad shoulders, but even he looked small next to the barrel-chested Germans. As the men climbed out of their boat, Maddie sidled up closer to Lucky and tried to keep from glancing at the tent, where she'd left the gold she'd found. Then avoided glances at her shovel, still half full of black sand and lying on the riverbank.

Smiling as he set down the saw he was using to cut a board in two, Lucky laid a hand on her arm. "Don't worry, darling. They're good men."

"I'll form my own opinion," she stated.

Lucky grinned and then made introductions. Abe, Albert and Tim. All three had curly blond hair and whiskers that said they hadn't shaved in years. Albert was the largest, but Tim, a few inches shorter, was the loudest. His booming voice rattled the insides of Maddie's ears.

"Gotta forgive my brother, Mrs. DuMont," Abe, the shorter one, who proclaimed to be the eldest of the brothers, told her in a rather normal tone while shaking her hand. "He lost most of his hearing when he fired off one of Pa's shotguns years ago and doesn't realize how loud he is."

Maddie nodded, while pulling her hand back. Her heart had fluttered oddly at being called Mrs. DuMont. Others had called her that, but after kissing Lucky, the name seemed to carry more weight.

"It looked as if the lady found something," Abe said to Lucky. "We thought we'd come see what it was."

Shouting as if they all stood a mile away, Tim declared, "We're hoping it was a nugget the size of a horseshoe. We ain't seen nothing on our side yet."

"It wasn't a nugget," Lucky said, "but some good dust and a few flakes."

"Promising stuff if I ever saw it," Jack added to the conversation.

The air in Maddie's lungs was growing stale, and when Homer had to stick in his bird squawk, "Gold," she huffed out a good amount.

Lucky hooked her hip with one hand, tugging her closer to his side.

"I'd say that calls for a celebration," Albert, the middle brother—in age—said. "I shot us a deer just this morning. I'll cook up enough for everyone."

Maddie glanced up at Lucky, expecting him to decline, yet the glimmer in his eyes said he wasn't opposed to a celebration.

Catching her gaze, he said somewhat unenthusiastically, "We need to get a sluice built."

"We'll help," Abe answered. "The faster you get it built, the faster you can get that gold out. We've been wanting to build one ourselves, but haven't taken the time yet."

"You help us build this one, and if it works, we'll help you build one of your own," Jack said.

Frustration was building inside Maddie, more so as the men continued talking about sluice boxes, and when Lucky agreed, saying it sounded like a good plan to him, she had to pinch her lips together to keep from proclaiming that it did not sound like a good plan. The Fenstermacher brothers rowing back across the river sounded good to her.

"While you're building, I'll be cooking," Albert said.

"I'll row you across the river," Tim shouted. "And bring back another saw and hammer."

"We have plenty of food," Maddie whispered to Lucky. "Tell them they don't need to cook for us, and we don't need their help."

"They're just being neighborly," Lucky whispered.

"Well, we don't need to be neighborly in return," she insisted.

"Yes, we do," he replied.

"Don't you worry about cooking today, Mrs. Du-Mont," Albert yelled while stepping into the boat. "I'll do it. Lots of food for everyone."

Abe, conversing with Jack a few feet away, turned toward her and Lucky. "Albert had rheumatic fever when he was little and Ma wouldn't let him out of the house afterward. He grew up cooking right alongside our sisters."

"That's why they brought me to Alaska," Albert shouted as the boat started across the river. "To cook while they mine gold."

Maddie didn't respond. As much as she didn't want company, she would admit—to herself—she wasn't overly fond of cooking, or very good at. Truth was, she really didn't know what to do with the things Lucky had insisted they pack in their bags before leaving Dabbler, or with what he'd hauled back from Bittersweet.

She'd never had much practice using store-bought things. Smitty had taught her how to snare rabbits and shoot grouse to roast over a fire. She'd shot a few deer, too, in the fall, and had made jerky to last them through the winter. Boiling that into a stew was simple enough. Beans, too, she knew how to boil, and she doubted there was a person alive who couldn't fry a fish.

She and Smitty had normally just eaten one meal a day, Lucky, though, even while on the trail had insisted on eating three times a day.

They'd already had breakfast, and not having to cook two more times today would give her more time to pan gold. Hiding it from the Fenstermacher brothers no longer mattered.

While the two brothers, Albert and Tim, rowed the little boat across the river, Abe, the third one, helped Jack carry more boards from the side of the cabin, and Maddie turned back to Lucky.

"I'm going to finish panning the dirt in my shovel," she said.

He grinned slightly, and the way he winked made her feel a bit sheepish for changing her mind so quickly.

"Do you need help?" he asked.

"No."

"All right," he said, picking up his saw. "Shout if you do."

She didn't shout, but did end up with a goodly sum of gold, which she carried into the tent. There she spooned the black sand and gold into a frying pan and left it on the table while she went outside to build the fire.

Lucky walked over a short time later, while she was using a stick to stir down the flames. Crouching down next to her, he asked, "You plan on cooking anyway?"

"Just my gold," she answered. "Gotta get the moisture out of the dirt so I can separate it."

Cole rocked back on his heels, sending up a silent petition of thanks. Not even on his deathbed would he admit he'd never tasted anything as horrible as some of Maddie's cooking. She tried and was doing her best, therefore he'd held his silence about that, just as much as he had with other things.

"How's the Long Tom coming?" she asked.

He might have had a hard time concentrating on it, but nothing much kept her focus off gold. "Good," he said. "With four of us working on it, the sluice should be finished this afternoon. We'll start assembling it as soon as Tim and Abe get the rest of the wedged riffles cut. I'll need a blanket then, to line the bottom."

"I'll get one for you," she said. "And some of the furs you got from Jack. Put those down beneath the blanket and we'll catch more gold. No doubt about it."

There were several things he didn't doubt, and Maddie's knowledge about gold mining was one of them. "Will do," he said and rose before the desire to kiss her again become so strong he'd have to act on it.

He was in a particular position. If Jack and Homer hadn't shown up when they had, he might have convinced Maddie to do a bit more than kissing. That couldn't happen. They'd found gold, and gathering as much as possible should have been his focus. Yet the faster they gathered it, the sooner they'd leave, and he wasn't ready to think about that.

A celebration with the Fenstermacher brothers didn't

just suggest edible food, it promised more time to figure out his next steps.

Less than an hour later, Cole entered the tent to gather the blanket and furs needed for the box.

"Got those ready for you," Maddie said, pointing to a pile on the floor as he entered.

She was sitting at the table, holding a tin can over her frying pan. "What are you doing now?" he asked.

"Separating out the gold," she answered without looking up.

He moved closer. "How?"

"Watch." She skimmed the bottom of the can over the gold-speckled sand and then carefully moved it over another pan that held nothing but gold. Almost magically, gold dust fell from the bottom of her can into the pan.

Amazed, he asked, "How are you doing that?"

She giggled happily and tilted the can so he could see inside it. "With this." Pulling on a string, she lifted a good-size magnet out of the can.

"I've read a lot of books, but never heard about that trick."

"Smitty taught me how to do it," she said. "I tied a string to the magnet, and when I drop it to the bottom of the can and hold the can over the pan, the magnet draws out the gold and holds it there." She demonstrated each action as she spoke. "Then when I move it to my other pan and lift out the magnet, the gold falls into that pan."

"That's pretty ingenious," he said, astonished at how well it did work.

"Works every time." A serene smile covered her face. "A new can was like a new pair of boots to Smitty." Lowering the can over the sand, she added, "I never saw him get a new pair of boots, but that's what he always said."

"He'd be proud of you, Maddie," Cole said. He certainly was. "Coming all the way up to Alaska."

"I know," she answered, focusing again on her gold. "And he'd be happier than ever with all the canned food you hauled with us." She released another splattering of gold into her second pan before saying, "When I'm done with this, I'll start gathering rocks so we can build a dam to channel water through the Long Tom."

Chapter Eight

The Fenstermacher brothers were in no hurry to leave. After everyone, including Maddie, Cole noted, ate until they couldn't take another bite that afternoon, they let their food settle with a hearty round of conversation that included the brothers sharing they were from North Dakota, where four more brothers and seven sisters lived. Then, with everyone working together, they'd built a dam out of the rocks Maddie had gathered as well as several more, and set the sluice box into the stream.

With Maddie directing exactly where to dig, Cole, along with Whiskey Jack and the brothers, carried shovelful after shovelful over and dumped them into the Long Tom. Cole was amazed, as were the other men, that Maddie knew what to do. She kept a watchful eye on the sluice box, making sure the riffles weren't clogging or the material building up on the edges, as she judged the flow of water by slightly adjusting the box or the rocks that created the dam.

When she announced they'd run enough dirt, Abe helped Cole lift the box out of the water and remove the riffles. Maddie had insisted she'd roll up the blanket and furs, since she knew how, but did let him help her set them into the tub of water she'd made ready.

She then rinsed out the blanket and fur like a washwoman well versed in her duties and scooped the water out of the tub, until little more than an inch covered the sand and grit in the bottom.

Even Homer went silent at the amount of gold glittering in the tub.

Cole wasn't sure if he was the first one to let out a whoop, but he was the one who gathered Maddie into his arms and swung her around like a kid in a play yard. He kissed her, too, smack on the lips not caring they were surrounded by others.

"We gotta build us one of those," Tim shouted, his loud voice roaring above everyone's laughter and shouts of glee.

Whiskey Jack broke out a bottle then—which was how he'd gotten his name years before—and passed it around.

"Should we put that box back in the water?" one of the brothers asked.

Cole was too busy holding Maddie to know which one, other than he knew it hadn't been Tim. He'd even forgone a chug on Whiskey Jack's bottle, not willing to let Maddie loose. "No," he answered when she opened her mouth. "It's getting late."

Disappointment flashed in her eyes even as she said, "I have to process what we found."

"Well, then, I'll warm up the food. So we can eat again," Albert said.

With everyone else in agreement, Cole chose not to argue, and other than setting the camp in order for the night, he sat near the fire talking with the other men.

"How'd you fare, girl?" Whiskey Jack asked when Maddie finally exited the tent.

"It's good gold" was all she said.

"Good gold," Homer squawked, and Cole used the bird's diversion—the Germans were quite smitten with the macaw—to move next to Maddie and drop an arm around her shoulders.

"Well, I'm ready to call it a day," he said. "How about the rest of you?"

Summer was about at its peak, with the sun not setting at all, and Maddie glanced toward the sky as she said, "We could run one mor—"

"No," he interrupted, "we can't. Or won't. It'll be here tomorrow." Though he knew it would be dangerous to be alone with her, he wanted just that. "It's late and it's been a long day."

She agreed with a nod, though somewhat solemnly.

"There's a kettle of warm water on the fire," he said. "I'll get it for you."

"I'll get it," she answered. Before doing so, she bid the others good-night and thanked them for the meal and their help. Incredibly, she seemed sincere, too, as if being neighborly wasn't as horrifying as she'd expected.

When she entered the tent, Cole said goodbye to Whiskey Jack and Homer and then assisted the Germans in loading their boat with the array of pots, kettles and tools they'd carted over and gave them a shove, setting the boat across the river.

He stirred down the fire and wasted a few more minutes washing up at the edge of the river, all the while questioning how miserable the cravings inside him had become due to the fact he knew he couldn't act upon them.

Lucky's resignation flared inside him as he flung his towel down on the tree branch. Maddie was worse than any woman he'd ever known, the way she'd weaseled her way right into his life. They had to come to some sort of understanding. One they both could agree upon. Living with her and not touching her couldn't keep happening. It was blocking his focus. He wasn't convinced a real marriage was what he wanted, but there had to be a happy medium.

Cole entered the tent with brisk determination, but his feet stuck to the floor as the door closed behind him. Maddie was sitting on the bed, brushing her hair, and the smile on her face was so adorable, he forgot all else.

"Can you believe it?" she said, setting the brush down. "All that gold?"

Shaking his head for clarity, he asked, "Did you think we wouldn't find any?"

"I knew we would." She stood and crossed the room. "I just didn't think it would be that easy."

"Easy?" he asked, resting his hands on her hips. "You think all this has been easy?"

She looped her hands behind his head. "Well, it certainly could have been harder."

"I suspect it could have been." He highly doubted it could have been harder on him.

Giggling, she turned her face toward the table. "I put it in two pouches. One for you and one for me. I figure we'll split it fifty-fifty, no matter who finds it." Turning back to him, she asked, "Does that sound fair to you?"

"That sounds fine to me," he answered, though at this moment he didn't give a hoot about the gold. It was her—them—he wanted to discuss. "Maddie, today, when you found the gold—"

"I know," she said. "I was being silly. The Fenstermacher brothers are nice men, and trustworthy, I suspect, just like you said."

"What made you change your mind so quickly?" Her hands were still on the backside of his neck. Her fingertips, gently massaging the area, felt heavenly as they teased his thinking.

"You," she answered. "Them, too, I guess, the way they set right in with helping you build the sluice box. And I've never tasted anything like that venison Albert made. It was so tender I barely had to chew."

He grinned and tugged on her hips, forcing her to step even closer. "So that's all it takes, a good meal, to make you change your mind?"

"I'm a terrible cook, aren't I?"

Cole wasn't about to go there. "You're good at finding gold," he said instead.

She laughed, but as the sound faded, her face grew serious. "Will you do me a favor?"

"Of course," he answered without thought. "What is it?"

"Kiss me." The heat that rushed into Maddie's face didn't stop there. It rushed around until every inch of her was warm and tingling. All day her mind had been on Lucky and kissing him again.

"Why?" he asked.

"Because I want you to." A moment later, she explained, "This has been the best day of my life. I don't want it to end."

"Maddie—"

An inkling of fear crashed through all her warm and tender sensations. She stopped it, though, with an inner willpower she hadn't known about. "I've been think-

ing about you all day. About us. About kissing and…"
She bit her lips together, knowing she didn't need to say
exactly what she'd been thinking.

He shook his head, but smiled. "You've been mining gold all day."

She shot a glance toward the bed. "But I was still
thinking about you. About us."

He lifted a hand and slowly, idly, twirled a lock of
her hair around his index finger. "What if it's not what
you want? If later you change your mind?"

Her skin turned overly sensitive, especially on the
side of her face, where his finger continued to tangle
itself into her hair, and her mouth grew dry. Tugging
her tongue off the roof of her mouth, she asked, "Did
you?" Swallowing a lump that formed, she continued,
"Did you change your mind?"

"No," he whispered near the top of her forehead.

His breath tingled her scalp through her hair and it
made her want to shiver, even though she wasn't cold
in the least. "I won't change my mind," she said. "I
know I won't."

His hands roamed up and down her back. "We aren't
married."

"So?" She tilted her head back to look at him. "I don't
want to get married, Lucky, ever, just like you, but we
don't have to be married to have adventures, do we?"

He grinned. "You're about the most adventurous
woman I've ever met, darling."

The words, the way he said it, floated through her
perfectly, as his hand caressed the small of her back.
Newfound boldness, which she'd only known during
anger or grief, swelled inside her. It was unique, this
strength growing inside her, and with it came another

memory of the months she'd spent with one of her father's mistresses. The owner of that house had often said, *Men don't know what women need. We have to show them. Don't ever be afraid to do that.*

She knew what she needed, and what she wanted, and wasn't about to wait any longer for it. Maddie undid the tie holding back Lucky's hair and combed her fingers through the silky strands, rubbing his scalp. "Are you going to kiss me or not?"

"Yes, I am."

Though she craved it, wanted it beyond all else, she was stunned by the soft warmth, the perfection of his lips gliding over hers. She closed her eyes in order to concentrate on the wonderful, astonishing pleasure. Playfully, his tongue teased her lips apart and darted into her mouth.

His hands were both caressing her back now, and the heat penetrating her dress was cruelly devastating, in a sweet, exciting way. When he slowed the kiss, it was to say, "I want to do more than kiss you, darling."

"That's what I want, too," she replied, and then squealed, caught off guard by the way he swept her off her feet and into his arms. It was amazing—being held by him—and anticipating what was yet to come made her giddy.

Lucky crossed the room, set her on the bed and then forced her to lie down by leaning over her, all the while stealing the smile off her face by kissing her breathless. Maddie didn't open her eyes when the kiss ended, but giggled when she heard two thuds, knowing he'd just kicked off his boots.

His hands settled on her sides and then moved, rubbing from her hips to her rib cage and down again. She had to open her eyes. The caress was so fascinating. Each pass of his hands had her body responding, her nipples tightening and a need inside her that she now understood.

"I want you, Lucky," she said, having no idea how else to explain the fierce yearning she felt.

"I want you, too, darling."

When he started to unbutton her dress, she watched in awe. It was a simple act, one she performed daily, but the way he undid each button inched up the excitement building within her. After the last button, when she pondered briefly about sitting up to remove her dress, he grasped her waist again. A moan formed in the back of her throat, and her nipples started to throb. His hands, big and gentle, and so wonderful, spread across her stomach and slowly made their way to her breasts.

The moan in her throat broke loose. His teasing strokes continued, and her desires turned more primitive. Lucky leaned forward, kissing her again and again while he slipped the dress over her shoulders, down her arms until her weight, pressed deeply into the soft comfort of their bed, prevented the material from moving any farther.

The boldness she'd found earlier was back, and she pushed at him, forcing him to sit up so she could wiggle her way out of the top half of her dress. Lucky untied her camisole and ran his fingers beneath the straps, pushing them over her shoulders all the way down to her elbows while kissing her chin and her neck. The thought of exposing herself to him sent a shiver of delight up her spine.

His smile said he was pleased by what he saw, and Maddie couldn't speak. What she'd heard in the past, what she knew, had left her with nothing but hints of what to expect. This, all this, she couldn't quite comprehend.

Lucky held her breasts, one in each hand, and twirled his tongue around each of her nipples, one by one. Maddie had to remind herself to breathe and wondered if she might go mad from pleasure as his lips closed around one nipple, suckling.

Gasping for air, she grasped his head, held him at her breast, certain she might very well die if he stopped right then.

Lucky's chuckle made her growl. "Good heavens," she said between short snippets of air. "I had no idea, I—" She stopped shy of saying she'd never imagined her breasts were capable of hosting such tremendous sensations.

"I did," he said, moving to the other breast. Before taking that one into his mouth, he added, "I knew you were perfect the moment I saw you."

"No one's perfect," she said, by habit only. Things were muddling in her mind, making no sense. She didn't mind, though, thinking straight was impossible.

"You are," he answered, tugging her toward the edge of the bed. When he stood, he pulled her onto her feet and held her as she wobbled. The stars in his eyes were as bright as she'd ever seen, and her last bit of propriety—the small amount she'd been holding on to—fell away.

About as frantic as someone with red ants in their pants, she pulled down the rest of her dress and then tugged at the stays holding up her pantaloons and petticoat. Lucky laughed again, folding his hands around hers. "Slow down, darling. We have all night."

The urgency, the yearning growing more feverish by the second, couldn't be quelled that easily. "I don't plan on wasting a minute," she answered, trying to explain.

"I don't, either." Lucky pulled her close and provided another star-shattering kiss.

A deep intuition said his desires were as strong as hers, yet he demonstrated restraint, and she truly wished she knew how he did that. His hands weren't clawing at her like hers were him—she couldn't seem to find the buttons of his shirt. Instead, his hands were slow and steady, roaming her back, her hips, with wide gentle circles that had her insides feel as if they were melting. A delicious feeling if she'd ever known one.

"Your skin is like silk from the Orient," he whispered near her ear. "And sweeter than sugar cane."

"You've been to the Orient?" she asked, though she already knew he had. What she really wanted to ask was if he'd take her there someday.

"Yes," he answered. "I have. But I've never seen anyone more beautiful than you." He set her back on the bed and knelt down to ease each of her socks and garters off slowly.

Lost in the wonderful world he was creating, it was a moment before she realized how rough and course the blanket was against her bare bottom. As if he knew that, Lucky took her elbows, pulling her onto her feet again. He tossed back the blanket, exposing the sheets he'd bought in town on his last trip. She'd thought it a ridiculous purchase; now, as he once again eased her back onto the bed, she stretched out her legs and sighed at the feel of the soft cotton. She'd never lain naked on anything, especially not a bed with sheets.

"Nice, isn't it?" he asked.

She giggled and reached up to take his face between her palms. "You or the sheets?"

His smile was more stunning than the gold specks in her pan had been.

"Both," she whispered, answering her own question.

He kissed her slowly, a tender, undemanding action that seemed to steady the cravings inside her while increasing their intensity at the same time. Lucky stood then, and Maddie shied away from sitting up to help him remove his shirt, though she wanted to. Waiting and watching, she deduced, gave her a distinct pleasure, too. Stripped down to a long set of drawers, he joined her on the bed. Lying on his side, he placed one hand on her bare stomach, and the heat of his palm caused another yearning to spring forth.

"Don't you need to remove your drawers?" she asked, not sure she could take much more.

"I will," he answered, "when the time is right."

"I do believe that would be about now," she answered, tightening her stomach muscles as his hand roamed lower.

"Not quite," he said.

Lucky kissed her again, and even while her tongue played with his, her focus was on the juncture between her legs. It had started to throb, as her breasts had done earlier. As his fingers eased over her thigh, her hips lifted off the bed. He caught the inside of one thigh, and Maddie couldn't say he tugged her legs apart, for she was already spreading them, craving his touch more profoundly than before.

He continued to kiss her. Her mouth, her chin, her neck, as his hand explored, stroking her lightly. His lips wandered downward, and when they found her breasts again, licking and suckling, his finger entered her. The sweet pleasure could have sent her into delirium if not for the new turmoil it created.

It had to be instinct, like knowing where to look for gold, but this time it was her very womanhood coming to life and unconsciously knowing exactly what to do. Her legs opened wider, her hips began to move and a powerful sense hinted that something grand and profound was on the horizon.

Lucky's lips returned to her mouth, teasing her with a kiss so playful and light, she had to question if his cravings were as grand as hers. She closed her eyes, tried to focus on maintaining an ounce of control. The moan rolling in the back of her throat wanted to be released, and the pressure had her tossing her head against the pillows.

Maddie hadn't realized Lucky had moved until moist heat seized her. Her eyes snapped open, but she'd already comprehended his mouth had taken over for his finger. Her mind shattered at the fiery intensity, and from that moment on she became lost in a world of glory. Her own blood, pulsing hard and fast, thundered in her ears like a raging waterfall, and she found herself in a more splendid place and time than she'd ever have imagined.

Her body seemed to know what it was doing, and she let it go, marveling at how the friction of moving against Lucky's mouth drove her toward a mysterious promise. Her heart was pounding, breathing almost impossible, yet nothing gave way.

Lucky's hands lifted her bottom, and her heels buried themselves into the bed, allowing her to arch into him as he continued to suckle, lick and drive her toward pure madness. A magnificent madness.

Suddenly a fiery freedom broke loose inside her like a celebration. Instantly filling her bloodstream, it spread through her so completely her thighs and legs stiffened and her toes curled as it continued to rush from one end to the other. Lucky eased her quivering bottom back onto the bed, kissing her stomach as her legs dropped. Much slower, the commotion inside her made a second pass through her body before it had her sinking deep into the mattress.

Her vision, her senses, returned gradually, peacefully. Perspiration covered her body, and a deep and profound sense of satisfaction left her lethargic and happy.

So happy.

"Oh, my." Having no idea how to explain the fulfillment swimming through her veins, she whispered, "That was as good as finding gold."

If he was as smart as he thought he was, Cole would stretch out beside her and find a way for his body to absorb the need burning inside him. Or he'd walk out the door and dive into the icy river. But the taste of her, as intoxicating as any spirits he'd ever sampled from one continent to the next, had his desires too intense to discount. He had to have her.

His common sense was intact, though, at least partially. Maddie was a virgin, and taking her hard and fast as his throbbing shaft begged would hurt her. So he shifted slightly and grabbed her waist with both hands to playfully dig his fingers into her sides for a good bout of tickling.

"As good as finding gold?" he teased.

Maddie twisted beneath him, trying to escape his

hands. Through her giggles, she squealed, "Better than finding gold."

Cole stopped tickling her to run a fingertip over her lips while the mischievous glint in her blue eyes had his throat growing thick. He'd never fall in love with a woman, and hadn't with this one, but Maddie had gotten under his skin. Deeply.

"That, I can agree with," he answered, having been quiet too long by the tiny frown forming on her forehead. He then leaned down to sample her nipples again. They were magnificent, as was the rest of her. While he rolled his tongue over one dark tip, he twirled the other between a thumb and finger. They both turned hard again, which made his ache almost excruciating.

Her low moan had the same effect on him, and he left her long enough to rid himself of his drawers. Returning to the bed, he positioned himself above her, holding his weight off her by resting his elbows and forearms on the bed. He did lower his hips, resting his hard length atop the smooth flesh of her stomach so she'd grow used to it.

She let out a sweet sigh, and the smile on her face toyed with everything inside him. Wrapping her arms around his neck, she tugged his face downward. Kissing her was beyond belief. She gave so fully, so completely, he couldn't explain the gratification he experienced knowing it was him she was kissing.

Her hands slid over his shoulders, down his back, where they firmly caressed his taut muscles. "Maddie," he said, tugging his lips off hers. His breath was ragged, his need more profound than ever.

"I'm ready for more, Lucky."

His insides soared at her honesty and enthusiasm.

"It might hurt, Maddie," he felt inclined to warn. "The first time usually does." He wasn't in the habit of taking virgins, had never done so, but had heard such things, and hurting her was the last thing he wanted.

"You didn't hurt me," she said.

"This time will be different," he answered.

"I imagine it will be," she chimed sweetly, seductively. "Considering you took your drawers off."

He grinned, yet said, "I'm being serious, Maddie."

"So am I." She tugged his head down again and drove her tongue into his mouth demandingly. As always, her courage was as tormenting as it was endearing.

Cole slid down, aligning his body with hers, and used a hand to position himself between her legs. "I'll go slow, darling," he said, hoping the words would stick in his mind. His need was explosive and burning, and it would take all he had not to thrust inside her and take her on a long, sizzling ride.

She was nibbling on her bottom lip as she nodded, but it was the trust he saw in her eyes that gave him the self-discipline he needed. Gradually he entered her, drawing air deep into his lungs at the intense, perfect heat of her moist, velvet-lined channel.

Waiting, he allowed her to stretch enough to accommodate him, and then withdrew to enter her again, inching in a bit farther. The slow, unhurried pace was more intense and gratifying than driving into her ever could have been. He repeated the action several times, and sensing the next thrust would breach her maiden barrier, Cole took her mouth in a tender, passionate kiss, hoping to keep her attention as he moved his hips forward again.

He slid all the way in and she gasped. Her fingernails dug into his shoulders, and he deepened the kiss until her hips, which had stiffened, relaxed. Then, slowly, gently, he began to move, in and out, over and over, until her hips were moving in time with his.

Maddie took to lovemaking like she did everything else, and he cherished her all the more for it. She accelerated with him. Her flawless, glorious body met his every thrust with generosity, taking as it gave, and she expressed her pleasure with lusty, rumbling moans that kept his passion at a piercing intensity.

During those moments of pure, heated passion, an unknown clarity flashed inside Cole, like a blinding lightning bolt. He tore his eyes open, and his gaze locked on Maddie. Beautiful, brave Maddie. She was rolling her head from side to side, and repeating his name over and over again, like a sweet, never-ending song, all the while smiling up at him with glowing eyes.

"Tarnation, Lucky," she said all raspy and breathless as her body bucked.

He grasped her hips, keeping their bodies locked tight as hers convulsed and her elation filled the air with sultry whimpers and gasps. It took tremendous willpower, for his pinnacle was near. Miraculously he held it off until, exhausted, she sagged beneath him, still repeating his name harmoniously.

With a somewhat frantic shift, Cole withdrew, and his splendid anguish ended with a shuddering greatness as his body released. Senseless and sluggish, he rested against her briefly and then rolled onto the mattress.

They lay there, winded and spent, until a few minutes later, when she asked, "Why did you do that?"

Cole flipped his legs over the bed, hoping they'd regained the strength to work. Testing one, then the other, he stood and walked to the water bucket she'd used earlier. There he gathered the washrag and walked back to the bed to wash her stomach.

"Because," he said, "this would be no place to bring a baby into the world."

"Oh."

Her response was soft and quiet, yet it kicked him internally hard. She'd given him everything, all without the security of marriage.

Once done with the rag, he tossed it at the bucket and watched as it plopped into the water before he crawled back onto the bed. "Come here," he whispered, pulling her close.

Chapter Nine

The little boat was once again so full Maddie could barely make out Lucky sitting in the middle, rowing the oars that were making the craft glide closer. The past few weeks had opened up a whole new world.

A grin overtook her face at the thought and she waved. Lucky held an arm up in return, making her heart skip several beats. The sigh that escaped her lips was full of splendor. Land sakes, some days she looked more forward to going to bed than she did getting up.

She'd changed in other ways, too. Lucky's attitude had rubbed off on her. Miners now lined the river on both sides, and she was no longer wary or suspicious of them all. She no longer looked over her shoulder continuously, either. There was no need. Mad Dog was thousands of miles away.

Jack had said they were all in this together, and she now understood what that meant. It was as if the camps up and down the river had formed a community, a town, with folks looking out for one another. She'd never experienced anything like it, and with Lucky's coaxing had become a participant, to the point she considered the Fenstermacher brothers friends. Real friends. The kind she'd never had. They often shared meals—which she appreciated as much as Lucky did, though he'd never admit it.

Maddie grinned again. Lucky never said a word about her cooking, but now that she'd tasted good food, she knew how bad hers was. All the more reason she needed to gather as much gold as possible, in order to hire a cook. Then Lucky would enjoy every meal as much as he did those that Albert brought over.

Slowing the water flowing into the Long Tom with her usual flat rock, she stood and wiped her hands on her skirt. The only part of her better-than-ever life that wasn't panning out so well was finding gold. The first few weeks their daily cleanouts were good—some days better than good, harvesting more than a hundred dollars—but lately, they couldn't seem to scrounge up five bucks worth of dust and flakes.

Lucky rowed closer and she wondered what he'd bought this time. Her list of other things she'd acquire had grown recently, but unlike him, she was waiting. Buying things now, when they wouldn't be staying here permanently, seemed useless and frivolous. They were here to find riches, not spend them.

Homer squawked and landed on the boulder a few feet away.

"You're a little late," she told the bird. "I already saw him." Digging in her pocket for a raisin, she added, "But that's all right. You're still a good lookout."

"Look out," the bird squawked. "Look out."

With Homer at her heels, checking to see if she dropped another raisin or two, Maddie walked to where Lucky pulled the boat ashore. "How was your trip?"

He took the time to kiss her—as she knew he would—before answering, "Good. How was your day?"

She followed him to the other side of the boat and lifted out a good-size bundle while telling him, "I think our honey hole has gone completely dry."

"An empty sluice again?" he asked, gathering several things to carry to the tents. They now had three. Tents that was. Mainly for the things he kept hauling home.

"Yes," she answered. Deep down, she couldn't quite believe it. That unexplainable sense that had come to life when she first picked this spot along the river was still there. Gold still had to be here, too. Maybe she wasn't digging deep enough. "Abe and Tim got a good-size nugget today, and Sylvester Whitehouse found some good color, but his rocker tipped over and cracked. I told him mining alone is difficult."

Lucky held the door open with his foot, waiting for her to enter first. "Did you help him fix it?"

Heat rushed into her face. A few weeks ago she wouldn't have cared a whit if another miner's rocker had broken, and Lucky knew that. "I had to," she justified. "He doesn't have anyone else to help, and the brothers were busy, having found that nugget and all." After setting the package she'd carried on the table, she changed the subject. "Albert made a ham today. He bought it off Wylie Roper. Wylie's going upriver and didn't want to haul everything with him. I'll warm it up for you. You must be hungry."

Lucky caught her by the waist when she turned to head toward the door. "I am hungry," he said in her ear, "but not for food."

Maggie giggled and leaned back against him. She'd never been in such good spirits, which, in truth, was rather spectacular. As was Lucky. The first time they'd come together as lovers she'd claimed it was better than finding gold, and had been right. All it took was one touch from him and her entire being grew more excited than gold ever made her.

"You think that's funny?" he asked, kissing her neck.

She tilted her head, giving him more access. "You're always hungry."

He twirled her around to face him, and she looped her arms around his neck, stretching on her toes for a soul-shattering kiss. The kiss hadn't yet ended when he started unbuttoning her dress.

Though it was what she wanted, she pulled her lips from his to whisper, "We have to finish unloading the boat."

Without slowing his deft fingers, he answered, "The rest can be unloaded in the morning."

The fear of theft no longer lived inside her nonstop, not with other thoughts overtaking her mind and body, yet she insisted, "We'd be better off to do it tonight."

"We'll do it tonight, all right," Lucky answered. Pushing her dress open, he added, "I thought about this all day. Coming home to you."

Shivering with delight as he dipped his head and kissed her from shoulder to shoulder, it was a moment before Maddie stated, "You say that every time you go to town."

"Because I mean it."

His fingers were now on the ties of her camisole, and Maddie wasn't sure if that was why her heart skipped several beats, or if it was because she believed him. "We really should unload the boat," she said, feeling as if she should at least attempt to pretend she'd thought of little else but him since he'd rowed down river this morning. The idea of doing exactly what they were right now lived in her mind day and night.

"We can't unload the boat," Lucky answered, hoisting her into his arms. "What I bought is too heavy for me to lift alone. I'll need one of the brothers to help me."

"I can help."

"It's too heavy for you to help."

Slightly miffed, Maddie pushed at his shoulders. "I can—"

"No, you can't," he insisted, and stopped any additional protest with a kiss.

His swirling tongue sent her senses reeling, yet indignation was still coiled in her stomach. She cut the kiss short to ask, "Why? What did you buy this time?"

A flash of frustration crossed his expression as he set her down next to their bed. "A stove."

"A stove?" Maddie took a step back as her annoyance increased. "Why on earth would you buy a stove?"

He sat down on the bed—which now hosted a mattress he'd hauled from town a couple of weeks ago—and tugged off his boots. "Because the days are already getting shorter—in a month or so we'll need the heat."

She knew all that, yet a stove had to have cost a fortune. A fortune they didn't have. "You're right," she said, "that we don't need to unload it. You can take it back tomorrow. We'll just dress warmer."

"Dressing warmer won't do, Maddie." He stood and shrugged out of his shirt.

The sight was as terrifying as it was pleasurable. He knew it, too, how easily distracted such things made her. Afraid of losing steam, she insisted. "We don't need a stove." Putting space between them, she crossed the room. "What we need is gold. At the rate you're spending it, we'll be in Alaska for years."

"No, we won't," he said. "I haven't spent an ounce of the gold we've found, but while we are here, I want us to be as comfortable as possible."

It was true, he hadn't spent any of the gold they'd found. That bothered her more than if he had. From all Jack had told her, Lucky had enough money and really didn't need any gold, which meant he didn't need her, either. "Gold mining isn't supposed to be comfortable," she said.

He'd crossed the room and pulled a paper-wrapped package out of one of the packs he'd carried in. "Here, maybe this will make you smile."

Maddie didn't want to smile. She didn't want a stove, either, or to be comfortable. Lately, she wasn't overly sure what she did want. Maintaining a focus on finding gold had grown hard, and dreaming of a future had grown blurry, too. He was the reason. Having what they had right now was what she wanted. Just being together. But that wasn't enough for him, and would never be. The way he kept buying stuff told her that.

Snapping the strings in two, he folded back the paper and then lifted out material, as yellow as sunshine, before her eyes. Her heart convulsed. It was a dress. The most beautiful one she might have ever seen. It had lace, too, thin and delicate, sewn in a V shape down the front and around the hem and cuffs. With smarting eyes, Maddie looked away.

"I don't need a new dress, Lucky. Whenever would I wear something like that?"

"Whenever you want."

"One trip to the river and the entire hem would be

stained," she said, "and it probably doesn't wash well, either, and most likely needs to be ironed."

"Then, I'll buy you an iron."

She walked away again, this time toward the bed. He'd turned her into a woman. That was what he'd done. At little more than a drop of a hat tears formed in her eyes, and she didn't like that any more than she did everything else. A woman. A silly woman who thought about nothing more than fancy dresses and places to wear them.

"Why do you have to be so stubborn about everything?"

The despondency in his voice struck her in her most vulnerable spot. Her heart. Shaking her head, she admitted, "I'm not trying to be stubborn."

He was behind her again and laid his hands on her shoulders. "Then, what is it?"

Even while mixed up and confused, his hands felt wonderful. Fighting tears, she admitted, "I don't know how to iron."

"I'll iron it for you." He spun her around and wiped the moisture off her cheeks with his thumbs. "I just want to make you happy, Maddie."

She wanted to say she was happy. That he made her happy. But that scared her. She didn't want a man to make her happy. Never had.

In the end, his kiss prevented her from speaking, and the tenderness of it played mayhem on her insides. Wanting him sparked anew and she gave in, wanting as well to forget her fears, her frustrations.

He made that happen in no time, with kisses and caresses that soon had her stretched out on the bed, in complete submission with arms open, waiting for him to shed the last of his clothing and join her.

The opportunities to indulge herself in actions for no other reason than pleasure had been few and far between in Maddie's life, up until meeting Lucky. It was still inconceivable, yet absolutely gratifying.

Rather than climbing on the bed beside her, Lucky went to the foot and parted her legs by grasping both ankles. He kissed his way up her shins, over her knees and along her thigh. By the time he reached her juncture, she was wild with need. In tune to her in ways she'd never understand, Lucky took her with his mouth with a feral roughness that had her thinking of nothing but the pleasure he provided.

Maddie was immediately swept into the throes of a promising journey. The hours of waiting for him, and her greed, played against her. His expertise brought her to the brink swiftly, and a matter of moments later she reached her breaking point. As the eruption sent her reeling over the edge, she bit her lips together to keep from shouting his name.

She was still in her downward spiral when Lucky eased on top of her. His entrance was divine, and she wrapped her arms around him. Every act of loving him thrilled her, but this was the most wonderful of all: when they became one. Pure, undiluted ecstasy. Two souls spiraling upward as a single unit.

This was what she wished would last forever. It confirmed she wasn't alone. That was what worried her like it never had before, and she wasn't sure why, expect for the fact Lucky had never promised he'd stay at her side. That they'd be together beyond Alaska.

A sense of despair gripped her, and Maddie wrapped

her legs around Lucky's, rising faster and harder against each of his thrusts. Their union grew more frantic, a pairing of wills as well as bodies, and it went on for a long time, reaching pinnacles and plateaus that sent her as close to delirium as anything ever could.

She fought her surrender, holding on until it was no longer possible. Her jubilation, coupled with wave after wave of fulfillment rushing over her body, was so stunning tears once more stung her eyes.

Lucky let out a low and lusty groan as their bodies swiftly separated, and Maddie held on to him with all the strength she could muster as his body shuddered a final time.

Shortly afterward, when he attempted to roll off her, she squeezed him again.

"Don't," she pleaded. "Please don't move."

"I'm too heavy," he answered. "I'll crush you."

"No, you won't."

He tucked his hands beneath her and held her tight. "Are you still mad I bought a stove?" he asked a few quiet moments later.

"Yes," she answered truthfully. "We don't need a stove."

His gruff laugh filled the air, and grew louder when she squealed at the way he rolled off her, pulling her with him until he was on his back and she was lying atop him. "Next month," he said, "you'll thank me for that stove."

Weeks later, long after the stove had been installed and used several times, Maddie was still mad, and Cole was wrought with frustration. He'd never let a woman put him in such a state before, and wasn't pleased it was happening this time. It was all a bittersweet situation. Maddie's anger seemed to increase her passion. Their almost nightly unions were heated and phenomenal, which left Cole as dangerous as a forest of dry timber. A mere spark, like a twinkle in her eyes or a playful giggle, ignited a wildfire of need to have her, possess her.

There was more, though. He couldn't help but admit he had it all—a beautiful, wonderful woman everyone thought was his. But she wasn't. Not really. And there wasn't much he could do about that.

He wasn't the only one fixated on Maddie. Every man for miles around smashed their fingers on purpose, just to have the chance for her to examine their injury. The older ones looked upon her like a long-lost daughter, doting on her endlessly, and the younger ones wanted to be him. They watched closely, hoping he'd make a blunder so they could step in. With the way they hovered, he couldn't let it slip they weren't married.

Cole was kicking himself for how he'd insisted Maddie be neighborly with the other miners. She'd taken it to heart, was now interacting with the others regularly, and with charm. He, too, acted hospitably, but mainly because it was the best way to keep an eye on the others, especially those who thought they might have a chance to gain her trust, or more—his place in her bed.

He should have asked her to marry him when he'd had the chance, but she didn't want that. All of her talk of life after Alaska, the big house she spoke of, complete with servants, never included him. He'd never wanted that in the past, and still didn't, but he did want Maddie. However, other worries were setting in.

Gold mining wasn't working out so well. They'd found a good amount, but when divided, his portion would barely put a dent in rebuilding DuMont Shipping, and his reserves were running thin. The amount of money he continuously spent in Bittersweet was part of what kept men trekking up the river, thinking he must be hitting it big. He hadn't, and going home broke was not an option. Never in his life had he worried about running out of money, but he'd put all his reserves in this investment. In making Maddie comfortable while finding a way to help his family.

That was the other part that kept men trekking past their camp. Word of the female miner—a beautiful one—had spread quickly. Truman said barely a miner entered town who wasn't talking about Maddie.

"We have to move," she was pointing out once again. "That's all there is to it."

They'd had this same conversation the past few days, but this morning, she was more adamant. Stomping around inside the tent while rain pelted against the canvas as it had for the past three days, she resembled a caged critter. He could relate. Everything was wet, damp and shrouded with an oppressing gloom left by gray skies.

"It's getting too late in the year to move camp," he answered, searching for a dry pair of socks. Not that it mattered; as soon as he tugged on his boots they'd be damp, too.

"No one's found anything for days. Weeks. Folks are heading farther upriver. That's what we need to do, too."

She was flapping her hands as she talked, and her animated actions had a grin tugging at his lips. Smiling might just set her off like a blasting cap, so he averted his gaze and moved to where his coat hung near the stove.

"We'd have to file on new claims. By the time we did that and moved all this," he waved a hand around the tent, "it'd be winter."

"If you hadn't bought all this stuff, moving wouldn't be any more work than coming here had been." She stopped near the stove and held her hands over the heat.

Grinning at how she enjoyed the stove while insisting they didn't need it, he kissed her cheek as he walked past. "There's still gold here, darling. Plenty more to go with the bags you've hidden beneath the floor of the outhouse." The outhouse was another thing she seemed to appreciate, though she never admitted that, either.

"No, there's not."

Cole shrugged into his coat. There had to still be gold here. Whiskey Jack was still finding color, and they would, too. He didn't regret spending almost every dime he had, but he was starting to worry. If he didn't find gold, lots of it soon, they'd barely have enough money to sail south before winter, and staying here was not an option.

"Where are you going?" she asked. "It's too wet to mine."

"I'm going to feed the animals, they—"

"The animals," she grumbled.

"You don't seem to mind eating the eggs," he retorted.

She rolled her eyes as if he was shooting blarney, and a chill of fury swept up his spine. "And you hover over that stove more often than I do. You don't seem to mind the fact we aren't standing in a foot of mud right now, either, like every other miner out here."

"If not for this wood floor, we'd be a mile upriver,

finding gold," she shot back. "Like every other miner out here."

"We're not moving upriver, Maddie," he stated firmly.

She huffed and glared and huffed again. "Fine, don't move upriver. I'll go by myself."

"No, you won't."

"Yes, I will, and you can't stop me."

He crossed the room and took her shoulders. "Yes, I can, and I will."

She twisted from his hold. "No, you can't. No man will ever stop me from doing what I want. Not even you."

Anger was blistering his insides, mainly because he knew her. Maddie didn't make idle threats.

For a split second he saw his grandmother in Maddie. Her fierce determination. *When you love someone, you find a way for both of you to be happy*, she'd once told him. Gran had done that. Found a way. She'd built warehouses to sell all the treasures his grandfather found on his sailing adventures. Though his grandfather had died long ago, his grandmother had never stopped buying and selling wares. Her ingenuity had built his family's dynasty.

Cole spun around. He was damn close to failing at finding the money to rebuild the family business, and he didn't like it.

"You're not going anywhere," he growled.

Hands on her hips and cheeks flushed, she held a defiant glare on him. "Just because we've—" Her gaze flashed to the bed and she started over. "I told you before I won't have a man telling me what to do."

Drawing in a deep breath through his nose to keep his temper intact, Cole smiled. "Fine."

Clearly stricken, the color in her cheeks heightened. "Fine?" she asked.

"Yes, fine," he repeated and pulled open the door.

"Where are you going?" she demanded.

Cole turned, and after eyeing her from head to toe, which darkened the color of her cheeks a bit more, he tipped his hat with a finger and thumb. "You don't want a man telling you what to do any more than I want a woman telling me what I'll do." With that thought screaming in his mind, he left. He didn't want a woman telling him what to do. That hadn't changed and never would.

Maddie flinched at the slamming of the door and swallowed hard, trying to dissolve the pain burning the back of her throat. Fine. She certainly didn't need him.

Anguish, stronger than ever, welled inside her, and so did anger, and she stomped one foot. A useless, silly action, but she couldn't come up with anything better. Damn him. All his talk about adventures, things he'd seen, made her want to see things she'd never even known about. She wanted things, too.

Like beds. Before meeting him, she'd never wanted a huge, soft bed, complete with pillows and sheets. She'd gotten used to them, though, and didn't want to go back to living without them. Floors, either, or outhouses or food that actually tasted good.

Maddie pressed a hand to her forehead. In truth, none of those things mattered. She'd lived without such luxuries before and could do so again. It was living without Lucky that had her insides feeling as if someone had just gutted her like a fish.

She could do it—live without him—she just didn't

want to. The truth of that filled her with a burning intensity and left her afraid to swallow. If she did, she'd start crying, and that she would not do.

Her hands, balled into fists, began to quiver as the pain in the pit of her stomach swelled. Refusing to be overcome, Maddie spun around, but then paused. It was only midday, but her chores were all done, and rain still battered against the canvas roof. Lucky would be soaked, could likely catch his death of cold.

"Good for him," she muttered in an attempt to battle with herself. It didn't work very well. Worry now joined everything else swirling around inside her. As did regret. She should never have said all she had. In actuality, she didn't want to move. Leastwise, not without him.

Chapter Ten

Hours later, Maddie froze in her pacing upon hearing Homer's screech. Heart tumbling at how the bird always signaled Lucky returning home, she rushed to the door.

Her shoulders drooped as Jack, holding Homer inside his dripping wet coat, hurried forward. Digging up a smile, she held the door open, silently inviting them in.

"I was hoping the rain would let up come nightfall," Jack said, putting the bird down before shedding his canvas coat.

Homer squawked and flapped his wings, ridding them of water.

"It's coming down harder now than before," Maddie pointed out.

"Nice and warm in here, though," Jack said, leaving muddy footprints as he meandered closer to the stove. "Cole knew what he was doing when he hauled this stove home. Everyone else is shivering and sopping wet."

"There's stew in that pot." Maddie pointed to the kettle on top of the stove. "Would you like some?"

Jack hesitated, which had her adding, "Albert brought it over earlier."

"Don't mind if I do," Jack said.

Maddie gathered a plate and two cups. Coffee she had learned how to make, and had grown to like it. The two of them sat at the table, and while Jack ate, Maddie fed Homer a few raisins, which were now quite hard, but the bird didn't seem to mind. She also forced herself not to ask if Jack had seen Lucky.

"I told Cole that Homer and I would come and check on you this evening," Jack said.

She lifted her gaze.

"When he borrowed the boat earlier," Jack explained. He frowned, though, as if he expected her to already know that. "I reckon he'll stay in Bittersweet until the rain lets up."

Nodding, she gave Homer another raisin.

"I sure was taken aback when he told me about the hurricane today."

Surprised, and confused, she frowned. "What hurricane?"

"The one that wiped out DuMont Shipping last year. Belmont started the company, Cole's grandpappy, but his grandmother, Annabelle, she's the one who built it. After Belmont died, Cole's father and Trig took over hauling in stores for Annabelle to sell. She did, too, sell things. Made a fortune doing it, but I guess it's all gone now."

Maddie bit her lips together. Lucky hadn't mentioned any of that.

Jack scraped the bottom of his plate with his spoon, gathering the last bits of stew. "Cole's other uncles are helping her, but they lost a lot, too. One grows cotton, the other sugar beets, so I guess that leaves it up to Cole and Trig."

"Leaves what?" she asked before remembering she was pretending to already know all this.

"Getting enough gold to rebuild the docks and warehouses." Jack shrugged. "Trig's ships run under DuMont Shipping. Half the South got their supplies from those shipyards. It's gonna take a lot of gold."

"I imagine so," she murmured, understanding much more than before.

His chair scraped against the floor as he stood and walked to the stove to refill his coffee cup. Jack held the pot toward her, but she shook her head. He set it down again. "That's how it is," he said. "Once a man builds a house, he has to stay there, take care of that house. Even when it all gets blown away." Sitting down at the table again, he took a swig from his cup. "That was never the life for me. Houses are for men who want to stay in one spot. That's not miners, or sailors."

The tiniest of shivers tickled Maddie's spine.

"Cole sure was lucky to find a wife similar to his grandma. She never tried to make Belmont stay put, and she gladly handed over money to those boys of hers to build their businesses," Jack said. "Seems only right they all help her out now." He sighed heavily then, and set his cup down with a thud. "I didn't know any of that when I invited Cole up here to go mining, but now that I do know, I'll be heading out with him, taking all the gold I can down to Annabelle to rebuild. She deserves it."

With so many things twirling inside her head, Maddie wasn't sure what to focus on. What to think. Other than what made her stomach turn. Directing her attention to Jack, she asked, "Heading out with him?"

"Yeah, I hope we hit Dabbler while ships are still sailing in and out."

Too frozen to do much, Maddie nodded.

"If only this rain would stop so I could investigate my one last hunch."

Not overly interested due to her concentration being on other things, she asked, "Oh, what's that?"

"I didn't tell Cole about it today, I wanted to wait until I'd panned a few more specimens, but since it's still raining, and I just dried out—" he gestured across the room "—and since Homer's set in a good roost on your bed post, I'll tell you. Considering we both want to help him."

Drawing her gaze off the big red bird perched on the log making up the headboard of her bed with his head tucked beneath one wing, Maddie turned back to Jack. All this time she'd thought about Lucky helping her, not the other way around. Yet that appealed to her. "What is it? Your hunch?"

Jack shoved aside his plate to use a finger to draw on the table as he started, "The river runs like this, with all these little tributaries coming into it."

She nodded.

"There used to be other tributaries, too, ones that were covered up by landslides over the years." He made two imaginary x's on the table. "I figure the hills behind your place and mine, well, that's where a couple of those creeks used to be, and I believe those were the ones that carried the gold into the river. If a man dug deep enough, he'd find those old creek beds and the gold lining them. Real pay dirt. More than enough to help Annabelle."

Maddie was intrigued. One of the books she'd read

back on the *Mary Jane* suggested the most gold would be found underground, but she also knew, just as Jack said, it would take money to get it out, and time. Not even two people digging all day and night would be able to sluice all the dirt and process it in one season.

"If it panned out, I'd have to hire men to help dig." Jack sighed then. "But it's getting late in the year."

Growing excited, Maddie insisted, "Not too late. How many men do you think it would take?"

"Well." Jack drew the word out as he scratched his chin. "Let's see…"

The two of them talked for a long time, and when Jack finally took his leave, the rain had stopped. He'd offered to stay, but she assured him that she'd be fine. The brothers were just a shout away.

Maddie prepared for bed and banked up the fire with new dreams dancing in her head. Which died quickly when she climbed into bed. Lucky had never been gone all night before. A fleeting thought of Mad Dog formed, but she ignored it. She wasn't fearful, just lonely, and that was worse.

At some point during the long and cold night, her mood turned dark and brooding as she speculated the reasons that Lucky had gone to town. In the past, he'd always made a list first, and asked if she needed anything. For whatever reason, probably because she missed his warmth in the bed beside her, she took to wondering about the women who had traveled on the *Mary Jane*. Similar ones lived in Bittersweet, and she couldn't help but wonder if Lucky had visited any of them.

The bright sunshine when she stepped out of the tent the next morning did little to brighten her mood. The rain, having fallen for days, had washed deep grooves into the hill the tent sat upon and had completely dissolved the neat set of steps Lucky had shoveled into the dirt for her to step upon while trekking to and from the river.

A glance across the river brought about a wave from Albert, Abe and Tim—all standing knee-deep in mud. "Good morning!"

She waved in reply and went about feeding the chickens and looking for any other damage. A large puddle had pooled on one side of the outhouse. The other side, though, still held the large pile of dirt from when Lucky had dug the necessary hole.

A sigh left her chest. As outhouses went, this one was rather charming. He'd built it large enough to also accommodate a washstand, where he shaved every morning. The bench itself, which held the required round hole cut out of the wood, was along the back wall. Lucky had even made a cover to put over the opening when not in use.

He'd also pulled up the first floorboard just inside the door for her to stash their gold beneath, claiming no one would look for it there.

No one might look for it, but the rain might have dislodged it. Lucky needed gold. Every last ounce. With mud clinging to her boots and more building up with each step she took, Maddie reached the outhouse. There was an opening cut high in one wall, so the space wasn't completely dark when she shut the door behind her, yet she lit the lamp hanging on the wall, knowing she'd need it to thoroughly inspect the area beneath the floor.

She lifted the board and leaned it against the bench

before unhooking the lantern and holding it over the opening. Some of the loose dirt from the pile had washed under the foundation and she bent down, scooping it aside to count the bags.

All ten little canvas sacks she'd sewn to hold their gold were still there. Thankful, she stood and set the lamp on the washstand to wipe the mud off her hand with the other one. That was when her heart shot into her throat.

Spending the night in town hadn't helped Cole one bit. If anything, he was more worried that Maddie might follow through with her threat. Bittersweet was a rough town, full of saloons and cutthroats. No place for a woman to spend the winter. Neither was their camp. Or one she might attempt to build farther upriver. He was more convinced of that after talking with Truman. The shop owner said last year the snow was so deep no one had traversed in or out of town for three months.

Provisions had run low, and some folks had taken to eating their mules. Cole's travels had taken him many places, but he hadn't encountered anything like that and didn't want to.

All in all, he was thinking harder about leaving, heading south. He'd have to convince Maddie of it, and didn't know how he might manage that. Competing for a woman's favors had never been something he'd considered before, but he had to conclude, fighting another man would be a hell of a lot easier than fighting gold. Especially where Maddie was concerned.

There was another thought he hated— that of failing his family. Staying meant gold. Leaving meant Maddie would be safe. He still had enough money to travel to

Seattle and wait until Trig arrived—if his uncle didn't take too long.

It was early in the day when he moored the boat at Jack's place. He'd only gone to town because of what he'd said to Maddie, and he hadn't purchased anything. Therefore, after conversing with Jack long enough to be courteous, Cole headed upriver. The other man said she'd been fine last night, but Cole wanted to know how she was this morning. Last night had been the loneliest of his life.

Rounding the last bend in the river before their camp, he saw Maddie working the sluice box, and his heart hit the bottom of his boots. As badly as he needed gold, he knew if she'd found another small vein, convincing her to leave would be next to impossible.

The flapping of wings overhead and Homer squawking, "Lucky, Lucky," caused Maddie to look up. After slowing the stream of water flowing into her box with a flat stone, she stood and, using her arms for balance, walked along the large boulders separating the Long Tom from the river's edge. Her black hair, which she usually tied back or tucked inside a hat, flowed down her back, twisting and curling in the wind that was also whipping her skirt around her ankles. Cole, watching, felt a hitch happen inside him. He hadn't forgotten how beautiful she was, would never be able to. It was the other thing he noticed.

She was glowing.

"You're just in time," she said as he walked closer.

It was there, all right. Her inner excitement. The shine in her eyes and the smile on her face proved it. She'd found gold again. And that had a chilling effect on his heart—which was still pumping blood from his feet.

"Oh?" he said.

She nodded.

"For what?"

"The first cleanout of the day."

His feet came to a halt, or maybe his heart did. Either way, Cole froze where he stood.

She moved closer, still smiling, eyes still twinkling. "I found it, Lucky. We found it. The bonanza."

"The bonanza?"

Nodding, she kept walking, coming closer with each step. "The mother lode."

Cole took a breath to prepare himself, but it wasn't enough, not when she leaped and landed in his arms. He stumbled backward, but managed to keep them both from falling.

"More gold than you can imagine, Lucky," she said, hugging him with both arms around his neck. "Pounds, not ounces."

If only he could contain the exhilaration that shot through his body like a bolt of lightning. Or if that thrill was because of gold instead of holding her. It wasn't. And he couldn't. So he kissed her, long and deep.

Her response was pure heaven, and he kissed her again and again, until she forced him to stop by pushing on his shoulders. With his hands still holding her hips, keeping her close, he asked, "Your honey hole again?"

She shook her head. "The outhouse."

Cole smoothed down her windblown hair, and then, stunned, or confused, held both of her cheeks in his palms. "The outhouse?"

After a swift, sweet kiss, she answered, "Yes, the outhouse. Let me show you."

She led him up the hill to where she'd dug deep into

the dirt that he'd already piled up while digging for the outhouse.

Cole's eyes locked on the dirt while his insides took to quivering. It was gold, all right. More than he could have imagined, and from the looks of it, more than enough to rebuild DuMont Shipping. Scooping up a handful, he let the dirt run through his fingers. How had he missed this?

A bolt of excitement shot through him. He leaped to his feet and grabbed Maddie. "You did it, darling. You did it."

She hugged him tight. "No, Lucky, we did it. We did it."

By the end of the day, they'd processed more than all of their other cleanouts put together. Maddie wanted to dance and shout for joy, but she didn't. There wasn't time for that. Lucky needed gold, and she was going to make sure he got it. Dumping the last pan of dried gold into a bowl, since she didn't have any more bags, she set the pan on the table and looked up to where Lucky stood next to her.

His gaze was on their gold. "I can hardly believe it."

A tiny giggle escaped; she just couldn't help it. Even though she'd told him several times how the find had come to be, she said, "I couldn't believe it when I looked at my hand. It was covered in gold. Covered."

He picked up a fairly good-size nugget—one of many. "I can't believe I didn't notice it while digging."

"Your mind was on other things, I suspect," she said, not wanting him to feel bad. "You were quite determined to get the camp set up before we started mining."

He set the nugget down and turned, taking her by the shoulders. Her heart skipped excitedly. It had only been one night, but she'd missed him terribly, and wanted to make up for it.

"My mind wasn't necessarily on setting up the camp," he said, kissing her forehead. "It was on trying to become so exhausted I'd be too tired to think about holding you." His lips touched the tip of her nose. "Kissing you."

"Are you too tired right now?" she asked hopefully.

"No," he answered.

Feeling a need to clear the air between them, she said, "I'm sorry about what I said yesterday."

"I'm sorry, too," he said.

"I like the stove," she said. "And the outhouse."

He laughed. "I suspect you do, darling. Especially now."

She giggled. "I liked it before I discovered the gold." Running a fingertip along the line of his jaw, she then admitted, "I do like eggs, too. Though I must admit, chickens stink."

"I'll agree with that."

She pressed a finger against his lips. "I like wood floors, too, and our bed."

He grinned. She wanted to ask why he hadn't told her about the hurricane, why he'd needed gold so bad, but in truth, it didn't matter. She knew now, and she was going to make sure he had the funds to help his grandmother.

Maddie started to unbutton his shirt. Even with all the gold, all the while they'd been working, one thing had been on her mind. Her unabashed actions brought a smile to Lucky's face.

"I missed you," he said.

"I missed you, too," she answered.

After unfastening his last shirt button, she led him

to the bed and there, she refused to let him take control. Not this time. He was masterful, though, pushing her hands aside at times to undress her as swiftly as she undressed him. When they were both stripped down to nothing but bare skin glistening in the moonlight, Maddie gave him a hardy shove, and laughed as he landed on the bed. He pulled her down on top of him, and enticed by the position, she stayed atop him as he scooted toward the foot of the bed, drawing his legs up from hanging over the edge.

She slid down then, until sitting on his knees, and stirred by all the times he'd pleasured her so, she knelt down and took him in her mouth. His swift intake of breath and low growl was all the encouragement she needed to continue. Knowing she was providing him the gratification he always gave her increased her pleasure.

Not until Lucky grabbed her by the arms and pulled her upward did she release him. Then she straddled his thighs, positioning herself above him as he had her many times.

Their coming together was exquisite, and Maddie arched her back, lowering onto him until their merging could go no farther. She pulled up then, drawing herself over him slowly and tightening her thighs at the perfection of him gliding inside her.

He growled her name, and she giggled, delighted beyond belief. When he reached up, played with both of her hard nipples, it was her turn to groan at the sweet glory his touch created.

Maddie, in the midst of transformation, overwhelmed by the thrill of being transported to another time and place through their union, continued to be the one to lead the way, rising and lowering herself onto Lucky.

As her inner journey climbed upward, grew more intense, she escalated her speed, bringing Lucky with her, and when her destination grew near, she held her breath and pressed deeply against him, locking them tightly together.

Lucky grasped her hips, but fully engrossed in her fiercely liberating moment, Maddie refused to allow their bodies to separate, and experienced a completely new sense of fulfillment when his muscles went hard and he bucked beneath her, giving in to his own release while they were still one.

Spent and exhausted, Maddie sank onto his chest and stayed there, still connected to Lucky in the most intimate way until sleep overtook her.

She found herself alone and chilled a few hours later. Instantly afraid, she sat up, but then sighed when she noticed him easing off the edge of the bed.

"I didn't mean to wake you," Lucky whispered. "The fire went out."

"We don't need it." She wrapped her arms around him. His body was so warm, so perfect. Sighing, she rested a cheek against his back. "We won't freeze to death before morning."

He twisted, wrapping his arms around her and tucking his legs back under the covers. "I suspect we won't."

"No," she agreed, "we won't."

Hours later, euphoric from spending a night in paradise, Maddie stretched her arms over her head as she watched Lucky build a fire. Her contented sigh had him looking toward the bed and smiling, causing her heart to swell. He was so handsome, especially when he smiled.

"Gonna stay in bed all day?" he asked.

"No," she answered. "Just until it warms up a bit."

His laughter had her cheeks growing flush. For the one who claimed they didn't need the stove, she certainly relished the heat it provided and he knew it.

Fully dressed, he lifted his coat off the back of the chair. "It'll be warm in a few minutes. I'll go gather eggs for breakfast."

Biting back a grin, Maddie nodded. When the door closed, she threw back the covers and dressed quickly, near the stove that was already giving off heat. She moved to the table then and, staring at the gold, drew in a long breath.

This was the mother lode. She just had to figure out a way to tell Lucky it might take them all winter to mine all of their outhouse gold.

Chapter Eleven

Cole questioned his sanity. Six weeks, at most, was all the time they had before winter set in. They had to be on a boat then, or soon after, while the waterways were still open. Turning about, he settled his gaze on Maddie. Face flushed and blue eyes full of pleading, she'd never looked more woeful or charming.

He had enough money to help Gran. More than enough. They'd already mined more gold than DuMont Shipping had made in several years. Maddie wanted to hire a tribe of men to mine all of the gold beneath the outhouse, and he'd do it. Hire the men. There wasn't much he wouldn't do for her, and he might as well accept that.

Aw, hell. Life would be a whole lot easier right now if she'd stuck to mining gold and left his heart alone. But she hadn't. She might as well put it in one of her little bags, for it no longer belonged to him. However, Cole wasn't ready to turn everything over to her. Not all of him. He was not going to spend the winter here.

"I'll make you a deal," he said after a bit more thoughtful consideration.

Her brows furrowed and she tugged the opening of her coat tighter across her chest. "What kind of deal?"

The wind was bitter today. Whitecaps rolled down the river. Cole turned to the hill where their camp sat. Leave it to Maddie to find gold beneath an outhouse. The one place no one would attempt to look. His grandparents had built a dynasty by taking advantage of the opportunities set before them. The pay dirt beneath that outhouse was an opportunity. One he couldn't ignore. "Thirty days," he said with finality.

"What happens in thirty days?"

He turned back to where she stood next to the tub. He'd just dropped in the blanket and furs out of the sluice box so they could rinse out the gold. All day yesterday and again this morning she'd talked nonstop about hiring men to work their claim. Jack had put the notion in her head. She told him all about that, too. It would work. With the right amount of good workers, decent weather and a bit more equipment, they could have a fortune that would last a lifetime and still head south.

"I'll hire the men needed to mine the gold," he said, "but only if you agree to leave with me in thirty days."

The excitement that momentarily flashed on her face turned to bewilderment. "What if we still have gold to mine?"

"It doesn't matter. We still leave. You and me."

"And go where?"

"South," he answered. "Leave Alaska. Take a boat from Bittersweet to the coast." That route was longer than going to Dabbler to catch a ship, but taking the overland trail so late in the year could be a death trap.

"Forever?"

Biting the inside of his cheek at how thunderstruck she sounded, he nodded. "Yes, forever."

Cole held his breath as her blue eyes bounced between him and the cleanout barrel, and willed his tongue to stay put. He'd made his ultimatum. If she chose the gold, so be it. At least he'd know. He'd know, too, what it had been like. Not being lucky for the first time in his life.

She folded her arms and tilted her head slightly to the left, looking at him thoughtfully. "I could stay here while you go south, and—"

"Yes, you could," he interrupted. There were several things he could point out, yet he simply stated, "But that's not the deal." His insides churned. He was making her give up her dream, just like his mother and Rachel had tried to make him, but this was for her own safety. That was different.

She sighed heavily and her gaze went back to the barrel. When she lifted her chin again, a grin had formed. "All right."

His apprehension collapsed, yet he asked, "All right? Thirty days?"

She nodded. "It doesn't give us much time, but thirty days it is. Then I'll leave with you."

Gold had little to do with the thrill that shot through him, and it ignited a burst of energy. Reaching forward, he grasped her waist with both hands, then lifted her into the air and spun around. Laughing. She laughed, too, and after a good, long and thorough kiss, he set her on the ground.

"You'll have all the gold your little heart desires, Maddie, girl," he said. "Enough to buy that soft bed, build that big house and hire those servants. I promise."

The smile slipped off her lips slowly as a dark and unhappy thought entered her mind. Her grin reappeared a moment later, as if she'd realized it had disappeared and caught it, but it wasn't as bright as before. "Well," she said, taking her hands off his shoulders and swiping them across her thighs, "if we only have thirty days, we best get started."

"We'll start by hiring the Fenstermacher brothers," he said.

"Yes," she answered, kneeling down next to the barrel, "and Sylvester Whitehouse, and Jack of course. It was his idea."

"Remind me to thank him," Cole said drily.

She glanced up and then grinned as she started swishing the blanket around in the tub. "Frank Harper seems like a nice man. His claim is next to Sylvester's, and Roman Carmichael hasn't found anything on his claim. He'd probably appreciate a job."

Cole swallowed a hint of uncalled-for bitterness. He'd been the one to encourage her to be neighborly, but Roman Carmichael wanted Maddie for himself in the worst way. "We'll need more equipment, too. Bigger equipment," he said, taking the subject off men to hire.

"It'll take a lot of money, won't it?"

"Don't worry," he answered. "We can afford it."

"But will it be a good investment?" she asked.

"We'll know soon enough." He nudged her aside. "Let's get this cleanout done so I can start hiring men."

Over the next few days, men appeared out of thin air. That was what it seemed like to Maddie, and though she tried to be neighborly—as Lucky called it—she found it hard. Not all, but some of the new men reminded her of those that had ridden with her father, and she took to tucking her gun in her pocket again. After months of it sitting on a shelf, it felt heavy and foreign. She'd use it, though, if needed, as she had in the past.

The gun, though, didn't help with the other things happening. While some men continued to use the small sluice boxes, others were building a much larger and far more elaborate one. The pounding and sawing never stopped, nor did the mining. Torches were lit and men worked around the clock.

Crews took turns sleeping and working, which meant the hustle and bustle never slowed. Albert was hired to cook meals for everyone and found two men to assist him, including one who stayed up all night, feeding those working.

The outhouse had been moved and though their main tent remained in the same spot, nothing resembled their old camp. Lucky said it was all necessary to harvest the gold. Though none of it was how Maddie had envisioned things.

Her fingertips were sure to be wrinkled permanently from having her hands in the cold water so much, and awaking this morning to three tubs awaiting her was troublesome rather than exciting. She couldn't grow lax on her duties, and wouldn't, but frustration gnawed at her, and she knew why.

She and Lucky no longer had any alone time. Not even at night. When he finally entered the tent it was to fall on the bed exhausted. It seemed the more men he hired, the more work he had to do. That was true of the gold, too—the more they found, the more work it made. The gold dust and nuggets could no longer be safely hidden beneath the outhouse floorboards. Instead, it had to be transported to Bittersweet to be refined into bullion for shipping.

Maddie accepted that, too, and how Lucky had to accompany the gold, but he'd barely been in bed a few hours. "If you wait until this afternoon, I'll have the gold collected that dried last night. You can take it with you, too."

Lucky grinned from where he sat on the edge of the bed, pulling on his boots. "Today's load can wait until the next trip." He stood and crossed the room. Stopping in front of her, he ran his hands up and down her sides.

Excitement filled her heart like it hadn't in days. Lately, they'd barely seen each other and had rarely been alone. Lucky hadn't touched her, either, not like he was right now, and she'd missed it. Missed him. Silly, considering they were still living together, but it was true.

"Having second thoughts?" he asked.

"About what?"

He shrugged. "Hiring all these men, making our operation so big."

Knowing he needed the gold, she answered, "No, are you?"

"Not as long as you keep your promise," he said against her lips.

"That we leave in thirty days," she said softly, leaning closer against him.

"It's less than that now," he whispered.

The kiss, their coming together had scarcely started when it was brought to an abrupt stop. Maddie had chosen to disregard the hard knock, and to her delight so had Lucky, but the opening of the door couldn't be ignored.

One of the new men—one who left her feeling uneasy every time he looked her way—entered. "Sorry, Cole. Ma'am," the man said. "I didn't mean to interrupt, but the boat's ready to be loaded."

Maddie removed her hands from Lucky's shoulders and turned to the table that still held their breakfast plates.

"I'll be out in a minute," Lucky answered.

"You haven't eaten breakfast yet," Maddie said. When Lucky's hand slipped from her waist, she pointed out, "You didn't have supper last night, either. You can't keep going without eating."

"I'll start carrying out the gold while you eat," the other man said.

A shiver of pure fear crawled up Maddie's spine at the thought of that man being in her tent. Maybe it was because of the gun in her pocket, but a deep foreboding had settled in her stomach. Maddie lifted her gaze, wondering if Lucky felt it, too.

He didn't, not according to the twinkle in his eye and the smile on his lips. Without taking his eyes off her, he said, "I'll be out in a minute."

"You want—"

"I want you to leave," Lucky interrupted the man. "Now."

The door slammed shut. Maddie didn't have a chance for relief to settle in before Lucky said, "What are you so afraid of?" He caught her beneath the chin. "I've seen you mad and sad, and happy and excited, but I've never, not even when you fell over the side of the mountain, seen fear in your eyes, not like what I saw a moment ago."

Maddie attempted to draw in a breath of air, but it lodged in her throat.

"Did that man do something to you? Say something when I wasn't here?"

She shook her head.

"Then, what is it?"

Telling him she didn't know what it was would be useless, other than it would give him one more thing to worry about, and that she didn't want. "It's nothing," Maddie said. "There have been so many changes, so much to do." Stretching onto her toes, she kissed his cheek. "And worrying about you not eating isn't helping matters."

He grasped her shoulders and tugged her close to fully kiss her, and no one knocked this time to interrupt them. Lucky ate his breakfast then, and afterward, Abe and Tim helped him haul the gold out to the boat.

The Fenstermacher brothers had been thrilled to join ranks in mining the gold and were as committed to the adventure as she and Lucky. More so, possibly. So was Jack, and Homer, well, the bird was just naturally happy. He squawked her name twice before landing on the ground next to her feet.

Lucky laughed and kissed her cheek. "We'll be home before dark."

Though she had the urge to hug him hard, she realized that was just her own jitters, so she nodded instead. "Be careful."

"We will," Lucky assured her. He stepped into the boat and nodded for Tim to shove them off the shore.

Maddie watched until they floated around the bend in the river, and let out a long sigh before turning around. "Come on, Homer, we've got work to do."

The bird flapped his wings and strutted along beside her. Tim had waited, too, and in his booming voice, declared, "Sunny day. We'll get a lot of work done today."

She offered a false smile and nodded, knowing he was just trying to lighten her mood. Nothing could really do that, though, not with how deep it became when she caught the man who'd knocked on their door earlier glaring her way.

"Don't worry about him," Tim said in what he must have thought was a whisper. "Cole told me to keep an eye on him. And I will."

Lucky was home before dark. Maddie met him at the water's edge and told him of the large cleanouts the day had provided. "I'll need a bigger magnet," she said as he hugged her.

Her whisper made him laugh, and he appreciated that. Not caring that all the miners could see them, Cole kissed her thoroughly. It had only been a few nights since he'd held her, loved her, but it felt like years. He'd known it would be like this. That the camp would be overrun with others and time alone would be nonexistent, but he hadn't expected it to be this agonizing. The fear he'd seen in her eyes this morning still gouged at him, too. No matter what she said, she was afraid of something.

There was no fear in her eyes when they separated—just the opposite, in fact. A part of him wished they hadn't found an ounce of gold. Then the camp would be empty except the two of them. As it was, not even their tent held enough privacy for what he wanted.

Disappointment flowed all the way to his toes. Cole

kissed her forehead and then turned her toward the tent. "Let's go eat supper."

"Tim shot a moose behind their old camp today," she said. "It took most of the day to haul it all over here."

A shiver rippled up his spine. He'd told Tim to stay at her side all day, and he damn well expected the man to do just that. "What was he doing across the river?"

"We went over there to dig up the last of Albert's garden," she said. "I was done with the cleanouts and asked Albert if there was anything I could help him do. When he suggested the garden, Tim insisted on going along with me."

Cole shook off the last of his frustration. That of thinking Tim hadn't followed orders, at least. Another thought occurred to him then. "A moose?"

She nodded. "It was huge."

"They are," he said. If moose were moving already, it meant winter was on its way, too. Possibly sooner rather than later. Men had gathered around the campfire, those who would soon take over the night shift, and Cole's thoughts once again shifted.

For the most part, he was satisfied with the men he'd hired to help them. The better part of them he'd already considered friends or acquaintances. In all, there were only two he hadn't met before. They'd approached the camp two days ago, saying they'd heard he was looking for men. Upon questioning them more scrupulously, he'd learned Truman had sent them up this way when they'd arrived in Bittersweet, after the creek they'd set claims on had proved void of any color. He confirmed the shopkeeper had given Elwood Reins and Butch Grimes directions to the mine while in town today.

The day's cleanout dominated the conversation while they ate. Cole kept a smile on his face and portrayed all the enthusiasm a mine owner should, even though he didn't feel it in his heart. He'd never been in such a place before. Normally when an investment paid off he was overly zealous and often started contemplating how he could repeat the action. This time, he couldn't wait for it to be over.

Night had completely fallen by the time the meal ended. The second crew had lit torches before taking over from the day crew, and all of them had moseyed over and eaten their fill of moose meat. Anticipation was high. The men were being paid percentages of each cleanout. Cole knew that would give them more of an incentive to mine the maximum amount than a daily wage would. It also meant he and Maddie wouldn't make as much, but he figured they'd already mined enough to be very rich when they sailed south.

That, too, was on his mind. Not going south, but what would happen once they got to Seattle. They'd have to wait for Trig's arrival—the port city was a frequent stop for the *Mary Jane*—and that was where his mind kept venturing. To what would happen after Trig arrived. Maddie would want to start building her big house, and Cole still couldn't accept living in one place for the rest of his life.

When Jack borrowed a lantern to light the trail home for him and Homer, Cole took Maddie's elbow and helped her to her feet. "Time for you to call it a day, too."

"What about you?" she asked.

"I'm going to stay out here for a while yet," he answered. "I want to make sure they shut down and swap out the blankets on the main sluice before the nuggets build up so high on those ripple boards that gold starts flowing into the river."

Disappointment flashed over her face, and though regret flowed in his veins, he was surprised by her reaction. She enjoyed their nights together, he didn't question that, but gold was her first and true love. There was no doubt in that.

"You won't be long, will you?" she asked.

Telling her he wouldn't retire until she was well asleep felt practically impossible, but he was back to where he'd been before—working himself until he was too tired to do anything except sleep once he crawled into bed beside her. This time was harder. He wasn't doing it because he thought it right, he was doing it because they lived amongst a pack of men and the walls of their tent were too thin.

"Will you?" she repeated.

Her tone was almost pleading and tugged at everything inside him. "I'll try to not be too late," he said. Pulling up a teasing grin, he added, "And I'll try not to disturb your dreams of that big house you're going to build."

Bowing her head, she nodded. "Night."

"Good night," he said, kissing her cheek.

He held the door for her to enter, and stood in the exact same spot after closing it behind her. His gaze roamed the camp. The tents, the sluice, the men working. If this, finding more gold than most men dreamed of, couldn't keep him in one spot, nothing would. Yet that was exactly what Maddie wanted. One spot. A big house. Since finding the gold under the outhouse, her determination to gather every ounce had tripled. So much she rarely slept.

"Cole! Come take a look at this!"

He lifted a hand and waved at Abe, signaling he'd heard before he emptied his lungs of pent-up frustration and started walking toward the sluice.

Chapter Twelve

Maddie was sick and tired. Sick of the mud covering the floor, and tired of scraping it up. She was tired of gold, too. Smitty would think her crazy. No one could ever get sick of gold. She was, though, but having no idea exactly how much gold Lucky needed, she couldn't stop.

"Just one more trip," Tim bellowed as he walked in the door, "and we'll quit tramping mud in your tent."

She nodded as he walked to the foot of the bed, where Lucky had stacked the gold to be taken to town today. The trips to Bittersweet took place every three days, rain or shine, and for the past two days it had been rain. Again. It seemed the sun only came out every third day or so.

As if he read her mind, Tim announced, "Clouds are breaking up. I'd say we'll have sunshine by midday."

Maddie merely nodded again, not just because the man wouldn't hear whatever she might say, but because she didn't have anything to say. Even if the sun did come out, it most likely would rain again tomorrow.

As Tim exited, Lucky appeared in the open doorway.

"The rain's letting up. I could fashion a tarp over the back of the boat if you'd like to go with us."

The longing to say yes added to Maddie's gloom. "No," she answered, turning back to the pans on the table waiting to be cooked down and separated. The days kept ticking by, and the end of each one brought her fear stronger to the surface. That of leaving. She hadn't felt this way in a long time, but remembered it well. Whenever her stomach had started churning like it was now, doom was approaching.

It was as if she'd lost control over everything all over again. Like it used to be when she'd lived with Bass. No matter how much she begged or pleaded, he'd always leave.

Lucky hadn't said what would happen once they left Alaska. She wanted to ask, but was afraid of his answer—that he'd go to his family and leave her. Leave her the first chance he got. That was what Bass had always done. She knew Lucky was thinking about it because whenever their leaving was brought up, all he'd talk about was the house she wanted to build. Her house, he called it. Not theirs.

In truth, that was the only part of going south that gnawed at her. Once she left Alaska, she'd no longer be safe. Neither would Lucky.

"There're other people who can do that," Lucky said.

"What?" she asked.

"Clean out the gold," he answered.

She'd tried so hard to be invaluable to him, yet seemed to have failed in that, too. No matter what she did, from cooking to cleaning out the gold, there was someone else who could do it just as well. Better in most cases. "And rob us blind," she said.

The door shut, but he hadn't left; instead, his hands

settled on her shoulders. His touch once so sweet and wonderful was now painful. Mainly because she missed it so much, and knew she'd miss it forever. Him forever. She shrugged off his hands and spun around.

His sigh echoed in her ears. "Why are you so suspicious of everyone again? No one will rob us. These men are more determined to gather gold than either of us."

"Exactly," she said. "They could pocket nuggets or decide to divide a cleanout between them if we're both gone at the same time."

"They wouldn't do something like that. Tim and Albert can oversee things." Taking her hand, he rubbed the back of her fingers with his thumb. "You've only gone to town a couple of times since we moved out here. Come with me today." Tugging her a bit closer, he said, "We could spend the night there, come back tomorrow."

Her heart fluttered at the thought of everything he was promising with his twinkling eyes. Maddie glanced toward the pans of gold on the table. Tim could clean it out. He helped her to do it every day. She could even wear her new yellow dress. Would have to, considering both the one she had on and the one waiting to be washed were crusted with mud. In town, she might even be able to sleep. Lately, every time she laid her head down old nightmares settled in. Terrible ones about Mad Dog finding her. They were worse now than ever. In these nightmares Mad Dog killed Lucky.

Escaping those dreams, if just for the night, would be heavenly. She was about to agree, to tell Lucky she would go to town with him, when he let go of her hand.

"Fine," he growled. "Stay here with your precious gold."

"I—" she started to explain, but he interrupted.

"Just remember in two more weeks you won't have a choice."

Anger at how he assumed her answer and how he wouldn't let her speak flared inside her.

"Don't forget that," he said, stomping toward the door. "Two weeks."

"You're the one who has forgotten," she snapped as he grasped the handle. When he turned, she folded her arms over her chest, where her heart was burning. "I told you no man will ever tell me what to do, and that includes you." It wasn't much, but it was all she had as a comeback.

"What are you saying?" he asked. "That you aren't leaving with me in two weeks?"

That, too, had kept her awake at night. Mad Dog wouldn't find her here, but once they sailed south, he would. Something deep inside told her that.

Overcome with frustration, with fury, Maddie spouted, "Maybe."

Her heart hit the floor at the way Lucky's expression went completely blank.

"We could build a house here," she said. "In Alaska, and—"

Without a word, he pulled the door open and left.

Maddie sank onto the nearest chair and laid her head on the table. Building a house here wasn't what she wanted, but neither was running from Mad Dog all over again. She didn't have time to contemplate any of it before a knock sounded on the door.

Wiping the tears off her cheeks, she stood and bid entrance.

Tim had cut holes in a canvas tarp and fashioned it as a raincoat, complete with a hood, and probably hadn't even heard her tell him to come in. He pulled the tarp over his head. "I'm here to help you. Cole said to."

Maddie nodded, and though her eyes were smarting so sharply it was hard to see, she withheld the tears, until that night, when Lucky didn't come home.

After delivering the gold and accepting his payment, Cole told the two men with him he had other business to attend to and would meet them at their boat in a couple of hours. He then went to the shipyard. Boats were scheduled to sail for Nome every day until it was no longer possible. He'd already checked on that, but today he'd buy tickets. Two of them. Actually, three— he'd promised Jack to arrange his passage when the time came.

The time had come, all right. He'd taken all he could of Alaska. He chose a date two weeks out and paid for first-class arrangements, having no idea what that might entitle. He went to the bank next, where he made his deposits and recorded everything in the book from his pocket. He'd set up accounts for each man in his employ and deposited their shares at the same time he did his and Maddie's. Theirs was a joint account. Mr. and Mrs. Cole DuMont. Seeing the names on paper stirred his already sour stomach.

Maddie was frustrated, he understood that, and in truth, that wasn't bothering him as much as other things. She hadn't been herself lately, and he feared something more than gold mining was causing it. She didn't want to leave Alaska, even though she'd promised she would. In a sense, he was doing the same thing to Maddie his mother had done to him. Instead of forcing her to stay, he was forcing her to leave. One was no better than the other.

Another understanding had formed inside him, and brought empathy along with it. For Rachel. He now understood she'd been so clinging, so insistent, because she'd wanted a man to love her above all else. That hadn't been him. He hadn't loved her, and he sincerely hoped she'd found that in James. It also made him understand his mother more. And, in a cheerless way, Maddie. She didn't need a man to love her above all else. Had claimed that from the beginning. The thing he'd admired about her was now gutting him.

Lost in his thoughts, Cole glanced around the alleyway that would take him back to the river when someone said his name. He pushed the dead air out of his lungs as his gaze landed on a man leaning against a building a short distance ahead.

Vaguely familiar, Cole responded when instinct told him to check his weapon by hovering one hand over his side.

"Remember me, DuMont?" the man asked.

The drawl put the slicked-back hair and beady eyes into clear perspective. "Yes, Ridge, I remember you," Cole answered.

"You stole something from me last spring, and I want it back."

Cole's insides went completely cold. "I never stole anything from you."

Alan Ridge pushed off the wall, and the cane in one hand proved he still had a bum leg. "A black-haired beauty," he said. "You must remember her. How you stole her from my men down in California."

"You've shanghaied boatloads of women, Ridge," Cole said, not about to admit Maddie was still with him.

"Yes, I have, and became a rich man because of it."

"I couldn't care less about your financial status," Cole replied. Ridge still wasn't within pistol distance and knew it. For every step forward Cole took, the other man backed up one, keeping just out of range.

"But you do care about Maddie." Ridge took a long draw on a cheroot before he flicked it onto the ground. "The woman you're pretending to be married to. I can't say I blame you. If that's what it took to get between her legs, I'd have done the same." Lifting his cane, Ridge waved it from side to side. "That little gal has led me on quite a chase, for years, but it's been time and money well spent."

Cole was fuming, and he was imagining strangling Ridge when movement caught in the corner of one eye. He felt a quick flash of relief the moment he recognized Elwood Reins, which dissolved when his glance in the other direction picked up Butch Grimes. Damn, he should have checked them out deeper. He hadn't expected this—Ridge and his henchmen following them all the way to Alaska.

He thought of going for his gun, but the men were moving in too fast. Spinning, Cole met one with a fist, the other with a heel, but it wasn't enough to deter them. Fists came in from all directions, driving into his jaw, his gut and the side of his face. He threw blows back just as fast, but couldn't keep up with the ones coming at him. A solid punch hit him in the temple, making his head spin, but whatever hit him in the back of the head was much more solid than a punch.

He saw stars, and then the image of Maddie's face before the world went black.

A sour, bitter taste coated his tongue, and every part of his head pounded. He couldn't have said which area hurt worse or why it felt so heavy. Cole couldn't say what had happened, either, or where he was. He tried harder to pull his eyes open. Eventually, he managed the task, but it left him winded and dizzy.

A single lit lantern sat on a table next to the bed, and the room smelled like Trig's cabin. Old socks and sweat-filled clothes. He wasn't on the *Mary Jane*, though; nothing was swaying, other than his stomach.

Memories hit like a gale wind. On the verge of heaving, Cole threw his legs over the edge of the bed. Wincing at the pain shooting across his rib cage and temples, he stood. It took a moment for his equilibrium to kick in, but when it did, he noticed his coat and gun belt on a nearby chair. His boots were there, too, and while putting everything on, he thanked his lucky stars Ridge—or his henchmen—were more foolish than he thought. Leaving everything in easy reach.

Pausing at the door, knowing that didn't make much sense, he turned the knob slowly, cracking the wood just an inch to listen. The voices he heard were familiar, and not one of them was Ridge's.

Cole eased out the door and down the narrow set of steps now comprehending he was in Truman's store. Fury overrode the pain of his injuries. Gun drawn, he raced down the last few steps and bounded into the kitchen. "Get your hands where I can see them!"

"What are you doing out of bed?" Truman asked, holding both hands over his head.

Ignoring his question, Cole turned to one of the other two men sitting at the table. "Are you in on this, too?"

Looking thoroughly stunned, Abe blinked. "In on what? Me and Sylvester found two men carrying you toward the river. We took chase, but stopped once we realized it was you they'd been about to dump in the water."

He was relieved, but, pressed for time, Cole turned back to Truman. "If anything happens to her, I'm holding you responsible."

"Who?" Truman asked.

Cole was already throwing open the door. "Maddie. Those men you sent to work for me were after her. Are after her."

"The hell you say!"

"We gotta get to the mine!"

Cole wasn't sure who said what. Finding each step he took harder than the one before, he had to grab the railing to make his way down the steps.

Truman rushed past him, yelling for Gunther. When the big man walked out of the barn, the shopkeeper shouted, "There're bad men after Mrs. DuMont!"

Cole's head started spinning and grew foggy. He rubbed his eyes, trying to focus. The next thing he knew, he was hoisted off the ground and flung over Gunther's shoulder.

"Take it easy," Abe shouted. "He has broken ribs."

Gunther was running, Cole was bobbing and Truman, jogging behind them, was shouting.

"I'd never put Maddie in harm. Never. They were just asking about jobs. They knew Trig was your uncle."

Cole attempted to lift the gun still clutched in his fingers, but his body wouldn't respond to his command.

They arrived at the river and Gunther set him down inside the rowboat about as gently as he'd hoisted him up. Abe climbed in next, picking up the oars, but Gunther, already in the boat, grabbed them. "Gunther row."

"Here," Truman said, handing another set of oars to Abe. "Sylvester and I will follow in my boat."

Both Abe and Gunther had arms the size of logs. Every rotation of the oars sent the boat flying over the water and Cole's stomach rolling. He took a moment to breathe and squeeze at his temples, where the pounding was excruciating.

"How long was I out?" he asked Abe.

"Hours," the man said. "The doctor gave you something for the pain, said you'd sleep until morning."

"No wonder my head feels as if it weighs a hundred pounds." Cole took a deep breath, which didn't help much. The sky overhead was black, but clear. It wasn't raining, either, which meant Ridge wouldn't have had anything to stand in his way of making good time to the camp.

Gunther stopped rowing long enough to grab the bucket from the bow of the boat. "Drink," he said.

"Drink what?" Cole asked.

"River water," Abe said. "Enough until you throw up. It'll empty your stomach."

Knowing he needed all his senses, Cole took the bucket and dipped it in the water. Even with both Abe and Gunther rowing, they wouldn't be at the camp until midmorning at the earliest.

The water trick worked. Once he cleared out his stomach, the haze left his mind, which also brought Maddie in crystal clear. Albert and Tim were there, as well as Jack, and every other man at the camp would watch out for her, too, but if she even went as far as the outhouse by herself, Ridge would find her.

More than nightmares had kept Maddie from sleeping. The fact Lucky hadn't returned yesterday was a real and current concern, not some conjured-up dream of her past. Her eyes stung as if coated with sand, and her heart might as well be a rock for as hard and heavy as it sat in her hollow chest.

Being a woman, one fraught with emotions that had her wanting to cry one minute and scream the next, was more than frustrating. Life hadn't taught her how to care about people, and now that she did—care, that was—she wasn't overly glad it had happened.

She'd promised Lucky she'd go south with him, and she would. Go as far as Seattle to meet up with Trig, but then she'd have to leave. Perhaps return to Alaska. It wouldn't be the same without Lucky, but nowhere would.

With both dresses needing to be laundered, she put on the yellow one. The softness of the material and the daintiness of the lace and ruffles made her feel like an impostor. Trying to be some fancy person she wasn't, but she wasn't going to mine gold today. She was going to town.

Upon hearing Tim's loud voice, knowing he and Albert were awake, she ventured outside. The men were busy preparing the morning meal, and knowing Tim wouldn't allow her to go anywhere on her own—Lucky had instructed him not to—she waited until breakfast was over before telling Tim she was walking down to Jack's place.

Tim insisted upon going with her, just as she suspected, and Maddie withheld the rest of her plan, figuring he'd start protesting before she even asked Jack if they could borrow his boat to go to Bittersweet. She couldn't ask Jack to accompany her. The last time he'd gone with Lucky, Jack had complained for three days how all the paddling had flared up his rheumatism, but his was the only available boat. The brothers used their boat daily and Lucky had taken the one he'd purchased.

She made sure her gun was still in her pocket before she and Tim took off walking along the gravel-lined shore. She'd spent plenty of time with Tim and liked the fact conversation wasn't expected. It gave her time to contemplate how she'd apologize to Lucky. Tell him she still wanted to go south with him. She'd figure out the rest later—how to make sure Mad Dog didn't pick up her trail again.

A shout interrupted her thoughts. They'd rounded the first bend in the river a short distance ago, so it couldn't be from the mine. The sound came again, and she turned to the hillside. Elwood Reins stood atop the hill near the timberline. She tapped Tim on the shoulder, and they both stopped, waiting for the man to join them. Elwood didn't move, just shouted again and pointed to the ground beside him.

"What did he say?" Tim asked.

"I don't know," she answered, blocking the rising sun with one hand. The trees and tall swamp grass still didn't allow her to see anything besides Elwood. "He's waving for us to come up there."

"You wait right here," Tim said. "I'll be right back. He probably shot a deer or something."

Maddie wanted to say she'd go on to Jack's place alone, but knew it would be useless. Whenever Lucky was away from the camp, Tim was glued to her side as firmly as the mud stuck to his boots. She turned instead, to gaze downriver, wishing Lucky would suddenly appear. The glistening water held nothing but a wave now and again. Alaska was a beautiful place, and she was going to miss it. The solitude she'd known before finding the outhouse gold was something she now longed for. Turning back around, she frowned and scanned the hillside, but was unable to find either Tim or Elwood.

A tremor let loose in her stomach as she took a step closer, peering harder.

"He's not going to save you, darling. No one is."

Old and mingling fears rushed forth with a frosty shiver that shredded her insides. Maddie swiveled slowly, to where the voice had come from.

"Hello, Maddie."

She swallowed hard in an attempt to dislodge her heart from the back of her throat, but it wouldn't slide down to her chest where it belonged. Instead, it settled there, beating frantically. His hair no longer hung onto his shoulders, straight and scraggly, and there were gray strands mixed in with the black. His face had more wrinkles, but his black eyes were the same. Menacing and cold.

"Aw, darling," he drawled. "You haven't forgotten me, have you?"

Willing her chin not to quiver, nor allow the memories to get the best of her, Maddie met his gaze squarely. "I remember you, Mad Dog."

He laughed. A bitter, cynical sound that turned her bones to ice. "Glad to know, darling, but I've changed my name."

"Isn't that a surprise," she sneered while questioning her choices. He was between her and the mine, and she couldn't knowingly lead him into Jack's place. He'd kill the old man for sure. The river was an option, but swimming in a dress wasn't. "An outlaw changing his name." Keeping him talking was a choice, too. Waving a hand at the black suit with a gold silk vest, she said, "That's a pretty dapper outfit for an outlaw."

He leaned on the walking stick, complete with a gold snakehead handle. "Who says I'm still an outlaw?"

Whether he was calling himself Alan Ridge or Mad Dog Rodriquez, he was an outlaw—always would be. A mean and evil one. Forcing her glare to remain as fixed as his, and as cold, Maddie said, "Once an outlaw, always an outlaw. I can't believe you weren't hanged with Bass."

"Now, that, darling, would have been impossible."

Maddie wanted to gag. When he called her darling it sounded ugly and wicked. Nothing like when Lucky said it. "Why's that? You were hiding in the bushes?"

"No, darling, I was the one that hanged him."

Her heart dropped. For years she'd told herself Bass had gotten what he deserved, yet he'd been her father, and she'd mourned his loss. Dying at the hand of the law was one thing, being murdered by a man in his own gang was another.

"I wouldn't have had to do it," Mad Dog said, "if he'd given me your whereabouts."

She knew exactly what he'd wanted. Knew he was the reason Bass had left her with Smitty, though she wouldn't give him that satisfaction. "My whereabouts? Why? I didn't have anything you'd want."

"Yes, you did." His beady eyes swept downward. "Still do."

Maddie's breath stuck deep her stomach, and she fought to keep her eyes from glancing around, searching for an escape route.

"Your father knew it. That's why he hid you in the hills with that miner after you shot me. I'd have found you long before now if Bass hadn't switched sides and sent that posse after me."

Try as she might, Maddie couldn't breathe. Switched sides? She couldn't faint, not now. Blinking, she caught sight of his cane.

"Yes, your bullet left me with a way to remember you every day," Mad Dog said. "But don't worry. It's not as bad as I make it look. It gives me an advantage. People feel sorry for a cripple."

"I should have killed you," she said without an ounce of remorse.

"Maybe you should have," he answered. "Then I wouldn't have hanged your papa. Of course, all he had to do was tell me where you were and I'd have spared his life." Mad Dog took a step closer. "But he wouldn't. Said he rather die than have me touch you."

A tremendous buzzing noise sounded in her ears. All the rage she'd kept bottled inside wanted out. Mad Dog was the reason she'd never been allowed to leave the mountains; even when Smitty had grown sick, needed medicine, she'd had to sneak into town wearing his old clothes to buy what was needed. Her hand slid into her pocket, and the cold steel felt as hot as flames.

Maddie was about to pull out the gun when a shout rang out behind her.

"You there! Get away from her!"

Fear rippled her spine, and when a squawk sounded, proving Jack was approaching, Maddie spun around to shout a warning. A hand grabbed her, pulling her backward.

She battled against his hold, but Mad Dog managed to wrap a thick arm all the way around both of her arms and waist. Brandishing a gun in his other hand, he shouted, "Stay there, old man, or I'll shoot you and her."

Maddie kicked and squirmed, but his hold was like an iron chain. Thrashing, throwing her head back to connect with Mad Dog was useless. He kept his legs apart, too, so she couldn't connect with a knee.

Jack was still approaching, and over his head Homer set his wings to dive.

"Stop, Jack!" she screamed. "He'll shoot!"

Another shout drowned hers. It was more of a growl, causing Mad Dog to spin toward the hill. Tim ran toward them so fast trees seemed to be moving with him. He was shouting, too, for Mad Dog to let her loose.

Everything seemed to happen in slow motion. Mad Dog spun forward again and fired twice. Maddie screamed as Jack went down and Homer fell from the sky.

The next instant, Mad Dog spun again and fired toward Tim.

Fury like she'd never known unleashed itself. Every muscle burned as she twisted and kicked. Mad Dog's grip slipped slightly, and she went wild. His gun went off again, but Tim kept barreling toward them and Maddie thrashed harder.

Her freedom came so quickly she fell, but leaped to her feet, gun in hand. All her fears were replaced by pure hatred. Outraged, she seethed, "Drop it, Mad Dog."

He paused momentarily, his beady eyes startled.

"You know I hit what I aim at." She leveled her gun purposely. "And I aim low."

His sarcastic laugh was the last straw. She fired.

Mad Dog went down, screeching. His gun landed near her feet and Maddie scrambled forward to kick it away.

"Untie me!"

Maddie spun to where Tim ran toward her, with a tree tied to his back, complete with roots holding clumps of dirt.

"They knocked me in the noggin and tied me to the tree," he said, arriving at her side and spinning around. "Untie me so I can take care of him. You go see to Jack."

The fury inside her turned into pain, and she glanced down the riverbank. Jack and Homer. Their bodies. Lying lifeless. Holding the tiny bits of composure left inside her, she asked, "Who hit you?"

"Elwood and Butch," Tim answered over his shoulder. "I knocked them both out." He grinned. "With the tree. They should have chosen a bigger one. With all this rain the roots let loose with no more than one good pull."

Her fingers shook and she dropped her gun in her pocket to work the rope. It still wasn't loose when Tim shouted, "Hurry, Maddie, he's getting away!"

As if he was half snake, Mad Dog slithered into the bushes. She grabbed her gun and fired again.

"Untie me!" Tim shouted. "I'll get him!"

Torn between firing again and undoing the ropes, she chose the ropes when she couldn't see anything moving in the bushes.

"Hurry," Tim shouted. "Hurry."

The rope finally let loose and Tim leaned back so the

tree tumbled away from them. "Go see to Jack," he said, grabbing Mad Dog's gun off the ground. "I'll get him."

Other shouts sounded as a crowd of men ran around the bend.

Tim starting barking orders at them and she turned, running toward the prone bodies of Jack and Homer.

Chapter Thirteen

Every step she took sent her heart lower, and tears stole a good portion of her vision. Yet, she could still see Jack and the red-feathered mass lying next to him. She'd never had friends like them.

Her knees wanted to give out, but she told her feet to keep moving, catching herself when she stumbled. Tears poured down her cheeks by the time she knelt down and laid a hand on Jack's shoulder. "Jack? Jack!"

He didn't move and her last bits of strength dissolved. She dropped her head to rest on his back, weeping. "Oh, Jack. It's all my fault and I'm so sorry."

Something rumbled against her cheek, and her heart fluttered. Going stiff, she held her breath, wondering if it was a moan she'd heard or the sounds of the men gathering. She held up a hand, hushing them and turned to the man on the ground "Jack?"

There it was again. A definite moan.

Trying to be careful, but with her heart racing, Maddie grasped his shoulder with both hands to turn him onto his back.

"Careful, girl," he groaned. "I must've hit my noggin."

With his help, she eased him over and then touched the lump on his forehead. Excitement rushed forward. Her joy was so great, she all but shouted, "You did hit your head."

"Shh…" he mumbled.

Biting a giggle, she shivered, and searched his chest for bullet holes. "He didn't hit you. Mad Dog's bullet didn't hit you."

"Bullet—" Jack sat up like a shot. "Where is that no good—"

"Shh." She pushed on his chest to keep him seated. "Tim has him. The other miners are there, too." Turning to where the men had stopped, she waved. "He's all right!"

They rushed forward, shouting their glee. As quickly as her happiness came, another wave of sadness hit. Someone had shouted Homer's name.

Maddie turned to the massive red wings sprawled across the sand. Her tears renewed.

"Get up, Homer," Jack snapped.

Homer's head popped up, and the next instant he was on his feet, fluffing his feathers and squawking.

Stunned, Maddie turned to Jack.

The old man shrugged. "I taught him to play dead whenever a gunshot sounded. Figured it might save his feathered hide if we ever got hit by pirates."

She kissed Jack's forehead and then whistled. Homer ran toward her, wings out like a child running to its mother. Laughing, she plucked up the bird and kissed the end of his beak. "You crazy bird."

"Crazy bird," Homer repeated.

Two men helped Jack to his feet, and another helped Maddie up. She still had Homer clutched in her arms.

Carrying him, she turned, now realizing it was Albert who had helped her stand. "Did Tim get Mad Dog?"

"He and some others took chase," Albert said. "They'll get him. Let's get you back to the mine."

They arrived to a gathering of men standing over Elwood and Butch near the fire, but she didn't see Tim and Mad Dog.

"Tie them to those trees," she instructed Albert, scanning the camp harder. "Where's Tim?"

Men all started talking at once. Saying they'd take chase, too. Tremors hit her again. Mad Dog was still out there. She willed her feet to stay beneath her, but all the noise sent her head spinning.

This was how it had been in Bass's camps, men fighting amongst themselves. She couldn't let that happen, and wished in so many ways that Lucky was here. He wasn't, and she was the one in charge.

The men's shouts were growing louder and angrier, claiming the outlaws must have wanted to steal their gold, and shouting who should stay behind. Maddie's head spun faster. Flashes of the past mingled with the present. One stuck. A vision of her father and how he'd gained control of events like this.

Maddie pulled her gun from her pocket and fired a shot in the air.

Silence happened immediately, and all eyes were on her. Except Homer's. Wings spread, he was lying near Jack's feet. As she lowered her gun, she nodded toward the bird.

Silent, as if he, too, was shocked by her behavior, Jack leaned down and tapped the bird on the head. Homer rose to his feet without a squawk and dashed behind one of Jack's legs. Peering around it, the bird looked up at her as questioningly as the men.

"Count out four men to send after Tim," she told Albert. "And another four to stand guard." Pocketing her gun, she kept her chin up and hoped it didn't wobble. Though she still had no idea what to do next, she said, "The rest of you have work to do. That gold won't mine itself."

Eyeing her with caution, the men started moving slowly, which allowed her a clear view of a boat that must have come ashore during the commotion. As Maddie watched Lucky step out of it, everything hit her all over again. Mad Dog's arms crushing her. Gunfire. Jack and Homer lying in the sand. Her past.

Suddenly Maddie felt weaker and more vulnerable than ever.

She heard nothing, saw nothing except how Lucky held his arms out. Her feet moved before she had time to think, and when solid, strong arms wrapped around her, she collapsed against him. Tears stung her eyes, but she wouldn't cry. Not now. Instead, she hugged him tighter.

Lucky seemed to flinch as he asked, "Are you all right?"

"Yes," she answered, slowly unwinding her arms from his waist to step back. A new bout of torment rushed forth. "What happened to you?" she questioned, gently cupping his face. His eyes were swollen and bruised, distorting his handsomeness. She took another step back to examine the rest of him. "Who did this?" she demanded. "Who beat you?"

"It was Alan Ridge and his men," Abe, who'd climbed out of the boat and stood nearby, said. "Broke a couple of his ribs, too."

The glare on Lucky's face said he hadn't wanted her to know that, and frustration, along with a plethora of other things, engulfed Maddie. She started to tremble. It was coming true—her nightmares were coming true. "He's here."

"Where?"

"Upriver," she whispered.

"Tim's chasing him," Albert said. He then began reciting the names of the men with Tim.

"Which way did they go?" Lucky asked.

"Into the brush," Jack said. "He tried to steal Maddie and kill me. Homer, too."

"Maddie shot him," Albert said. "He couldn't have gotten far."

Albert went on to tell the story in a no-nonsense way, and though Maddie was grateful for that, her attention was on Lucky and the one hand he held against his ribs. If she'd known Mad Dog had done this to him she'd have aimed for his heart, not his leg.

When the questions and answers were done, Lucky glanced down at her before he instructed, "You heard the lady. Set up guards around the perimeter, and the rest of you get back to work." He then twisted her toward the tent, but she heard him whisper to Albert, "I'll be right back."

She dug her toes into the ground and spun. "You aren't going after him."

He didn't answer, but his silence said more than words could have.

"You aren't going after Mad Dog," she repeated.

Lucky frowned. "Mad Dog?"

"Yes," she answered staunchly. "Mad Dog Rodriquez. He changed his name to Alan Ridge, but that's all that's changed about him. And you aren't going after him. Not with broken ribs."

Though he still held his rib cage with one hand, a hard glint appeared in his eyes. "You know him?"

Conscious of the change taking place in Lucky and the men casting curious gazes their way, Maddie lowered her voice. "Yes, I know him. Or knew him." Searching for something to make him understand he couldn't go looking for Mad Dog, she added, "And I didn't spend all summer finding enough gold to save your family's shipyard just to have him kill you."

"Enough money to what?"

His tone was colder than the wind had been last night. She hadn't meant to let that slip. Unable to take it back, she explained, "Jack told me. But I figured it was something like that, why you'd want gold when you already had money. Why Trig would want gold, too. Why he made such a deal for it."

"Trig? Deal?" Fear of Ridge harming her resided in Cole's thoughts, along with a great deal of pride in how she'd taken control of the men, and now a strong bout of anger flared along with everything else. He grabbed her arm.

She refused to move. "Yes, Trig. He gets fifty percent of my gold if I don't deliver you to him, safe and sound. I'm not about to lose fifty percent of my gold."

"I'm sure you're not," Cole growled, tugging hard enough so she was forced to move.

"Looks as if the lady doesn't want to go with you."

Cole pivoted, and let his gaze roam up and down Roman Carmichael. The man stood a foot or two ahead of the rest of the horde once again gathered together. If he didn't know the men as well as he did, he'd expect to see pitchforks and torches. "I thought I told all of you to go to work," Cole said, putting himself between Maddie and the crowd.

Jack finagled his way closer, shoving broad shoulders aside. "Tell them it's a lie, Cole."

"What's a lie?"

"Elwood's claiming you and Maddie aren't married," Jack said.

Cole's entire being sagged on the inside. On the outside, he stood tall as he glanced down at Maddie, who'd grabbed his arm. Her eyes were wide and startled, and he wasn't exactly sure how she'd want him to answer. Slowly, with intent, he let his gaze roam the crowd. He'd never seen so much hope in all his born days. Though some held anger and disbelief, most were hoping he and Maddie weren't married, leaving a chance for one of them to gain her love.

He'd be damned if that would happen. "How would he know if we were married or not?"

"That's what I said," Jack replied, nodding.

"He says you stole her from Alan Ridge down in California, swept her aboard your uncle's ship in the middle of the night and then brought her up here so no one would find the two of you," Albert said.

"And you believe him?" Cole challenged.

"She's not wearing a wedding ring," Roman Carmichael said, as if that was proof.

"That don't mean nothing," Jack argued. "Sea captains marry people all the time, with or without rings." Waving a hand at the group, he continued, "I've known Cole since he was born. His uncle, too. If he says he and Maddie are married, they're married."

All eyes landed on him while Roman asked, "Are you married or not?"

A shout from the river saved Cole from having to reply. A good thing, too, since he hadn't come up with an answer. He reached back and pulled Maddie forward, tucking her to his side. He still had a head full of questions for her; though he might not be impressed with her answers, right now she needed his protection, and she'd have it.

Letting his glare cut a path, he walked through the men as they parted. He arrived at the shore the same time Truman and Sylvester rowed ashore, followed by a second boat filled with men dressed in black-and-red uniforms.

"Did you catch them?" Truman asked. "Those outlaws?"

"They're here," Cole said, gesturing to where Elwood and Butch were tied to a tree. "Ridge got away, but we have men chasing him down."

A third man stepped out of Truman's boat. "You most likely don't remember me," he said. "I'm Dr. Westphal. I saw to your injuries yesterday. Truman asked me to ride along in case others were hurt."

"Ridge took a bullet," Cole answered. "But everyone else is fine."

The doctor retrieved a leather satchel from the boat. "How about you?"

"I'm good," Cole said, watching the Mounties land their boat and begin to climb out. A fifth man, not wearing a uniform but a winter coat and wool pants, was the last to exit the boat.

"Mr. DuMont?" the man asked.

"Yes."

"My name's Curtis Wyman. I spent ten years as a sheriff in Wyoming. I'm a federal marshal now, tracking down an outlaw." He nodded toward the uniformed men. "We've joined ranks. Outlaws from both Canada and the States think they can escape to Alaska. That may have been true at one time, but let me assure you, it's not that way anymore."

Maddie had shivered when the man had said his name, and Cole tucked her tighter to his side.

"From what I hear, the man you encountered may very well be the man I've been chasing for years," Wyman said.

"Alan Ridge?" Cole asked.

Wyman nodded. "Also known as Mad Dog Rodriquez."

"I just discovered that," Cole said. The way Maddie trembled beneath his arm had Cole wondering if she'd go down at any moment. Half-afraid he wouldn't be able to carry her with cracked ribs, he suggested, "Would you join us in our tent, Marshal? As I said, there's a posse on Ridge's trail right now." Cole wanted answers and, just like the lawman, wanted Ridge caught. "Albert there can fill your men in on what happened here."

Wyman agreed with a nod, and assigned men to stand guard over Elwood and Butch. He directed others to question Albert, before gesturing that he'd follow them toward the tent.

Cole kept one arm around Maddie and took her elbow with his other hand. He sensed her fear and her wish to stop shaking as hard as she was. His insides were quivering, too. The entire time they'd been up here, she'd been in danger. Ridge could have gotten to her a hundred times. Back in California, and Seattle, too.

Once inside, Cole encouraged Maddie to sit on the bed. "Have a seat—" He paused to admit, "I'm not sure if I should address you as a marshal or a constable."

"Either, or," Wyman said. "I'm sworn in as both." Turning a chair away from the table, he said, "But I do prefer Curtis, or just Curt."

Cole liked the man's attitude, and now that she was inside, he liked the fact Maddie's strength was returning. She'd lifted her head, eyeing the marshal with all the attitude she held toward most men.

"If that is Mad Dog Rodriquez, he has a list of charges that cover most every state west of the Mississippi," Curtis said.

"It's him," Maddie said.

"You know him, Mrs. DuMont?" Curtis asked. "Rodriquez?"

"She shot him," Cole answered, surprised at how much pride he had for her actions. Though it had to have been dangerous, she'd taken on the outlaw with all the gusto and stamina she'd displayed from the beginning.

She glanced up at him, and color touched her cheeks as she said, "Mad Dog used to ride with my father. Bass Mason."

For a moment, Cole imagined he looked as taken aback as Wyman did. He shook it off to frown. "Rode with your father?"

Before she answered, Wyman asked, "Bass Mason? You mean Boots Smith?"

"Yes." Lifting her gaze, she shrugged slightly. "He changed his name, too. Outlaws do that."

"Outlaws?"

Cole's question happened at the same time the other man asked, "You're Smith's daughter?"

She nodded.

"The same one who lived in the mountains north of Cutter's Gulch with an old miner?" Wyman questioned.

She nodded again.

"I'll be damned," the man muttered.

Cole had the same sentiment.

"Sorry, ma'am," the marshal apologized. "I'm dumbfounded to say the least. I was part of a group that searched those hills for you for years."

Cole's insides were growing cold and bitter. "Why?"

"Smith, or Mason, kicked Rodriquez out of his band of outlaws after—" Curtis cleared his throat "—a disagreement. A year or so later, Smith turned himself in. He was granted amnesty upon his agreement to help capture Rodriquez."

Maddie's head had snapped up. "Amnesty?"

Curtis nodded. "Yes, ma'am." The man then met Cole's gaze. "Perhaps you and I should step outside."

"No." Maddie leaped to her feet and crossed the room to grab his arm. "I should have told you, but please, Lucky, I need to know what he has to say."

The desire to shield her was great, figuring what Wyman had to say wasn't going to be pleasant, but he also knew Maddie. She'd want to know every detail. "You're sure?" he asked.

"I'm sure," she said.

"Go ahead," he told Curtis.

The man nodded, but it was a moment before he spoke, probably to curtail some of the details of his story. "Rodriquez had never been a kind man, but after leaving Smith's gang, he turned bad. Real bad. Carnage littered his trail. Mainly soiled doves. He'd been shot in the thigh and infection had set in, causing him to lose…" The lawman's face took on a red hue. "Certain abilities."

Cole had no doubt what abilities Curtis referred to, and that shocked him. He'd always assumed Alan Ridge sampled the girls he shanghaied.

"I shot him," Maddie said, "a long time ago, in Colorado after a train robbery when they were all celebrating. He—"

"Shh," Cole said, rubbing her shoulders as he led her back to the bed. Her desire for that big house, one full of food and servants so she'd never have to leave, made sense now. She wanted a fortress, one Mad Dog—or Ridge—couldn't penetrate. Her distrust of men, people in general, made sense, too.

"I shot him today, too," she said softly.

Cole sat down beside her and rubbed her back.

"Good for you," Curtis said. "I'm sure you had no choice, ma'am, and you did the world a favor. Your father would be proud."

She shook her head. "My father was—"

"Was, Mrs. DuMont," Curtis said. "Your father was an outlaw, but he died with a badge pinned on his chest. Not so unlike this one." He pointed to the one on his shirt.

In an effort to make her hands stop trembling, Maddie folded them in her lap. She couldn't comprehend, not fully, what the marshal was saying. There was no way her father could have died a lawman. "How?"

"Shortly after Rodriquez went on his rampage, your father turned himself in. He explained how you'd shot Mad Dog. Smith knew Rodriquez was set on finding you, and was willing to do whatever was needed to keep that from happening. He said he'd hid you in the mountains, but feared you'd be discovered. The judge was more than happy to enlist your father's aid. Rodriquez had stolen the judge's daughter. Your father aided in the capture of several of Rodriquez's gang, but unfortunately, lost his life before Rodriquez was captured."

Maddie covered her mouth to keep in a sob before she whispered, "Mad Dog hanged him."

"Yes, ma'am, I'm sorry to say he did." The marshal sighed heavily. "Rodriquez seemed to disappear then. Most likely he saw the badge on Smith and the others he hanged that day. Knowing the law was so close to catching him, he went into hiding. We heard tales he'd gone to Mexico and others that he'd gone to Canada."

"It was neither," Lucky said. "He'd gone to California."

Maddie nodded in agreement. "And changed his name."

"We know that now," the marshal said. "But it took a few years before it was discovered. He went down through Mexico and worked his way back up to California."

"He ran henchmen up and down the coast, stealing young girls and selling them, mainly to ship captains who took them to Mexico or farther south," Lucky said.

"He's like a chameleon," the marshal said. "Blends in so well he practically disappears whenever the law gets close." He then asked, "How long have you been in Alaska?"

"Since spring," Maddie answered. "Smitty, the miner I lived with in the mountains, died last fall and gave me enough money to go to California."

Lucky stood up and started pacing. "Ridge tried stealing her. My uncle had partnered up with a local woman who hid girls Ridge and others like him pursued. We'd sneak them out of town and take them north to Seattle."

Maddie held her breath, waiting for the lawman to ask if they were truly married like the men outside had. Even with everything else she'd just learned, it was that thought that still plagued her.

The marshal nodded. "I've heard that, how ship captains were helping those girls. I trailed Rodriquez to Seattle, and when I saw the boats sailing north, figured this is where he'd gone. I'll catch him. Have no doubt about that, ma'am," he said, addressing her with a steady gaze. "I suggest when you go south again, you stop in Clear Springs, Wyoming."

"Why?" Lucky asked.

"Smith captured several men, and each one had a bounty on their head," the marshal answered. "There's a bank account in his and your name, ma'am, a pretty hefty one."

Curtis Wyman appeared to be an honest and knowledgeable man. His eyes were kind, too, and his smile friendly, and he'd certainly been sincere while sharing information about her father, yet Maddie couldn't help but point out, "Outlaws can't claim bounties, or lawmen."

"The judge insisted, ma'am. Your father rescued his daughter before Rodriquez sold her to a band of renegade Indians."

Chapter Fourteen

A thick fog had formed inside Maddie's head. For so many years she'd remembered her father one way, and couldn't quite work her way around all the lawman said. Other memories, things she'd forgotten because she hadn't wanted to remember them, were filtering in, too. How Bass had moved her and Smitty several times that first year, and how the last time she'd seen him, Bass had looked at her differently. His parting words that day had been to tell her everything would have been different if she'd been a boy.

All the time, she'd thought he'd been disappointed because she wasn't a son who could have followed in his footsteps. Now she had to wonder if he'd said it because she'd been his daughter and he'd had to change his life because of her.

It was as if all she'd ever known, ever believed, had changed, and she wasn't sure what to do about that.

The opening of the door snagged her attention. "Wait," she said, jumping off the bed before Lucky could follow the marshal out the door. "Where are you going?"

Lucky said something quietly to the lawman before closing the door. "I won't be gone long," he told her. "I'll have Albert stand guard at the door."

His face was swollen and he held one hand against his ribs. She shook her head. "You aren't going anywhere."

"Maddie, I know you're scared, but—"

"Scared? I'm not scared. Not of Mad Dog." She wanted to move closer, explain her only true fears concerned him, but his standoffish attitude stopped her. "I've shot him twice, and I'm not afraid to do it again," she declared. "Mad Dog's a lot of things, but he's not stupid. He won't come back here, not in the light of the day." She thought about saying Mad Dog was lying, that her first bullet hadn't rendered him incapable of anything, but that would only make Lucky more determined. Maddie knew, too, that her second bullet hadn't done much damage, either. Rubbing both arms, she tried to ward off a sickening chill. "He'll find a spot to hide, maybe even gather his men together, and then wait."

Beneath the swelling, Lucky's eyes grew hard, his features rigid. "Start packing."

Thrown by his command, she questioned, "Packing what?"

"Your things," he barked. "You're leaving."

"No, I'm not." Maddie spun around to wave a hand at the table, where everything was set up for the day's cleanout. "We still have two weeks to mine gold and I—"

"Maddie, you're leaving." Lucky grabbed her arms and spun her around. "You said yourself Mad Dog won't return in the light of day. That he'll wait. Come back at night. We can't take that chance."

Even angry, his sincerity, his concern, touched her. Maddie wanted to lay her head on his chest, but his injuries made her afraid to touch him. "Maybe Tim already caught him," she offered hopefully.

Lucky shook his head. "No, he'd have already been back." He took her arm and ushered her toward the boxes holding her possessions. "Start packing. I'm taking you to town."

"You can't row in your condition," she argued. "Besides, we can't stop mining now. Our payouts have been—"

"Don't worry about your precious gold, Maddie," he growled. "I'll see to it."

She wrenched her arm from his hold. "You'll see to it?" Fury matched concern. "It's my gold, too, and I'm not leaving without you. We either both leave or we both stay."

The door flew open and Jack stuck his head in the tent. "Cole, you best get out here."

Lucky moved to the door, but before stepping out, he glowered at her. "You take one step out of this door and I'll paddle your backside."

She opened her mouth, but clamped it shut when his glare increased.

"I mean it, Maddie. I'll paddle you in front of all those men."

As furious as his statement made her, she had to remember he hadn't broken a promise, not yet. Not even with broken ribs. She slapped her arms across her chest, glaring back.

Lucky turned around, and moments before slamming the door shut, he shooed a squawking Homer inside the tent.

"Don't say a word," she snapped at the bird.

Homer hopped and flapped his wings, crossing the room to stop before her, where he promptly stuck his head under one wing.

She rolled her eyes, but went to the shelf and pulled down the bag of raisins. After dropping a pile on the floor, she went to the door and opened it a crack. A broad back, Albert's no doubt, completely blocked her view.

"Don't make me lock you in, Mrs. DuMont," he said without turning around. "But know I will."

She shut the door and let out a few choice words, which Homer repeated verbatim.

It was a damn nightmare. That was the only way Cole could describe it. Ridge or Rodriquez, whatever his name was, had gotten away. Once persuaded, Elwood Reins confirmed they'd hidden a boat in one of the tributaries. With all the rain lately, what had been little waterways were now deep enough to sustain boat travel, and several of those creeks weaved around the mine.

There was but one choice.

Upon seeing the parameter secured by his most trusted men, Cole drew Abe, Albert and Tim into a huddle. His ribs were killing him, his mind was a mangled mess, but the brothers refusing his request was the last straw.

"Why not?" Cole demanded to know. "It's a hell of a deal."

The brothers glanced at each other. Abe was the one who spoke. "What about Maddie?"

Impatient and irritated, Cole asked, "What about her?"

"The mine's half hers. Does she want to sell it?"

Cole glanced toward the tent. No, she wouldn't want to sell it. She didn't want to leave it, either. But she would. Even if it meant dragging her kicking and screaming all the way to Bittersweet. That he could do—drag her out of here—but selling the mine, he couldn't. "Let's make another deal," he said. "A partnership."

The brothers were more amicable about that, and Cole agreed to the changes they made to his offer. His mind was more on getting Maddie to safety than money. He wasn't so sure he'd ever felt that way before, but didn't waste time contemplating it. Convincing Maddie it was time to leave was not going to be easy, and that was what he kept his focus on.

He entered their tent with a gut full of determination and a head full of reasons to combat her refusal, only to be taken aback by the canvas sacks—packed full—sitting on the bed. She was stuffing things into another one.

"What are you doing?"

"I'm making sure Trig doesn't get fifty percent of my gold," she said, acting too busy to look up. "I've worked too hard to let you go chasing down Mad Dog and getting yourself killed."

"I'm not—" Cole stopped. She'd made up her mind to leave, which was precisely what needed to happen. Yet he couldn't discount the fact he was forcing her to leave—to do something she didn't want to do. That she didn't want a man telling her what to do. Stepping forward, he turned her around by her shoulders. The apprehension in her eyes snagged his heart harder than a grappling hook. He brushed her hair back from her face and tucked strands behind both ears. "Trig made me promise the same thing."

"To give him fifty percent of your gold?"

Cole bit the inside of his lip. Shaking his head, he answered, "That I look after you. Make sure nothing happens to you."

"I'm fully capable of looking after myself," she said.

Fully resigned not to argue, Cole nodded. "I know, but Trig didn't know you as well as I do."

She nodded and diverted her gaze. "I'm sure you have enough gold to help your family. If not, I'll give you some of mine." Staring up at him again, she said, "Mad Dog will come back. I know he will. We need to leave."

That snagged at him, too—the want to catch Ridge still had a hold on him. Electing to ignore that for a moment, he asked, "What about the Big Bonanza?"

"I've been thinking about that," she said. "I think we should sell it to the Fenstermacher brothers."

Cole withheld a grin. "What if they don't want to buy it?"

"Not want to buy it?" she asked. "They'd be fools not to. We've barely tapped into that vein. The Big Bonanza will be profitable for years to come."

"Yes, it very well could be," he answered. "Are you sure you want to sell it?"

She laid a hand against his cheek. "To save your life, yes."

"So Trig doesn't get fifty percent?" Cole had no idea why he asked that, other than he truly wanted to know if that was her only reason.

Shaking her head, she stretched upward and planted a tiny kiss on his chin. "I'd give him a hundred percent if it guaranteed your safety."

He pulled her into a hug. "There's no worries there, darling."

"So we're leaving?" she asked. "Going to Bitter-sweet? Now?"

"Yes," he said. "We're leaving."

Maddie wanted to leave, but when it came right down to it, she was torn. Saying goodbye to the Fenstermacher brothers was much more difficult than she'd imagined, and though she kept her tears hidden, the big men didn't. All three of them had moisture welling in their eyes as they hugged her goodbye. The fact they now owned a major portion of the mine could have been partial cause, but considering they hadn't started sniffling until it came time to say farewell told her differently.

"You'll come back?" Tim asked, his voice uncommonly soft and broken. "To see us?"

Maddie couldn't bring herself to speak. Her tears would break loose if she did. Instead, she stretched onto her toes and kissed his cheek.

"You be sure to make arrangements with the bank," Albert told Lucky while pulling her from Tim's arms for another hug. "So we know where to send your share of the profits from the Big Bonanza."

Maddie grinned. She had no doubt the brothers would assure the mine continued to be profitable, and was more than pleased with the agreement they'd made. The brothers hadn't even seemed surprised when she'd approached them, and she was overly thankful for that. She certainly didn't have time to haggle over details.

Getting Lucky away from Mad Dog as soon as possible was her one and only focus.

"I'll see they do," Abe answered, taking a bag from Sylvester and setting it in the boat. "Won't let them get on the ship until they do."

"You take care of yourself," Maddie told Tim as he took her hand to help her into the boat. Of all the brothers, she'd miss him the most.

Tim let out a barrel laugh. "We will. You take care, too." He gave her a wink then. "Don't worry, we'll see each other again someday."

"We'll get word to you," Lucky said, taking her other hand. "Let you know where Maddie builds her big house."

Maddie's heart skipped a beat. She'd told the brothers about her goal, her big house, but now, leaving them, that house had lost some of its appeal. Actually, it had lost most of its appeal over the past few months. That, as well as the fact she didn't know what would happen after they sailed south and met up with Trig, made her stomach flip. She knew one thing, though. Mad Dog would follow wherever she went. Leaving here would mean the miners were safe, and that was what she'd have to do after paying off her debt to Trig. Leave. That would be the only way to keep Lucky safe.

He aided her steps over the sacks containing their possessions, and the tears she'd been holding at bay burned harder. Yet the way he was still holding his ribs with one hand told her this was how it had to be.

As Lucky settled her onto one of the bench seats, she turned her blurry-eyed gaze to the boat beside them. Jack was piling stuff into Truman's boat, and Homer had already made himself comfortable on the pointed front of the boat. She was glad they were leaving, too.

The boat rocked slightly as Lucky sat down next to her. Sylvester and Abe gathered up the oars in the front and back of the boat while Tim and Albert gave the craft a mighty shove, sending it out to catch the southbound current. The two then pushed out Truman's boat, with him and Gunther rowing and Jack, Homer and the doctor as passengers.

Maddie waved at the men lining the shore and cracked a smile as Homer squawked a garbled farewell. She tried to hold the grin on her face when Lucky looked at her, but it wobbled and she had to close her eyes against the tears that still persisted.

He wrapped an arm around her and encouraged her to rest her head on his shoulder. She did so, too distraught not to. Mining had been a tremendous adventure, and she'd found gold. Lots of it. She'd found other things here, too. Friends. People she cared about. Yet in reality, she was no different than the girl who had left Colorado. She was still running from Mad Dog. That, it seemed, would never end.

It was almost dark when they arrived in Bittersweet, and from the looks of him, Lucky was hurting. The doctor noticed it, too, and didn't listen to Lucky's protests. With Maddie's persistence, Lucky finally held still long enough for the doctor to check the bandage wrapped around his ribs.

"I don't think they're broken," the doctor said. "But you're mighty bruised up. One or two could be cracked. A few days in bed is what you need."

"I'll be fine," Lucky insisted.

"They'll be staying at my place, Doc," Truman said.

"I'll see he gets some rest. You can stop by tomorrow and check on him."

Grateful for the other man's kindness and support, Maddie smiled at Truman as she took Lucky's arm. It was a fair way to the store, yet she said, "It's not far. We'll go slow."

"I'm fine," Lucky told her before he said to Truman, "Make sure Gunther follows us."

The marshal and his men had stayed at the mine, still searching the woods and creeks for Mad Dog. Maddie now wished they'd rowed to town, to keep an eye out here. Gunther, as well as everyone else, including her, had their guns handy, but Mad Dog was sneaky.

Sylvester managed to secure a team of mules hitched to a wagon, and once all of their belongings were transferred from the boat, she pleaded with Lucky to climb onto the wagon seat. He refused, but finally conceded to sit on the tailgate. They'd barely gone a few yards when he leaped off. She jumped off, too, taking his arm.

When Sylvester slowed the wagon, Lucky waved him on. He turned to her then. "It's easier to walk than ride on that bumpy thing."

It was good and dark by the time they arrived at Truman's store. While the men unloaded the wagon, Jack helped her get Lucky into the cabin.

"You two can stay here," Jack said. "Homer and I will bed down in the barn with Gunther. So will Abe and Sylvester. Truman only has one bed in his place."

Maddie didn't protest as she pulled back the covers, preparing a spot for Lucky to lie down, and she assisted in removing his coat. His deep sigh as he lowered onto the bed told her just how bad he was hurting. Jack started a fire before he left, and she used the time to pull off Lucky's boots and tug the covers up to his chin.

His eyelids fluttered open for a moment as he said, "Thanks, Maddie. I just need to rest for a minute."

The tears were back, smarting as sharply as ever. His bruises were turning darker, and both eyes were swollen. There was a cut in the corner of his mouth, too, and all she could think about was how it was her fault. All her fault. She should have known Mad Dog would follow her. The past two years she'd thought Bass had quit visiting, but she now knew Mad Dog had hanged him. During that time, she'd grown lax, and had worried more about Smitty's illness than Mad Dog finding her. An inner chill made the hair on her arms stand. Smitty had said Mad Dog had gone down to Mexico, and until this moment, she'd never questioned how he'd learned that information. Now she wondered if he'd also known about Bass. How he'd turned himself in to catch Mad Dog. To protect her.

A knock on the door interrupted her musing, and she hurried to open it. Truman walked in, followed by Jack. Both men had their hands laden with plates, cups and a coffeepot still steaming.

"Gunther's boys brought over some stew, and I made coffee," Truman said. "You'd best try to get some food in that boy before he falls to sleep. He hasn't eaten since yesterday."

Maddie helped set everything on the table, other than the coffeepot. Truman set that on the stove.

"Don't you worry," Truman said as he turned to leave. "We got the place well protected. That outlaw won't get within firing range of this cabin."

* * *

Tired and sore, all Cole wanted to do was sleep, but saying no to Maddie was impossible, so he ate. He kept his ears pricked, too, listening to the voices outside. The thick logs of the cabin muffled actual words, but he'd recognized the voices. Jack. Truman. Albert. Sylvester. Gunther. They were good men. Better than he could ask for. And not one of them would let harm come to Maddie.

He set the spoon in the bowl, and smiled his thanks when Maddie took the bowl. She'd removed her coat, and he couldn't help but appreciate how lovely she looked in the yellow dress he'd bought for her. It fit her like a glove, like he'd known it would, enhancing all her mystical curves perfectly. The same curves he'd enjoyed exploring, and longed to do so again.

"Come lie down," he said, missing her more than ever.

"No, you're hurt."

"It's late and you're tired," he said. "Blow out the lamp and come to bed." Maddie, being Maddie, would argue, so he added, "I won't sleep until you're beside me. I've grown too used to it."

Her lips curved into a tiny smile. He scooted over, making room, and watched as she stacked the dishes and stoked the fire before blowing out the lamp. His eyes adjusted to the darkness in time to see the yellow dress slip from her shoulders and down her back. She folded it over a chair and then removed her socks and shoes.

Extremely slow and cautious, she eased onto the bed, hardly making the mattress move, and his grin broke free. Barely moving himself, he slid his arm under her head.

"I'm sorry," she whispered.

"Shh." He shifted slightly to kiss her temple. "Just close your eyes and go to sleep."

She snuggled closer. "I'm afraid to touch you. I don't want to hurt you."

"Your touch will never hurt me." He pulled her arm across his chest.

Cole didn't remember falling asleep, nor did he know what woke him. It was still dark, stars twinkling outside the tiny window. An electrical jolt shot through him as Maddie snuggled closer. Her hand, soft and gentle, was rubbing his chest. If there was any pain in his ribs, it disappeared beneath her touch, and he became fully aware of what had awakened him. He slid a hand inside her pantaloons, caressing the smooth, silky skin of her backside.

She let out a husky little moan.

He kissed her closed lids, the tip of her nose and then her lips. Her response was all he'd hoped, until she pulled her lips from his.

"You're hurt."

"Who told you that?" he teased, running his hand lower into her pantaloons.

She arched against him and folded a knee over his thigh. "I saw it for myself."

"That's only on the outside," he said, nibbling on the side of her neck. "On the inside I'm as good as ever, and I want you."

Her groan was adorable and intensified the deep throbs of his desires. She was perfection from tip to toe, and finding her sweet spot all warm and moist was better than any gold they'd discovered.

"Lucky, we can't," she insisted.

He laughed at how halfhearted she sounded. "We'll be quiet."

"It's not that," she said. "You're hurt."

"I'm hurting for you." He teased her more thoroughly. "And it's mighty painful."

She tilted her head up, kissing him deeply at the same time her hand ventured past his stomach and caressed him though his drawers—the specific part that wanted her more than his lungs needed air. His throat grew thick and a growl rumbled its way up and out.

She giggled as she pulled her tongue out of his mouth.

"Aw, darling, I've missed you."

"I've missed you, too," she whispered.

Easing his hand out of her pantaloons, he suggested, "Then, let's get rid of these clothes."

Her pause said she was going to protest again, so he kissed her until she was rubbing against him with the same amount of fervor pumping in his veins. He wanted to take the time to truly appreciate the splendor of her body—the firm breasts, the warm, moist heat between her legs—but he was pushing his luck in convincing her to make love. Her hand had moved back up to his ribs, where it was gingerly checking for injuries.

"I'll lie still," he whispered. "Let you do all the work."

The steady stare she settled on his face wasn't one to reckon with. Though passion glittered her eyes, concern was there, too. "You promise?"

"I promise," he answered, tugging at her underclothes.

She brushed aside his hands. "I'll do that. You lie still."

If this was his reward, Cole vowed to crack a rib regularly. She slid out of her underclothes and then folded back the blankets and drew his drawers down so slowly, so enticingly sweet he was ready to explode from the need thumping through his veins. Her skin glistened in the darkness, and he reached to run his hands along her arms, but she pulled them away.

"You lie still," she whispered.

"Maddie," he growled. "You're torturing me."

She giggled. "No, I'm not."

Yes, she was. Her hands roamed up his legs, over his knees, along his thighs, teasing his very being to agonizing heights. When she wrapped her fingers around him, his breath locked in his lungs. She played him like a gambler does a full house, until Cole swore at his own desperation and grabbed her arms, pulling her onto him.

Cracked ribs didn't stifle his stamina as much as she did, and when she slid over him, her velvet channel taking him fully, he tensed every muscle to simply relish in the sweetest pleasure imaginable.

Cole had no choice but to accept the steady and even course Maddie set. It was pure perfection and propelled them forward steadily, sweetly. The flawless union suited him beyond all other sailing he'd experienced. Her thighs, parting and joining as she hoisted upward and glided downward, set loose an imaginable force he could no longer resist. When her head flung backward, her breasts arched into the air as her fulfillment neared, Cole grabbed her hips, holding her to him as his own completion hit.

Her lips were clamped together, muffling her cries of victory into whimpers, and Cole grasped her neck, tugging her down to kiss away the groan bubbling in the back of his throat.

Afterward, as she slowly moved off him, he wrapped an arm around her and pulled the covers over both of them with his other hand. "I do believe, Maddie, girl, finding gold is only one of the things you're tremendously good at."

She giggled, nestling her head on his shoulder. "Go back to sleep," she whispered. "You need your rest."

Thoroughly sated, he kissed the top of her head. "That was more healing than sleep."

"Go to sleep," she demanded sweetly.

Despite what they'd just shared, how he'd witnessed her body was unharmed, Cole's thoughts shot to Mad Dog. How the man had laid his soiled and cruel hands on her, and that he was still out there, somewhere.

Cole kissed the top of her head again. It was going to be hell, but it was what he had to do. Leave. He didn't want to, but getting her to safety meant more to him than anything else. She'd changed that about him. Putting someone else's needs before his.

Tilting her head back, she looked up at him with those star-filled eyes, and half-afraid she'd say something, he pressed his lips to hers. "Go to sleep, darling, and dream about that big houseful of servants you're going to build."

She stiffened slightly. Cole kissed her again and then pressed a finger to her lips, and kept it there until her body had relaxed enough to know that she was sleeping once again. He, on the other hand, lay awake for hours.

Chapter Fifteen

Maddie was torn again the following day when Lucky insisted they board a ship heading for Nome. She'd assumed they'd stay in Bittersweet, at least long enough for him to heal; yet at the same time, she wanted to get as far away from Mad Dog as possible.

After meeting with the banker and signing papers along with Albert, they returned to Truman's, where she grew heavyhearted again while saying goodbye to the shopkeeper and Gunther. Albert helped transport their possessions on board a ship smaller than the *Mary Jane*, but equipped to haul passengers, which meant she and Lucky had a private cabin. So did Jack and Homer.

Maddie stood near the railing, waving goodbye to Albert as the boat set sail, and once again she questioned all that had changed inside her since arriving in Alaska. Mainly her perceptions. Not all men were untrustworthy.

Lucky, standing at her side, took her hand and led her toward their cabin as Bittersweet disappeared. There, he warmed her, inside and out, until she completely forgot about everything except him.

* * *

The weather turned colder, and the day they arrived in Nome, snowflakes danced in the wind. The town was larger than Bittersweet, but to her surprise, the buildings were similar, built of rough lumber and tents. Lucky insisted upon purchasing things for their ocean voyage. Maddie shook her head at the armloads of items he hauled onto the much larger ship they were now passengers on.

Their cabin was much larger, too. Thank goodness. "I certainly don't need all these clothes," she declared, running her hands over the softness of a remarkable blue velvet dress he'd bought for her.

"It'll be a long voyage," he said. "We won't be able to wash clothes until we get to Seattle."

He was right, of course, and Maddie had worn all of the half-dozen dresses he'd purchased as well as all the underthings by the time the boat docked in Seattle the first part of December.

All her life Christmases had come and gone with little notice, so seeing an entire town decorated from end to end for the approaching holiday was fascinating. Lucky learned the *Mary Jane* was due to arrive after the New Year and acquired accommodations in a fancy hotel in the heart of the city. Jack found separate lodging in a simple boardinghouse closer to the shoreline that welcomed Homer.

"We could have stayed at the boardinghouse, too," Maddie said after they'd seen Jack settled and returned to their suite. It not only had a huge bed, but a separate bedroom, complete with an attached bathing room, and a sitting room with two sofas.

"Yes, we could have," Lucky answered, removing

his tie. He'd purchased himself several suits, which he looked extraordinarily handsome in. "But I like this place better." He caught her waist and pulled her up against him. "We have a lot more privacy."

She looped her arms around his neck. "I like that, but the prices here are outrageous."

"You are worth every dime," he insisted, kissing her.

Ever since that night back in Bittersweet, the only disruptions in their lovemaking had been due to her monthlies. Sometimes he loved her slowly, sweetly, and other times it was so swift and wild she was left in a dizzy, spiraling world. His kiss right now said this would be one of those encounters, and her heart leaped into her throat, ready for the adventure to sweep her away.

Maddie was swept away, and enjoyed every caress, every moment they spent in the big fancy bed. It was afterward that hurt. When another part of her heart broke off, knowing as soon as Trig arrived she and Lucky would go their separate ways. He'd go south to New Orleans to help his grandmother. She'd been at the bank with him the first day they'd arrived, where he wired money and sent messages saying he'd be home as soon as possible. He hadn't asked her to go with him, and she hoped he wouldn't, for she didn't know how she'd tell him no.

She would have to, though. If needed, she'd ask Trig to help her, even offer him his 50 percent to take Lucky to New Orleans.

She'd go to Wyoming then. That was what she figured, to the judge who wanted Mad Dog. The outlaw would follow her, and she hoped the judge would help set a trap for him. Wyoming was the opposite direction from New Orleans, and that was the most important thing. To keep Mad Dog as far off Lucky's trail as possible.

Part of her wished Trig would never arrive, and another part wished he'd hurry up and get here, so she could get on with things. There wasn't much she liked about Seattle. The vast number of people was overwhelming and made keeping her vigil, of watching for Mad Dog, more difficult than ever.

Word had spread of their mining success, and people flocked to them, right to their hotel room, wanting to sell things or buy shares in the Big Bonanza. Maddie gladly let Lucky talk to the visitors, but unfortunately he also accepted invitations from them. To an array of parties and dinners, things she'd never attended before. It was frightening at first, since she had no idea how to act or what to say, but Lucky told her not to worry, to just follow his lead.

She had, and soon knew exactly what fork to use when, and how to pretend she was having a wonderful time when she clearly wasn't. By the second week, she wished she'd never learned such things so she'd have an excuse not to attend any of the lavish gatherings.

She continued to go, though, because Lucky wanted her to. He'd hired men, too, who followed her every step. He, too, knew Mad Dog was out there. Word had arrived by a ship that Wyman had tracked Mad Dog clear to Dabbler, but lost him there.

From across the room, Lucky's statement penetrated her deep musing. Turning, she frowned. "I thought we were going to spend Christmas with Jack and Homer at the boardinghouse," she said.

"We will," he said, tying his tie. "Tomorrow. Christmas Day. Tonight we'll attend a party at the mayor's home. Jack will be there, too."

"A party," she repeated drily. That was not what she called them. So far none of them had been close to the happy celebrations they'd had back in Alaska, with Albert cooking venison and everyone chatting endlessly. Happily. People talked here, but only about money. Either how much they had or how much they wanted.

She'd discovered something else, too—something she'd always known. Men didn't have to be outlaws to be treacherous. The rich ones they kept encountering would rob a man blind while looking at them. At least an outlaw did it on the sly.

The women here were just as bad. And, to her way of thinking, rather mindless. She wouldn't trust a one even on a lead rope. To her face they were kind enough, asking where she'd gotten the dress she wore or some other article of clothing, such as the never-ending jewelry or shawls Lucky kept buying her, but that was where their eyes always were. On Lucky. Leaving her with a great desire to draw her gun and force them to keep their distance.

She didn't draw her gun, but did keep it handy—a little derringer Lucky had bought that she could keep hidden most anywhere.

"Yes, a party," Lucky said, picking up a fur shawl he'd purchased for her a few days prior. "Are you ready?"

She turned, letting him drape the garment over her shoulders, and picked up the matching muff. The fur was luxurious and she felt pretty wearing them, which left her sickened, knowing she was as bad as all the women she detested. "Where are we going now?"

"To buy you a dress for this evening."

Stopping midstep, Maddie shook her head. "I have dresses. Lots of them. Some I've only worn once."

Lucky propelled her toward the door. "A rich woman never wears the same dress to a party."

"That's a waste of money, if I've ever heard it."

"Maybe," he said. "But it's how high society works." He opened the door. "That's what you wanted. To be a rich woman with a big house and servants." Leading her along the hallway, he continued, "The mayor's house is the largest in town. Many of the other people we've met will be there tonight, and they'll remember what you were wearing last night and last week."

Maddie frowned but quickly hid it. Lucky did seem to enjoy escorting her about and acted as if each event excited him as much as the one before. Deep down, she had her own reason for continuously accompanying him. They'd soon be parted, and she wanted to spend every moment possible with him.

The day was surprisingly warm and sunny—a rarity. Before Lucky had a chance to direct the man near the front door of the hotel to find them a carriage, she asked, "Can we walk? I feel as if I haven't done anything except sit for months."

"All right," he said. "It's not far."

"What isn't?"

"The dress shop. I'm told Agatha Foster's gowns are the most popular and highly sought after."

For a moment, she'd forgotten where they were going. Once again his excitement prevented her from commenting, but two hours later, after having tried on several gowns, Maddie couldn't maintain her silence. "Don't you have anything that buttons up the front?"

The shop owner, Agatha Foster, had bright red hair and a crooked nose she looked down even while kneeling to check a hem or seam. It was her haughtiness that had rubbed Maddie the wrong way from the moment she'd stepped into the shop full of gowns covered with ribbons and lace. The shop owner had two young assistants, and rather than talk to them, Agatha Foster clapped her hands toward the girls to send them scurrying after whatever she wanted.

"Surely you have a dressing maid to assist you," Agatha Foster said.

"No." Even without the woman's obvious scorn, Maddie didn't feel like furthering her explanation. Once she and Lucky were parted, she wouldn't have anyone to fasten any of the lavish gowns he'd already purchased.

"To answer your question," the woman added snootily, "no. Fashionable gowns do not fasten down the front."

Maddie turned and glanced in the long mirror. "Well, then, this one will do." The gown was rather lovely. The shiny material was dark green, and rows of gold stitching formed decorative swirls on the cuffs, hem and at the waist. A heavy sigh escaped. She hardly recognized herself, and wasn't sure she liked that.

"Very well." The woman glanced toward the heavy curtain separating this room from where they'd left Lucky. "Mr. DuMont said you will need a few other gowns."

"He was mistaken," Maddie said, done dress shopping. She disrobed and retrieved the blue velvet gown—her favorite—that she'd put on this morning.

"How about undergarments?" the woman asked.

"I have plenty of those, too." Maddie wasted no time

in buttoning her gown, which did fasten up the front. "There is nothing else we need here."

"Very well. I'll make the slight alterations needed and have the gown delivered to the hotel, if that is to your liking, Mrs. DuMont." There was definite disappointment and a hint of reprimand in the woman's tone.

"That will be fine," Maddie said, parting the curtain. She waited impatiently while Lucky settled the bill, something he always insisted upon doing, and practically ran out the door when he opened it.

Once on the boardwalk, he took her elbow. "I secured us a coach. I want to show you something."

Holding in a tremendous sigh, she asked, "What is it?"

"I've arranged for us to tour a couple of homes," he said. "To give you some ideas for the house you want to build."

"I don't want to build a house here," she said.

Cole did his best to keep a smile on his face. This was the life she wanted, and he was trying his best, but it all reminded him of the things he didn't miss. Gran had hosted lavish balls and galas, and as the eldest son, it had been his duty to escort his mother after his father had died. He was using that, his experience, to make them fit in now. Had to. He had an ulterior motive. Mad Dog was still on the loose, and Cole wanted the outlaw to know where to look for Maddie.

Not find her, but look for. He was using their mining success to make them the most popular people in town and wanted word spread that they were building a house—the house she always wanted. "I'm not suggesting we build one here," he said. "It'll just give you an idea for when you choose where you want to live."

She nodded and allowed him to escort her into the carriage, but the smile on her face looked as strained as his felt. He couldn't share his plan with her, but hopefully afterward, when all was settled, she'd understand why and forgive him.

He'd sent messages to both his grandmother and mother, saying he'd be home as soon as possible. That was part of his ploy, for everyone to know they planned on sailing south when Trig arrived. Whereas, in reality, it was all to set a trap for Mad Dog.

He was setting a lot of hope into the plan, as well as what happened after apprehending Mad Dog. If the scenarios that rolled in his head played out, Maddie would never have to worry about the outlaw again. Then they could truly start their life together. It was now what he wanted. He couldn't imagine spending the rest of his life without her. If that meant building a big house and setting down roots, so be it. The happiest days of his life had included her, and something deep down and foreign had convinced him that that would be enough.

He'd just have to be sure to never tell her what to do. Cole almost cracked a grin. Not telling Maddie, the stubborn woman she could be at times, might prove to be more fun than Lucky had originally expected. He'd figured out a lot of things, many of them concerning women, since meeting her. She wasn't so different from his mother and Rachel, not when it came right down to it. The number one thing women wanted was to have things their way. Unlike Rachel and his mother, when it came to Maddie, he wanted her to have things her way. Even if it wasn't what he wanted. That was what happens when a man loves a woman above all else.

He did. Love her above all else. Cole wasn't sure exactly when that realization had happened, but had come to accept it, and in truth, he liked loving her.

She was gazing out the side window and turned, sensing him watching her, no doubt. She smiled and leaned her head against his shoulder. "I've never seen such decorations. There are even red bows on the lampposts."

He kissed the top of her head. "My mother and grandmother decorate their homes for the holidays," he said. "And we always had a huge tree full of candles." He'd taken to talking about his home a lot lately, just so she'd be convinced he was missing it and wanting to return soon.

"You did?"

The sadness of her tone wrestled inside him. He wouldn't mind seeing his family again, but in truth, if Maddie didn't want to go to New Orleans, they wouldn't go. Not telling her that stung. "Yes, we did," he answered. He now understood why she wanted that big house. The security it would provide. Having grown up as she had, the daughter of an outlaw, being pursued by a killer, left her with no one to trust. No one to shelter her from all the evils of the world. He wanted to promise he'd give her that more than he wanted anything else, but he couldn't—not just yet.

She was worried. Very worried. He sensed that. There wasn't anything he could precisely put his finger on, but it seemed as if he'd lost half of her someplace along the line. He'd tried to convince her she had nothing to be ashamed of when it came to her father, the life she'd had, but that hadn't seemed to help. The only time she was really herself was at night, when they were alone. The fiery, passionate Maddie came forth

then. That thrilled him, and he wanted to see the lus-
ter in her eyes during the day, too. Every day, for the
rest of her life.

She sighed heavily, and he squeezed her shoulder.
"I'm sure the mayor's house will be quite festive tonight."

"I can't wait to see it," she said.

That was about the biggest lie she'd ever told. However, Cole kept his thoughts to himself. Not going would
put a kink in his plan. He had hired men lining the
docks, watching every ship that landed for Mad Dog,
and they needed to know where he was every minute
of the day. Changing his schedule could leave him not
knowing if Mad Dog was in town or not.

She let out a heavy sigh. "Do we have to go to the
mayor's house tonight?"

As much as he'd like to say no, he said, "Yes."

"Why?"

He wanted to say because it was the only way to assure her safety. Instead, he dived into a softer explanation. "The gold rush to Alaska has been good for
Seattle. The city has started proclaiming itself as the
gateway to getting there, and we've become the proof it
can happen. That anyone willing to take a gamble has
the chance of making it rich."

Cole had been surprised that the entire town knew
of their mining success before they'd landed, but it had
given birth to his plan. Before then, he'd planned on securing her a hotel and heading north again, in pursuit
of Mad Dog.

"Jack's hoping to find a buyer for his claim tonight,"
Cole said, glad he had one solid truth to tell her.

"Do you wish we'd sold everything to the Fenstermacher brothers, instead of just making them partners?" she asked.

"No," he said honestly. "My grandmother once told me that a smart man invests in things that will keep working for him long after he walks away. The brothers are good men, and with their leadership, I believe the Big Bonanza will continue to make us money for years to come."

"Me, too." She glanced out the window. "So we're going tonight because of Jack?"

Cole held in his own sigh. "The party is sure to have people chomping at the bit to acquire an already promising claim."

The carriage stopped, and Cole waited for the driver to open the door before escorting Maddie down the steps and up the walkway of an impressive brick home. He'd lined up these tours in hopes to put a fire inside Maddie. Get her talking about future plans at the parties they attended.

Though Maddie was kind and pleasant, she barely muttered a word. Knowing he couldn't cut the tours short, Cole continued as planned, but was brooding as deeply as Maddie by the time they were over.

On their way back to the hotel, they passed a rather large and elaborate church, and he recalled another thought, one that was never far from his mind. He and Maddie had never discussed what Elwood had told the miners, not fully.

Displaying little emotion, Maddie said, "Don't worry. I haven't told anyone we aren't really married here, either." Turning away from the window, she went on to say, "If they find out differently, and they will, considering how fast word spreads here, they'll start to question other things, and that could ruin Jack's chances to sell his claim."

He didn't want her to be right, but she was, and the set of her jaw said she wasn't open to discussing any of it. She seemed to react that way to everything lately. Refused to talk about the future, of where she wanted to live, to build a house. All she'd say was they'd discuss it after Trig arrived and she paid off her debts.

Growing more frustrated by the heavy silence growing between them, Cole asked, "Do you want to go shopping?"

"We went shopping yesterday," she said without glancing his way. "And this morning. Let's just go back to the hotel. I want to read the newspapers."

"You've read every paper they have," he snapped. "From all across the nation."

"Mr. Harms promised to collect any new ones that may have arrived this afternoon," she said, turning back to the window. "I like reading about new places."

I don't, he wanted to bark. He liked seeing new places, exploring new places, which was the one thing he was having a hard time giving up.

Chapter Sixteen

The mayor's house was more elaborate than the ones they'd visited earlier in the day. Maddie attempted to be impressed, to be awed by the decorations and the furniture and the servants, but she wasn't.

She wasn't impressed with Lucky, either. Shortly after returning to the hotel this afternoon, he'd left, giving her strict instructions to stay put, as always. She didn't mind him telling her things like that; he was just worried. Besides, it wasn't as if she had anywhere to go. That was what was driving her crazy. At least when she'd been in hiding with Smitty, she'd been outdoors. Able to breathe.

Mr. Harms, the man behind the front desk at the hotel, had delivered new papers, but they hadn't held her attention. Instead, she'd questioned things. Like how long it would be before Trig arrived. Though she didn't want to be parted from Lucky, she did want Mad Dog caught, and that wouldn't happen as long as Lucky was at her side. It wasn't safe for Lucky, and with all the people he had guarding her, Mad Dog might never approach her. And knowing that he was out there somewhere, waiting, was worse than having him actively chasing her. An oddity, but a reality.

When one of the girls from the dress shop arrived with the green gown, Maddie had let her in and accepted help in getting ready, since Lucky wasn't there to button the back of her dress.

In the end, Maddie had even let the girl, April had been her name, curl her hair with a piece of iron the shape of a gun barrel and hot enough it made her scalp sizzle. Maddie still wondered if she'd ever find all the pins April had shoved into her head to keep the curls in place.

She wasn't impressed with the mayor's house, or Lucky, but the mayor's wife really aggravated her already raw nerves. Normally Maddie welcomed Lucky's touch, and his nearness, but this evening, the way he kept his palm in the small of her back, urging her forward to say hello to people she had no desire to meet, made her want to stomp on his foot.

She wouldn't, though. Not because he'd given her another lecture on being neighborly, either. He no longer did that. She wished he did. It was easier to understand. She understood the concept of being neighborly. The concept of being a rich woman was what she didn't understand. Rich or not, no one needed to be rude. The mayor's wife was. Rude. Mean. And ugly.

Maddie bit her lip, knowing her reactions to the other woman were just as bad mannered. Perhaps that was what happens when a woman has money. Their lives became so boring and empty they took it out on everyone else. She'd once thought all she needed was money and her life would be wonderful. It wasn't so.

However, Maddie was smart enough to know deep

down that wasn't what bothered her. For as long as she could remember, she'd wanted things. Things that would make her life better. Reasons to get up in the morning, and it hadn't all been about money.

Pulling her gaze away from the young serving girl the mayor's wife had just reprimanded in public, Maddie turned to accept the glass of punch Lucky held toward her. Trying not to let her anger show, she said, "Thank you."

"You're welcome," he said, sounding as icy as she had.

He'd seen the scolding, too, and she knew he wasn't pleased. A warmth settled in her chest. Not only did he look overly handsome in his dark green suit jacket, but he was also the most down-to-earth person in the room, so unlike all those other snobbish and superficial men. All the gold in the world wouldn't change Lucky.

Several of the men at the party reminded her of Mad Dog—how he'd put on fancy clothes, masquerading as someone else, when deep down he was still a no-account, low-down, mean outlaw.

A jovial laugh had her turning again. Nothing changed Jack, either. Though he was wearing a three-piece black suit with a red silk vest and tie and his hair and beard had been trimmed short, he was as boisterous as ever.

When her gaze settled on Lucky again, she had to admit gold wouldn't change Lucky, because he'd grown up with it. With all this. He was as comfortable amongst this finery as he had been living at the mining camp.

He took the cup of punch from her hand, which she hadn't even tasted, and set it on a nearby table. "Would you care to dance?" he asked, nodding toward an adjacent room where couples were sashaying around a dance floor.

"No, thank you."

"Come on," he coaxed, tugging on her elbow.

She kept her feet planted. "I don't know how," she whispered through a painful and false smile in case anyone was looking.

"I'll teach you."

Though his whisper tickling her ear sent a delightful shiver down her back, she shook her head. "I don't want to learn."

The disappointment in his eyes formed a hard knot in her stomach, and she considered giving in, but the maid—whom the mayor's wife had chastised—was approaching with a plate of bite-size delicacies, and Maddie couldn't stop staring at the girl.

"Would you care for one?" Lucky asked, gesturing toward the tray.

Maddie didn't respond. The girl looked vaguely familiar. She'd met many people since arriving in Seattle and wasn't sure if this was one she'd seen recently, or some time ago. Considering the maid worked for the mayor, and Maddie had never been in the house before, she wondered if the maid just resembled someone else.

Lucky took one of the tidbits and thanked the girl before popping it in his mouth.

The maid gave a curtsy and smiled before turning to walk away, and that was when recognition hit. "I know that girl."

"Of course you do," Lucky said drily. "The entire room does after the tongue-lashing the mayor's wife just gave her."

"No," Maddie said. "I know her from Mrs. Smother's. She thought you were handsome."

He lifted a brow, and when his gaze went to follow the girl across the room, Maddie wanted to stomp on his foot again. When he slowly turned to look at her again, he asked, "How would she have known me?"

"You rescued her the year before."

He nodded as if it didn't matter and folded his hand around her elbow again. "Are you ready to dance now?"

Maddie let her gaze follow the girl again. The plate she held was almost empty. "I'll be back in a minute."

His hold tightened on her arm. "Where are you going?"

"I want to talk to her."

"Why?"

"Just because I do."

Lucky shook his head. "Servants aren't allowed to speak to guests."

"I've figured that out already," she said, watching the girl leave the room. "I'll be right back."

"Maddie   "

"I'll be right back," she insisted, tugging from his hold. A burning desire said she needed to talk with the maid.

Maddie found the girl in the kitchen, refilling the plate along with several other servants, who all stopped talking when she entered.

"Are you looking for the *facilities*, Mrs. DuMont?" one of them asked.

"No," Maddie said, walking up to the girl. "I'd like to speak with you."

The maid turned red.

"I'm sorry, ma'am, that would be most improper," an older woman said, most likely the main housekeeper.

"I know," Maddie said, holding a stern and steady gaze on the older woman. "This will only take a moment."

The housekeeper eventually nodded toward the young maid, and Maddie took the girl's arm, which trembled beneath her touch. "You haven't done anything wrong," Maddie assured her, leading the girl out the door.

Down the hallway she found a quiet corner, away from the traffic leading in and out of the kitchen. Unsure why her heart was skipping beats, Maddie said, "I remember you from Mrs. Smother's."

"I remember you, too," the maid answered. "Mrs. Smother was in a tizzy when you came up missing. And again when those men came looking for you."

"Alan Ridge's men?" Maddie asked, her insides churning.

"Yes. I'm glad to see they didn't find you."

The sincerity of the girl's tone touched something soft inside Maddie, yet she muttered, "They found me, all right."

"But we all told them we didn't know where you'd gone."

Maddie laid a hand on the girl's arm. "I'm not saying they found me because of you." Unsure what to say next, she asked, "How old are you?"

"Fifteen."

She'd assumed the girl was much older when meeting her last spring. Maddie then asked, "How old were you when Lu—when Mr. DuMont rescued you, took you to Mrs. Smother?"

"Thirteen."

Maddie held her breath for a moment. "He rescued you from Ridge, didn't he?"

"Yes, ma'am."

With Maddie's prodding, the girl shared a harrowing story of how Mad Dog overtook her family wagon, killing her parents and capturing her and her sisters. The maid, named Ilene, had escaped and eventually ended up at Hester's, from where Lucky had whisked her away to Trig's ship.

"What about your sisters?" Maddie asked.

"I don't know what happened to them," Ilene answered. "But I will someday. As soon as I've earned enough money to pay off my debt to Mrs. Smother."

Maddie's head was spinning. She had no way of knowing just how many girls Mad Dog had captured over the years. It was a moment before Ilene's statement entered her thoughts. "What debt?" Trig had told her he paid Mrs. Smother to educate the girls, giving them a new start.

"For my training and room and board."

"Captain DuMont paid for that."

Ilene shook her head. "Only for the first month."

Maddie highly doubted that was the deal Trig made with Mrs. Smother. "Do you know of other girls indebted to Mrs. Smother?"

"Yes, ma'am. Several. Some of them work here, for the mayor, and others for his friends."

Maddie's spine quivered. "And they were escaping from Ridge?"

The maid nodded. "Or others like him."

"Maddie?"

She spun at the sound of Lucky's voice and held up

a hand, telling him she'd heard him, but silently asking that he not come any closer.

"You were lucky, ma'am," Ilene said. "Getting away, going to Alaska and marrying Mr. DuMont."

Turning back to glance at Lucky for a moment, Maddie let her thoughts flow in several directions, yet they settled on one. The man looking at her curiously. "Yes," she said. "I was lucky. I am lucky."

"You've given the rest of us hope." Ilene blushed slightly. "That if we have a mind to, we can change our status in life."

The emptiness Maddie had felt the past few days dissolved. "That's right," she said, squeezing Ilene's hand. "You can. Anyone can." She felt a tide of purpose rise within her. She had changed her status in life. Lucky, Trig, even Jack, was who she had to thank for that, as well as the Fenstermacher brothers and other miners. Lucky most of all, though. He'd changed a lot of things about her.

Months ago she'd recognized he'd turned her into a woman, but at the time she hadn't known exactly what that meant. It was more than crying at the drop of a hat or wanting to wear clothes that would make her look pretty. In truth, Lucky had allowed her to become who she wanted to be. At the time, she'd thought that was to have money. Make it rich so she'd be self-sufficient. There was more to it, though. Lucky had made her believe in herself. That her dreams weren't just dreams, but goals, and that she could succeed in whatever she chose.

Right then and there, Maddie realized he'd done that by loving her. He'd never told her so, just as she'd never told him. Mainly because she hadn't known that was what it was.

Love.

Her entire being grew warm, and when she glanced down the hall, saw him still standing there, waiting for her, her heart skipped several beats. With him she was capable of everything. Anything.

Her greatest perception happened then. She didn't have to change. Didn't have to become someone she didn't want to be. She didn't mind having a man tell her what to do, either, not when they were partners. Happiness welled, and Maddie turned to Ilene. "I'd like you to come to the Empire Hotel tomorrow, around one."

The maid frowned. "It's Christmas Day tomorrow."

"I know."

"But I have to work."

"I'll arrange it with the mayor," Maddie said. A lot of clout came with being a rich woman, and she was about to start using it. "One o'clock at the Empire Hotel."

With a newfound spring in her step, Maddie walked down the hallway, and when she stopped in front of Lucky, she stretched onto her toes and kissed him, heedless of the traffic going in and out of the kitchen.

He grinned. "What was that for?"

"Because I'm lucky," she said.

"You are?"

She nodded. "Your luck rubbed off on me. Which was what I hoped would happen the night we met." Hooking his elbow with hers, she added, "And it did."

"Maybe yours rubbed off on me," he said.

She laughed. "Maybe it did." Leaning her head against his shoulder as they walked, she said, "We make good partners, don't we?"

"The best."

Maddie drew a breath so full of contentment it made her lightheaded. She still had to take care of Mad Dog, see he was captured so no more girls like Ilene and her sisters were harmed, but she had now accepted that task would be easier with Lucky's help than without it.

He stopped before entering the party area again. "What did that girl say to you?" Reaching up, he twisted a ringlet of her hair around one finger. "What's going on in that pretty little head of yours?"

The twinkle was back in his eyes, and the excitement bubbling inside her let loose a giggle. She stretched up to kiss him again. "You and I are going to talk about that," she whispered against his lips, "right after I talk to the mayor."

Lucky caught her by the hips when she'd have turned for the door. "The mayor? Why do I have a chilling sense I should be worried?"

She giggled. "Probably because you know me."

He muttered a slight curse. "You don't have your gun with you, do you?"

"Just the derringer," she admitted. "Besides fastening up the back, this gown doesn't have any pockets."

"Thank God," he muttered, though the twinkle in his eyes flashed brighter when he asked, "Where's the derringer hid?"

Biting her lip to hold back a rather boisterous bout of giddiness, she said, "I'll show you at the hotel."

He groaned teasingly, and she released a full laugh. "Come on. I've decided I do want to learn how to dance."

After meeting with the mayor and securing a meeting time for the following day with Ilene, Maddie gladly let Lucky lead her onto the dance floor. He was an excellent dancer and soon was whisking her about. Fully intoxicated by him and the music, she promptly refused offers to dance from other men who tapped him on the shoulder.

Delighted by the woman he knew back in Alaska, the one who wasn't shy and purposefully adamant about what she wanted, Cole couldn't erase the grin that sat on his face. Maddie had returned. He wasn't sure what had happened, but his chest had never swelled with such pride as when she informed the mayor she'd be meeting with one of his household staff on the morrow and that the girl would not be docked in pay or time.

Not used to being talked to, especially by a woman, the mayor did attempt to stand his ground—insisting the next day was Christmas and all of his household staff would be needed—but Maddie shot him down as swiftly as if she had drawn her pistol.

The mayor had been left speechless, which had left Cole grinning. Maddie was more than he'd ever have imagined a woman could be, and the ring in his pocket was burning a hole in his skin. Upon leaving the hotel this afternoon, he'd passed a jewelry shop and hadn't been able to help venturing in. He'd give it to her tonight and ask her to marry him. She was right—they made good partners. Together there wasn't much they couldn't tackle. Even outlaws.

Dancing with her, holding her close and sensing her as intimately as when they lay together in bed though the room was crowded, Cole accepted that living in her big house until he was old and gray, never traveling again, wouldn't be hard at all. In fact, it would be all the adventure he ever needed.

As the music ended, he let her loose and gave her his best elegant bow. A blush covered her cheeks, but being Maddie, the woman he loved—that was no longer as scary as it had once been, either—she threw her head back and laughed, and then looped her arms around his neck and kissed him on the lips.

He returned the kiss, while whispering, "You are supposed to curtsy."

"Who cares?" she asked.

"Who indeed," he answered. Taking her hand, he turned to escort her off the dance floor. His heart stalled in his chest upon recognizing a man standing near the door, gesturing.

Jack interceded just then. "I've been looking for you two. I've got me a buyer for my claim."

"You do?" Maddie asked.

Cole responded, but eased away as Jack started to explain, making his way toward one of the men he'd hired to watch the docks. For a moment, he'd forgotten Mad Dog, and how the outlaw threatened his and Maddie's happiness.

"Your uncle Trig's ship was spotted in the bay over an hour ago." The man gestured toward the front doors. "May be docking by now. They didn't want to let me in."

The distinct chill that had assaulted his insides eased a portion. "Thanks," Cole said.

The man parted moments before Maddie arrived at his side. "Who was that?"

"A man from the docks," he said. "The *Mary Jane* is about to set port."

Her face fell, but she caught it and squared her shoulders. "That's good news."

"Yes, it is," Lucky said, silently questioning her disappointment. "Yes, it is."

They took their leave of the party and Lucky instructed the driver to take them to the seashore before climbing into the open-top carriage. Looping an arm around her shoulders, he pulled her close with one hand while covering their legs with the blanket. The stars overhead reflected in her eyes and he couldn't stop himself from kissing her long and hard.

When the kiss ended, she sighed, and then snuggled closer against him. "That maid I talked to," she said quietly, "was one of the girls you saved from Alan Ridge."

"I know." He'd recalled the event earlier, while Maddie had been talking with the girl. "That was the night Ridge almost caught me."

"He did?"

"Almost," he said, kissing her furrowed brow. "I'm lucky, remember?"

"Yes, you are," she said. "And so am I."

"That you are, darling," he said, kissing her again. "That you are."

She cut the kiss short. "I have something I want to tell you, but I can't do it if you keep kissing me."

Still wondering about the way she'd reacted to hearing the *Mary Jane* was docking, he ran several small kisses along the side of her face. "Is it that important?"

She giggled, but still said, "Yes."

"All right," he said, sitting up straighter. "What is it?"

"Well—" she twisted to face him "—first off, I'll go to any frivolous party you want me to attend, live in any fancy house you want, wherever you want it to be, but first—"

"Whoa up," he interrupted, "I never said I wanted live in a fancy house. You did."

She opened her mouth, but closed it and frowned before asking, "You didn't? But that's how you grew up."

"I know, and I'll gladly live that way again, if it's what you want."

She grew so quiet, so thoughtful, his insides started ticking. "Maddie?"

"What if…" She grew silent, looking up as the moon slipped out from behind a cloud. The yellow beams shone down on her and she continued to gaze up as she often did, letting the rays bounce off her face as if gathering strength or something from the light. A moment later she smiled and turned back to him. "What if I want to be Mrs. Cole DuMont in truth, not pretend?"

His heart was in his mouth. Even though he'd bought the ring, he hadn't been overly sure she'd accept it. Agree to marrying him. "I want that, too, Maddie. Have for a long time."

"Why haven't you told me that?" she asked.

"Because that's not what you wanted. From the beginning your dream was to build a big house and have servants."

A stomping of hooves came from behind them and the carriage driver pulled to the side of the road, letting a fast-moving coach surrounded by riders whisk past them. "What's that all about?" Lucky shouted to the driver.

"Don't know, sir, but that's a police wagon. Something must be up at the docks."

Chapter Seventeen

Another group of riders galloped past before the driver could set the carriage forward again. Maddie clutched onto Lucky's arm. "What do you think it is?"

"I'm not sure," he said. "But I want you to—"

"Oh, no, you don't," she interrupted. "Don't try telling me what to do right now, Cole DuMont."

He let out a curse. It was under his breath, but Maddie heard it. She didn't need to say more, though; Lucky was already shouting to the driver. "Step it up!"

Not sure what they might see ahead, Maddie had the greatest desire to say one last thing. "I trust you, Lucky. I know no harm will come to me when I'm by your side."

He looked startled by her admission.

A tear slipped out of the corner of one of her eyes. "And I don't mind you telling me what to do some of the time, because I love you."

The carriage was bouncing, jostling them about, and he grabbed her face, held it firmly before his. "That's good, darling," he said. "Because I don't mind you telling me what to do, either, once in a while."

She bit at the smile forming on her lips.

"Because I love you, too, Maddie," he said, touching his lips to hers. "I love you like I never knew I could love someone."

Maddie's heart threatened to explode. She'd never imagined hearing him say it would have such an impact. She should have known, though; that was how he'd turned her into a woman. By loving her.

Between the rough ride and a ship's horn echoing through the night, their kisses were short and lopsided, and came to a stop when the carriage skidded to an abrupt halt.

"What's happened?" Cole asked one of the men creating a barricade. Pointing at the ship with deckhands scurrying about to drop the gangplank he said, "That's the *Mary Jane*. My uncle's ship."

"That ship has a notorious outlaw on board," the man said. Having heard her gasp, the man glanced at her. "Don't worry, ma'am, we're here to escort him straight to jail."

"Who is it?" Cole asked. "The outlaw, who is it?"

"Goes by the name Alan Ridge, but he's really Mad Dog Rodriquez," the man said. "And he's one evil outlaw. Wanted in most every state in the nation."

A shiver shot through Maddie, and Cole's arm, which was wrapped firmly about her shoulders, tightened.

"How do you know?" Cole asked the man.

"The captain sent a rowboat ahead to send for us, secure the area before he docked."

It took a moment for Maddie's mind to fully comprehend what the man had said, and then she had to be sure. "Mad Dog Rodriquez has been captured?"

"That's my understanding, ma'am," the man said. "The sailor said there's a federal marshal on board, too."

"Curtis Wyman?" Cole asked.

"That's sounds right," the man answered.

The plank had been lowered, and the moon overhead shone brighter, giving Maddie plenty of light to see that the man being escorted off the ship was definitely Mad Dog. Chains connected his legs, and his hands were behind his back. She made out the marshal, too, and Trig.

The coach was indeed a police wagon, complete with metal bars on the windows... Mad Dog was loaded into it, the door slammed shut and men mounted on horses surrounded the wagon. Maddie watched as it rolled past, intuitively knowing it was the last time she'd ever see the outlaw.

"It's over," she whispered. "It's over."

Lucky caught her beneath the chin with one finger, turning her face to look at him. "Yes, it is. It's over."

Turning toward the wagon again, she thought of Ilene and all those other girls. "Almost," she said. "It's almost over."

"What do you mean?" Cole asked.

She didn't have time to answer. Trig had spotted them and jogged toward the carriage. "Cole! Maddie! Did you see who that was?"

"We saw," Cole answered, climbing out of the carriage. He helped her down, and by then Trig, Robbie and Marshal Wyman were standing next to the rig.

Trig instantly set into telling them how Robbie had first spotted Mad Dog when he'd gone ashore in Dabbler, looking to see if Cole and Maddie were in town, ready for a ride south.

"We'd decided to sail out of Bittersweet rather than take the trail back to Dabbler," Cole interrupted to tell them.

Robbie jumped in to say, "I caught sight of Mad Dog at one of the establishments the women we'd taken to Dabbler had set up. I thought he looked familiar. But it was the next day, when Marshal Wyman boarded the *Mary Jane*—informing all the ship captains that a wanted man might try to arrange passage—that I knew it had been Alan Ridge I'd seen. He was still there, and we hauled him aboard the *Mary Jane*."

"I thought you were only making the one trip to Alaska this year," Cole said to Trig.

"We made out so well on the first, thought we'd try a second one," Trig answered, "Glad we did, too."

Marshal Wyman finally got a word in then, and he turned straight to Maddie. "Mrs. DuMont," he said, "I told you I'd catch Rodriquez. I'm taking him all the way to Wyoming, and I'm sure the judge will issue you the reward money."

Maddie shook her head. "You caught him."

"But the bullet you put in his leg is the reason I was able to. He needed some doctoring by the time he got to Dabbler. He promised that dance-hall gal a lot of money to patch him up. She was a bit put out to learn the shooting hadn't been accidental and he wasn't the owner of a very profitable mine up by Bittersweet."

Maddie wasn't sure how to respond and was saved from doing so when Trig announced the success of the Big Bonanza was the talk of Alaska. A short time later, when the storytelling slowed, she issued an invite to Marshal Wyman. "We'd like to have you join us for Christmas, Marshal. At our hotel, the Empire. Around three?"

"I'd be honored, Mrs. DuMont," he said, tipping his

hat. "Truly honored. Right now, I have to see to my prisoner."

A silence settled around them as the marshal walked away, joining a few other lawmen that had been waiting on him.

"So you two are still pretending to be married?" Trig asked then.

Maddie's cheeks burned, but Lucky grinned. "We'd like you to rectify that," he said.

"How?" Trig asked.

"By marrying us," Lucky said, looking down at her with a sky full of sparkles in his eyes. "Tonight. Right now."

Maddie's heart soared, but then her entire world collapsed when Trig spoke again.

"I can't," he said.

"Why not?" Lucky asked, pulling her to his side.

"Because I'm not authorized," Trig said. "Everyone believes ship captains can perform marriages. In truth, we can preside over funerals when there is a death at sea, but, Cole, you know most ships only carry men. Marrying people never really happens on the high seas."

"But," Robbie piped in, "I know someone who can. We have a preacher on board. Picked him up in Dabbler, too. The winters were too much for him. He's not planning on going ashore until morning."

As Robbie ran toward the dock Lucky asked Trig, "Are you becoming a passenger ship?"

Trig shook his head. "We will be if your brother has his way."

"Will he be discreet?" Maddie wanted to know. Though Jack had found a buyer, she didn't want the news of their marriage to hamper the deal.

Trig laughed. "I'll talk to him," he said, leaving the two of them alone.

"We can travel to a neighboring town," Lucky suggested. "Or take the first train heading east, get married somewhere along the line."

So touched was she in his willingness to marry her, that Maddie felt bad for having to shake her head. "There are things I need to do here in Seattle. I can't leave right now."

"A Christmas party?"

"Among other things," she said. The sullen look on Lucky's face had her adding, "But I want to marry you. As soon as possible. Tonight."

"All right." With the arm he had around her shoulders, he escorted her toward the *Mary Jane*. "As long as you marry me tonight, I'll do anything you want, stay here as long as you want."

She giggled, though she was smart enough to know better. "I have a feeling I'll have to remind you of those words—that you'll do anything I want." Smiling up at him, she added, "Often."

The ceremony was held on deck, beneath a moon that shone down on her brighter than sunshine, and Maddie was once again convinced Smitty was still looking out for her, sending a beacon to light her way. There was also a part of her that wondered if Bass wasn't up there, too, beside Smitty, watching her.

As soon as Lucky placed the gold band on her finger Maddie became so full of happiness, she feared she might burst. Although his kiss was as heart-stopping as hundreds of others had been, this one thrilled her to no end. She truly was Mrs. DuMont. No other adventure would ever compare.

Afterward she invited Trig, Robbie and the minister to join them at the hotel the following day to celebrate Christmas, asking them to arrive before one. When she said Jack would be there, too, and Homer, Lucky pointed out that the hotel didn't allow pets of any kind. She told him to let her handle that, at which point he assured Trig and Robbie the bird would be in attendance.

They took their leave then, traveling back to the hotel in the open carriage, with the moon lighting the way.

"Why do I have a feeling tomorrow is more than a simple Christmas celebration?" Lucky asked while unlocking their hotel room door.

She crossed the sitting room and entered the bedroom to place her fur shawl and muff in the wardrobe and then sat down on a bench to remove her dress shoes and stockings. "I'm going to give Ilene, and the other girls she knows from Mrs. Smother's place, enough money to pay off their debts and find their families."

"What debts?"

He was removing his clothing, too, on the other side of the bed, and she explained about Mrs. Smother's charging the girls.

"Trig's not going to like hearing that," he said before asking, "How do you know how much money that will take?"

"I don't," she admitted. "But I have to start somewhere." She crossed the room. "When I saw Ilene, I realized that could have been me working at the mayor's house. And when she told me about her sisters, I realized if not for you, who knows where I might have ended up. Ilene told me I was lucky, and I am, because of you." She stopped in front of him. "Mad Dog started stealing girls because of me."

He took her hands. "That wasn't your fault, honey."

"I know it wasn't my fault," she said, unsure how to explain the understanding that had blossomed inside her. "But since arriving in Seattle many of the people we've met reminded me of Mad Dog, all dressed up in fancy clothes, pretending to be Alan Ridge, whereas underneath he was as evil as ever, if not more so."

"Clothes can't change people, Maddie. Money doesn't, either. If they were evil before they had it, they're still evil afterward."

"I know." She squeezed his hands. "You made me understand that. You're no different no matter how you dress or where you live. I want to be like that. I want to be me, no matter where I am. No matter how much money I have or don't. I never want to pretend to be something I'm not."

He folded his arms around her. "I don't want you to be anyone but you, either. Ever." Holding her close, he asked, "That's what's been bothering you the past few weeks, isn't it?"

She nodded, then shook her head, and then nodded again.

He frowned.

"I didn't fit in," she said, "but I didn't want to fit in, either." Looking up at him, she admitted, "I didn't realize that until tonight. But what bothered me was leaving you."

"Leaving me?"

"Yes. I planned on setting a trap for Mad Dog. To see he was captured, but I didn't want you to get hurt again. Once you left for New Orleans, I was going to go to Wyoming and ask that judge to help me catch Mad Dog."

"You thought I'd just leave you?" he asked.

"No," she said, all along knowing that would be the tricky part. "I was hoping to convince Trig to take you away."

He laughed and then kissed her smack on the lips. "Everything I've been doing, from going to parties to showing you houses, was to set a trap for Mad Dog."

"It was?"

"Yes, it was."

"Why didn't you tell me?"

A devilish grin appeared on his face. "Because you don't like being told what to do."

She frowned, yet had to smile. "I don't mind you telling me what to do sometimes. We're partners."

He twirled her around and started unfastening her dress. "Yes, we are, darling. Forever." At that moment, Maddie had to admit she didn't mind something else: how fashionable gowns fastened down the back.

He was taking his time with each button and his due diligence had her simmering like a pot to boil. "You said you don't mind me telling you what to do, either," she said, "in the carriage tonight."

"Yes, I did," he said, kissing the back of her neck. "And I don't."

Excitement flared inside her. "Will you hurry up, then?"

He laughed, but didn't speed up his movement. Instead, he kissed the other side of her neck. "I bought the ring on your finger this afternoon, fully intending to ask you to marry me tonight."

Her insides melted. She attempted to turn around,

but he wouldn't let her. "No," he whispered against the back of her neck while pushing the gown off her shoulders. "I'm not done."

"You did?" she asked, even while she wanted to insist he hurry.

"Yes, I did. I love you, Maddie, and will forever."

When the dress pooled around her feet, he lifted her camisole over her head and then slid a fingertip all the way down her spine to the base of her back before sliding his hands inside her pantaloons and around her stomach to untie them. "But, darling, there's something you should know."

"What?" she asked, holding her breath, both because of the sensations erupting inside her and because she had no idea what he might say next.

"I'd never have left with Trig. Not without you."

She giggled, even as her breath caught in her throat again when her pantaloons fell to the floor. "I don't know about that. Trig is somewhat easily manipulated," she finally managed. "Rescuing girls he didn't know, paying their room and board."

"Aw, yes," Lucky said, keeping her stationed with her back to him while he kissed her shoulders. "But he's also sly. He did convince both of us to take care of the other one."

His hands roamed over her midriff and upward, toward her breasts, which had grown heavy and full. Maddie nodded in agreement. "I guess you're right about that."

Lucky fondled her endlessly, sweetly, until she was trembling with desire so great her legs wobbled.

"Remind me to thank him for that," Lucky whispered. Then he picked her up and slowly, gracefully, swung around and laid her on the bed. His eyes were twinkling, full of stars brilliant enough to make wishes upon. There was love there, too, sparking brightly, and Maddie wondered how she'd never recognized it before now.

She lifted her arms, looping them around his neck. "I will, and I'll thank him, too." Kissing the center of Lucky's chin, she added teasingly, "He drove a hard bargain with that fifty percent clause."

"I'd have had to pay him a hundred percent if you didn't return with me."

Maddie was taken aback, and the glimmer in Lucky's eyes didn't tell her if he was teasing or not. He didn't let her ask, either, not with the way he kissed her.

Lucky took his time then, loving her at his leisure. Kissing, caressing and pleasing her until her scalding release could wait no longer. She'd barely regained her senses when he began again. Just as slowly, just as patiently. Maddie dug her hands into the tangled bed covers and held on. He was so relentless she might float up into the heavens, into the vast dimension overhead filled with the stars like the ones in his gaze, and never return to earth.

He was unyielding in withholding his own satisfaction, even when another spasm tore through her, signaling she'd reached her limit yet again. When he finally disrobed and positioned himself over her, entered her, he continued to hold back, bringing her to yet another peak, encouraging her to tumble over the edge while he forged onward.

She was beyond reality, and at his complete mercy, no longer able to control a single muscle when he let out a husky groan and went stiff. Her body was there, too, driven to another pinnacle, fully glorifying in one more bright and astonishing union he'd perfectly orchestrated.

Astounded by her own stamina, she held on to him as her final release proved to be the most earth-shattering of them all.

When he relaxed, rested upon her briefly, he whispered, "I love you, Mrs. DuMont."

Maddie was too spent, too exhausted to do much more than smile as her heart went rather wild. She vowed to tell him how much she loved him as soon as her strength renewed.

That didn't happen until morning when she opened her eyes to a room already awash with light. Maddie reached for him, but her arm encountered an empty pillow. Spinning to the other side, she grinned, seeing him sitting in the chair.

"Good morning, Mrs. DuMont."

"Good morning, Mr. DuMont," she replied in return while scooting up in the bed.

"I was hoping you'd wake up soon." He hoisted a tray off the table. "I had breakfast delivered, and it's getting cold."

"You and your three meals a day." Pointing to the tray, she said, "You can leave that on the table, but you can join me."

It was an hour before they ate a very cold breakfast, and after reading the newspaper, Maddie had to hurry through a bath in order to make her way downstairs to inform the manager that Homer—bird or not—would be celebrating Christmas in the hotel. She also ordered a rather lavish meal to be delivered to their suite at four o'clock and then told the man there would be several visitors coming that day and that he was to see them escorted up directly upon their arrival.

Trig, Robbie and the minister arrived first, and upon listening to her story, all three were set to hear her entire proposal to assist the girls that had been rescued from Mad Dog—and men like him.

Their involvement solidified her plan. When Ilene arrived and Maddie explained why she'd asked her to the hotel, Ilene cried. And again when Maddie assured Trig would speak with Mrs. Smother and that she would speak to the mayor if Ilene was uncomfortable turning in her resignation in order to start looking for her siblings immediately.

Ilene and the minister were invited to stay for the afternoon, and when Marshal Wyman arrived, he, too, agreed to assist, and pledged to inform the judge of how Maddie's reward money was to be spent. The holiday celebration turned into the most joyous affair Maddie had ever attended. Then again, Homer had a knack for making affairs festive and entertained everyone by the mess he made of opening his Christmas gift—a bag of raisins.

It was late when everyone left, and Maddie sat down on one of the sofas.

"Tired?" Lucky asked.

"Happy," she said, smiling up at him.

He sat down next to her and placed an arm around her shoulders. "So what are our plans after we travel to Colorado to buy headstones for Smitty and your father?"

She glanced his way, not quite believing he was leaving their plans up to her. "We'll go to New Orleans, to see your family."

"What then?" he asked.

"You won't want to stay there?"

"Will you?"

Maddie frowned. "What about your grandmother, the rebuilding of DuMont Shipping?"

"My grandmother is a very independent woman." Lucky withdrew a piece of paper from his pocket. "This arrived earlier. It's a telegram from her, thanking me for the money, and telling us to visit when we can, but to never stop living our own lives." He unfolded the note and read, "'Because of you, DuMont Shipping will rise to its glory again and always be here, I'll see to that. You keep seeking your adventures. It's what you were born to do.'"

"I think I'm going to like your grandmother," Maddie said.

"I know she'll like you." Lucky set the note aside. "So where do you want to go? Where do you want to build that big house?"

Nibbling on her bottom lip, Maddie lifted her hand and gazed at the solid gold band on her finger. Twirling the ring with her thumb and middle finger of the opposite hand, she said, "I do believe this is the final piece of gold I'll ever need." She glanced up to see if Lucky was watching her. He was, and a familiar zing rippled her insides. "And I'm not so sure I want to build a house just yet, but how do you feel about diamonds?"

"Diamonds?" He shrugged and kissed the end of her nose. "If you want diamonds, I'll buy you diamonds."

She shook her head. "I don't want you to buy them."

"How else does one obtain diamonds?"

Stretching, she lifted the newspaper off the table. With her other hand she pointed to an article she'd read that morning. "Mine them. A man in Arkansas discovered diamonds on his property last month."

"Really?"

A definite thrill shot up her spine at the excitement in his tone. "Yes, really."

Cole leaned his head against the back of the sofa and let out a roar of a laugh. A happier man couldn't possibly exist. He caught Maddie's chin and gazed into her eyes. He couldn't believe he was this lucky. This profoundly lucky. But he was.

"Diamonds?" he asked. "In Arkansas?"

With her black hair glistening in the lamplight and her ocean-blue eyes sparking, his adorable wife nodded her head.

"It sounds like an adventure to me," he said. "When do you want to leave?"

"Tonight?"

He laughed while rising to his feet and then he swept her into his arms. "Tomorrow. We're busy tonight."

"All right," she agreed.

Maddie and Cole soon discovered there were diamonds in Arkansas, and finding them was more of an adventure than the gold in Alaska had been.

* * * * *

COMING NEXT MONTH FROM

H HARLEQUIN®

ℋISTORICAL

Available May 19, 2015

WED TO THE MONTANA COWBOY
by Carol Arens
(Western)

Rebecca Lane has always felt unlovable. But that all changes when she heads West to her grandfather's ranch, where cowboy Lantree Walker is there to protect her!

RAKE MOST LIKELY TO REBEL
Rakes on Tour • by Bronwyn Scott
(1830s)

Viscount Amersham has come to Paris to prove his expert skill with the blade. Yet feisty, stunning Alyssandra Leodegrance is not the opponent he was expecting...

A MISTRESS FOR MAJOR BARTLETT
Brides of Waterloo • by Annie Burrows
(Regency)

Major Tom Bartlett is shocked to discover the angel who nursed his battle wounds is darling of the *ton* Lady Sarah Latymor. One taste of her threatens her reputation and his career!

WHISPERS AT COURT
Royal Weddings
by Blythe Gifford
(Medieval)

French hostage Marc de Marcel wants only to return home, so he makes an unlikely alliance with enticing Lady Cecily. But what will happen when their pact leads them to scandal?

HHCNM0515

REQUEST YOUR
FREE BOOKS!

H HARLEQUIN®

HISTORICAL

Where love is timeless

2 FREE NOVELS PLUS 2 FREE GIFTS!

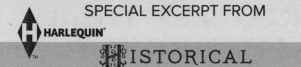
*Viscount Amersham has come to Paris on his
Grand Tour to prove his expert skill with the blade.
Yet feisty Alyssandra Leodegrance is* not *the opponent
he was expecting…*

Read on for a sneak preview of
RAKE MOST LIKELY TO REBEL
an exciting new offering from
Bronwyn Scott
and the first in her new quartet
RAKES ON TOUR.

It was darker now. There were fewer lanterns and even
fewer guests in this remote corner of the garden. Her pulse
began to leap. They'd reached their destination—somewhere
private.

"It seems we have reached the perimeter of the garden,"
North commented, his eyes full of mischief. "What do you
suppose we do now?"

Alyssandra wet her lips and turned toward him so they
were no longer side by side but face-to-face. "I've talked
for far too long. You could tell me about yourself. What
brings you to Paris?" She stepped closer, drawing a long line
down the white linen of his chest with her fan. She would
genuinely like to know. She'd spent the past three weeks
making up stories in her mind about what he was doing in
France.

But she'd not come out to the garden to acquire a thorough history of the Viscount Amersham. That would come in time, as those layers came off. Tonight was about making first impressions, ones that would eventually lead to…more. Even so, she rather doubted her brother had expected "more" to involve stealing away to the dark corners of Madame Aguillard's garden with somewhat illicit intentions.

"I *could* tell you my life story," he drawled, his eyes darkening to a deep sapphire. "Or perhaps we might do something more interesting." Those sapphire eyes dropped to her mouth, signaling his definition of *interesting*, and her breath caught. *Something more interesting, please*.

It was hard to say who kissed whom. *His* head had angled toward her in initiation, but *she* had stepped into him, welcoming the advance of his mouth on hers, the meeting of their bodies; gentian blue skirts pressed against black-clad thighs, corseted breasts met the muscled firmness of his chest beneath white linen.

Her mouth opened for him, letting his tongue tangle with hers in a sensual duel. She met his boldness with boldness of her own, tasting the fruity sweetness of champagne where it lingered on his tongue. Life pulsed through her as she nipped his lip and he growled low in his throat, his arm pressing her to the hard contours of him. She moved against his hips, challenging him, knowing full well this bordered on madness; desire was rising between them, hot and heady.

THE WORLD IS BETTER WITH

Romance

Harlequin has everything from contemporary, passionate and heartwarming to suspenseful and inspirational stories.

Whatever your mood, we have a romance just for you!

Connect with us to find your next great read, special offers and more.

f /HarlequinBooks

🐦 @HarlequinBooks

www.HarlequinBlog.com

www.Harlequin.com/Newsletters

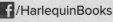

A *Romance* FOR EVERY MOOD™

www.Harlequin.com